350

Praise for the Historical Romances of Jaclyn Reding

White Mist

"Rich historical detail, endearing characters, compelling stories—Jaclyn Reding has it all. This is a writer to watch."
—Linda Lael Miller

"With endearing characters, murder, mysticism, and vivid imagery of the Scottish Highlands, *White Mist* brings the reader an emotionally intense love story."
—*Romantic Times*

White Knight

"I'd be a damsel in distress any day if this white knight was in the vicinity! Don't miss Reding's latest."
—Catherine Coulter

"Jaclyn Reding spins a tale of love like no other! Highly recommended!" —*Under the Covers Book Reviews*

White Magic

"Charmingly written, witty, [and] sure to please."
—*Romantic Times*

White Heather

"An exciting and passion-filled love story that has a cleverly and intricately twisted plot line." —*Rendezvous*

"Fabulous . . . a must read for fans of historical romance." —*Midwest Book Review*

"Captivated me from the start . . . a magical journey to romance." —*Scottish Radiance*

P9-CIV-041

HIGHLAND HEROES:

The Pretender

JACLYN REDING

A SIGNET BOOK

SIGNET
Published by New American Library, a division of
Penguin Putnam Inc., 375 Hudson Street,
New York, New York 10014, U.S.A.
Penguin Books Ltd, 80 Strand,
London WC2R 0RL, England
Penguin Books Australia Ltd, Ringwood,
Victoria, Australia
Penguin Books Canada Ltd, 10 Alcorn Avenue,
Toronto, Ontario, Canada M4V 3B2
Penguin Books (N.Z.) Ltd, 182–190 Wairau Road,
Auckland 10, New Zealand

Penguin Books Ltd, Registered Offices:
Harmondsworth, Middlesex, England

First published by Signet, an imprint of New American Library,
a division of Penguin Putnam Inc.

First Printing, March 2002
10 9 8 7 6 5 4 3

Copyright © Jaclyn Reding, 2002
Excerpt from *Highland Heroes #2* copyright © Jaclyn Reding, 2002
All rights reserved

 REGISTERED TRADEMARK—MARCA REGISTRADA

Printed in the United States of America

Without limiting the rights under copyright reserved above, no part of this publication may be reproduced, stored in or introduced into a retrieval system, or trans-
mitted, in any form, or by any means (electronic, mechanical, photocopying,
recording, or otherwise), without the prior written permission of both the copyright
owner and the above publisher of this book.

PUBLISHER'S NOTE
This is a work of fiction. Names, characters, places, and incidents either are the
product of the author's imagination or are used fictitiously, and any resemblance to
actual persons, living or dead, business establishments, events, or locales is entirely
coincidental.

BOOKS ARE AVAILABLE AT QUANTITY DISCOUNTS WHEN USED TO PROMOTE PRODUCTS OR
SERVICES. FOR INFORMATION PLEASE WRITE TO PREMIUM MARKETING DIVISION, PEN-
GUIN PUTNAM INC., 375 HUDSON STREET, NEW YORK, NEW YORK 10014.

If you purchased this book without a cover you should be aware that this book is
stolen property. It was reported as "unsold and destroyed" to the publisher and neither the author nor the publisher has received any payment for this "stripped book."

FOR JOSHUA,
MY BONNIE PRINCE

May your life be the grandest adventure

The Skye Boat Song

Speed bonnie boat
like a bird on the wing.
Onward! the sailors cry,
Carry the lad that's born to be king
O'er the sea to Skye.

Loud the winds howl, loud the waves roar,
Thunderclaps rend the air.
Baffled our foes stand on the shore,
Follow they will not dare.

Though the waves leap, soft shall ye sleep,
Ocean's a royal bed.
Rocked in the deep, Flora will keep
Watch by your weary head.

Many a lad fought on that day,
Well the claymore did wield.
When the night came, silently lay
Dead in Culloden's field.

Burned are our homes, exile and death
Scatter the loyal men.
Yet, 'ere the sword, cool in the sheath
Charlie will come again.

Speed, bonnie boat,
like a bird on the wing.
Onward! the sailors cry,
Carry the lad that's born to be king
O'er the sea to Skye.

Chapter One

Early one summer's day in 1746 . . .

Dawn broke softly on a peaceful Northumbrian morning in May, wrapped in the gossamer warmth of a rose-colored sunrise and stirred by the gently warbling lyric of birdsong, until—

"Preposterous! That's what this is. Utterly preposterous!"

Alaric Henry Sinclair Fortunatus Drayton, fourth Duke of Sudeleigh, shook his head and grumbled over a breakfast plate heaped with his favorite buttered eggs and mutton ham. He stabbed a chunk of melon with his fork, and from the expression on his face as he chewed it—the bitter twist of his mouth—one would have thought the fruit had gone foul.

At the opposite end of the table sat her grace, Duchess Margaret, a striking woman of regal demeanor, straight nose, and high forehead, with thick chestnut hair only slightly sprinkled with silver. This particular morning she wore it *à la tête de mouton* beneath the frilled tippets of her lacy lingerie cap, haloed by the sunlight pouring in through the window behind her as she calmly poured a steaming splash of pekoe into her husband's tea bowl. In contrast to the duke's thundering moments before, the duchess presented the very picture of tranquility.

Her husband's outburst hadn't given her even the slightest turn, for over these five-and-twenty years past—the whole of their married life together—she had learned to take the duke's sudden fits of temper in stride. Though at times he was hot-headed, Alaric rarely did any real damage.

"What is it this time, dear?" she finally asked, knowing he was stewing, waiting for her to respond.

"Bah!" he answered immediately. "It is another installment of that ridiculous journal, *The Female Spectator*." The duke waved a small, printed booklet through the air. With his graying auburn hair and starched collar, he looked quite like the local vicar pontificating at his pulpit. "A waste of the very paper on which it is printed."

The duchess took a small sip of tea, glancing sidewise at him. She noticed a loose button on the lapel of his morning coat and made a mental note to have it attended to. She quite liked that coat. The color brought out the flecks of green in his eyes. "Wherever did you find this one?"

"I heard of it from Lord Polson, who had it by Lord Gwynne, who first learned of it from Lord Bainesford, who actually came across his wife discussing it at tea!"

"Leticia had it at tea? I always thought her a most sensible woman. . . ."

The duke rallied on. "So I sent for a copy myself from

the bookseller in Newcastle. They tell me it is all the talk at the coffeehouses in London. A disgrace to king and country! I say, just look here on the first page, Margaret. 'A Letter in Favor of Woman's Equality to Man.' Equality! A woman to a man? Have you ever heard such nonsense?"

The duchess, who knew when it was best to keep her own views to herself, simply shook her head and concentrated her attention on the spreading of a thin layer of marmalade over her breakfast toast. "No, dear. I should say I have not."

"Who on earth would write this foolishness?"

"I really cannot say, dear."

"*A Lady of Quality*, that is what it says here, but I cannot imagine anyone of our acquaintance doing something so extreme as this. I'm told there is wagering into the thousands as to just who the author of it might be. Everyone from serving maids to duchesses—even the queen's name has been bandied about, treasonous a notion as that may seem. More than likely the unruly chit is the natural offspring of some Whig bast—"

Any resemblance he'd borne to the vicar ended right there.

"Alaric! The girls . . . kindly curb your tongue."

The duke swallowed his oath, frowning so deeply that it made his jowls droop over the tight knot of his lace cravat like a pudding. He dropped the pamphlet onto the table in front of him, took up his tea, and swallowed a vigorous gulp of the fragrant brew. He then spent the next several moments glaring sullenly at the square silver buckle on his left shoe.

His silence on the matter, however, didn't last for long.

"I say if she dares to write such a thing, this self-proclaimed 'Lady of Quality,' then she ought to at least have the conviction to attach her name to it. Let everyone in the kingdom know exactly who she is so they can shame her husband or her father or whoever else it is responsible for her into bringing this indecent rebelliousness into line."

"Yes, dear," the duchess replied a sigh.

"Discipline, Margaret, that is what it is lacking there." He shook his finger at his wife's nose. "I've always said there needs to be discipline in every household. You scold me for keeping such a tight rein on our girls, but you could wager your favorite pair of silk stockings that *our* daughters would never be found authoring such twaddling trash. *Our* daughters know the proper order of things, a woman's place and what not."

The duke looked from his wife to the display of feminine grace arranged prettily along both sides of the long mahogany table. Five pairs of eyes, demurely cast in varying shades from brown to green, peered back at him.

"Is that not true, girls?"

"Yes, Papa," came a chorus of singsong voices.

The duke measured out a breath to steady himself. Indeed, he thought as he stared at them all, even to someone without his biased opinion, they were a veritable feast of female perfection. Had there ever been such grace, such unembellished loveliness? A credit to England they were, for there could be no truer examples of polish and good breeding in the land. Completely forgetting the pamphlet that had so provoked him moments before, the duke actually smiled beneath the fringe of his powdered periwig, contented as a cow as he looked from one daughter to the next down each row, ranging in age from eight to twenty-four.

Caroline, Matilda, Catherine, Isabella, and Elizabeth; they'd named them for some of the finest queens in English history. Each in her own way was as unique, as intelligent, as undeniably refined as royalty—legitimate royalty, that is—even the little one, Caro, who drank her breakfast tea quite as if she were dining at Kensington Palace.

And, oh, how very close they'd come to doing just that.

It had begun nearly two centuries and a quarter before, with an obscure little scrap of a baggage named Eliza FitzJames. Of all the women the eighth King Henry had wedded, bedded, and even beheaded, none had managed to successfully deliver him a surviving male heir—none except the quiet, unassuming Eliza, a distant cousin to the king several generations removed, and one of his longest-lasting mistresses.

It was on a quiet autumn day back in 1521 that Eliza gave birth to an infant son, one who bore both the trademark red-gold hair and the fiery temperament of his legendary sire. She dubbed the child Fortunatus in hopes that he might elude the sickness and calamity that had befallen the king's other offspring, and indeed the babe grew into a strapping young lad of whom the great king only grew more fond each day.

But history had already been written and Henry was yet wed to the Spanish Catherine of Aragon, leaving him unable to claim the child as his own. So he did the only thing he could to secure the boy's future, wedding his sweet Eliza to one of his most devoted courtiers, Sinclair Drayton of Parbroath. In exchange for a fortune and a noble title, Drayton agreed to raise young Fortunatus as his own while turning a blind eye to his wife's lifelong liaison with his sire.

And on the son who would become Henry's only male child to survive to adulthood, one never able to inherit his crown, the king bestowed the highest honor he could—the dukedom of Sudeleigh.

So it was that two centuries later, Fortunatus's great-great-grandson Alaric now sat among his own progeny, puffing up his barreled chest beneath his brocaded waistcoat in a manner quite like that of his regal forefather. Though denied by fate a kingdom now in the hands of a distant Hanoverian cousin, Alaric had made it his life's duty to continue the lineage of his own near-regal dynasty through his daughters, whom he would see allied with fine husbands of good English stock—earls, marquesses, perhaps even a royal prince.

He looked on them now, poised like delicate blossoms around his breakfast table, at the heart of which sat his duchess, his pride, his meaning. Closest to her, always at her side, sat Caroline—their youngest, his daisy, innocent and bright as a star with her pale blonde hair and sparkling blue eyes constantly seeking the sunlight. Next came Matilda, or Mattie as she preferred, pretty as a pansy, the flower of thoughts, or so Hamlet's Ophelia had said. She more than the others was the image of her mother with rich brown hair, her eyes flecked with gold and most often turned onto the pages of a book. Catherine, his middle daughter, was the wallflower and ivy, not because she wasn't as lovely as the others, not at all. Katie was a vibrant flower with her dark red-orange hair and deep green eyes, but contented most to blossom away from the dazzle of sunlight—quiet, unassuming, a waft of fragrant scent carried gently on the summer's breeze. Across from her sat his sweet violet, Isabella, with a sweep of dark hair and damson-blue eyes—the romantic, tender, and virtuous. And with her Elizabeth, his eldest, his wild rose—vivid, fragile, lovely beyond compare, delicate yet still barbed.

When he came to the eighth chair at the table, the only vacant one, the duke found himself giving in to a familiar sigh. Much as he loved his daughters, beamed with fatherly pride whenever he looked at them, just like old King Henry two centuries before him—

—Oh, how he longed for a son.

It was the very worst of dilemmas.

Alaric Henry Sinclair Fortunatus Drayton, the wealthiest and most influential duke in all England, was without a direct male heir. Should he kick off this mortal coil by the morrow—perish the thought—his beloved wife and daughters would lose everything they had ever had, the home they'd always known, the comforts to which they were accustomed. Their clothing, even the bedsheets they slept upon, would fall to the present Sudeleigh heir, the son of his father's youngest brother. In doing so, his wife and daughters would become financially dependent upon a person who at last count had reached an age all of fourteen years.

It was this thought which kept Alaric awake through many a long night, chasing shadows as he paced along dark corridors when he couldn't sleep. It was this thought which caused him to dread each approaching new year. The older he grew, the further his hopes for his family's future flagged. But if he had a son . . . ah, yes, if he had a son.

Alaric stole a glance at his wife as she sat listening to their daughter Catherine chattering about her latest art lesson. Even though the other girls were all eager for their mother's notice, Margaret gave the child her undivided attention. She'd always had that way about her, he thought as he watched her, that way of listening to someone, making that person believe, truly believe whatever it was they had to say was the most interesting topic of discussion there was. Even something as commonplace as the intricacies of papier-mâché . . . or which particular periwig best complemented his bottle-green waistcoat. It was one of the many things he loved about his duchess.

Alaric had married Margaret Leighton, daughter of the Earl of Fiske, when he was just a young man of one-and-twenty, and she little more than a child of thirteen fresh out of the nursery. It was a match that had been long in agreement between their two families, but as a gentleman of the world, Alaric had been less than pleased at the prospect of taking on a child bride. He'd only just left university. He hadn't yet visited a brothel or fought in a duel. So Alaric had departed for his gentleman's tour of the Continent scarcely before the ink had dried on the parish register. He returned some five years later to find himself in possession of a wife who was suddenly a woman grown, and the toast of London as well, a lady who made his breath catch in his throat the moment he first beheld her.

He would never forget that night more than twenty

years before when, having just returned to London from the Continent, he had been to the opera with friends and had spotted her sitting in a nearby box, looking as delicate as a pearl.

"Who is she?" he'd asked aloud to whomever happened to be closest by. "Surely she must be someone's wife."

His companions had confirmed. "Yes, she is indeed a wedded woman."

"To whom?" he'd asked.

"To you, for she is none other than the Duchess of Sudeleigh . . ."

Alaric had scarcely been able to believe that the young miss he'd left five years earlier had blossomed into the elegant beauty who sat so poised, so lovely in that theatre box. He'd wasted no time, no time at all, in assuming his role as her husband and consummating their marriage posthaste.

Not very long afterward, the duke and his lovely duchess had begun filling the Sudeleigh nursery with wailing little bundles of newborns—one after another a daughter. With each successive birth, Alaric had noticed Margaret looking on him with increasing anxiety in her eyes, as if some small part of her actually feared he'd follow in the footsteps of his formidable ancestor Henry and send her to the chopping block.

"'Tis a wife's duty, after all," she would say, "to deliver her husband a son."

But Alaric could never fault her for fate's folly. They had, after all, been given the gift of five beautiful, healthy, and intelligent daughters. And just who, he thought hopefully, who had proclaimed their family yet complete? At four-and-forty, Margaret was yet of an age to bear another child successfully. He himself had only recently passed his fiftieth year, well capable of siring again . . . and again if need be. True, it had been five years since they had lost their last, and too early to tell what it might have been. But perhaps they might have time yet, even if only to give it one last try.

And *oh,* the sport they'd have of it trying.

The duke was so caught up by these sprightly thoughts he failed to take notice of the hazel-eyed stare of the young woman sitting at the left end of the table from him. It was a stare that a more observant man might have termed *dangerous.*

Elizabeth Regina Gloriana Drayton was the eldest of the duke's daughters, and by far the most like him. Head-strong and assertive from the very day she'd been born, she had been christened after King Henry's daughter Elizabeth, the Virgin Queen of England. With her straight auburn-blond hair and milk-pale skin, it was a name this daughter seemed fated to bear. Taller than most other women, Elizabeth had grown into the very image of her royal namesake, with a striking manner of carrying herself that drew stares whenever she walked with her distinctive brisk pace through a room. Educated far above her gender, Elizabeth—or Bess, as her father liked to call her—could converse in a mixture of languages, was fond of dancing and the theatre, and was as proficient with the needle and thread as she was at the pianoforte. She rode a steady sidesaddle with the reckless-ness and spirit of a man, and could debate any topic with a conviction worthy of the House of Lords. And it was her father's high dudgeon over the pamphlet that morning which had brought that particular characteristic astir. She waited, however, until she was certain the duke was deep into his morning newspaper before she chose to speak.

"Papa?"

"Hmm?" the duke responded without moving from behind his newssheet.

Elizabeth pushed away her plate and threaded her slender fingers together on the table before her. "I was just thinking about what you said earlier, of that pamphlet you read."

"Yes?"

She glanced once at Isabella, the sister closest to her in age, who gave her a small dissuasive shake of her head.

Elizabeth, however, pressed on.

"I believe you stated that the pamphlet was 'foolishness' and 'a waste of the paper on which it was printed . . .'" She paused, staring at the wall of his newspaper. "I wondered, though, mustn't there be some interest in such writings if the publishers of these pamphlets are printing them?"

The room went silent. Conversation ceased as all eyes turned to gape at Elizabeth. A moment passed. Then two. Everyone, including the footmen, and even her mother's pet pug, Ming, braced themselves for the outburst that was sure to follow.

But the duke simply lowered his newspaper, peering at his eldest daughter over its top. "What did you say?"

Elizabeth sat up straighter in her chair, squaring her shoulders. "I simply wondered why anyone would go to the expense and trouble of publishing works such as the one you mentioned if they truly were unworthy of print."

The duke's eyes, the same hazel color as hers, narrowed.

"After all," she quickly added, "I am merely a woman and so do not have your grasp of such matters."

Her sarcasm, disguised in humility, went lost on the duke. He lightened. He even smiled. One could almost hear the others in the room breathing a collective sigh of relief.

"Ah, my pet, you are too young, too innocent to grasp the true concept of scandal and controversy. You must therefore allow me to enlighten you."

Elizabeth nodded.

"It is an unfortunate reality that two things—scandal and controversy—alone sell more newspapers and books than the greatest examples of literature and learning combined. The more shocking the subject matter, the more copies, I am afraid, go into circulation. It doesn't so much matter if any of it is true. What it comes down to is that so long as the public continues to devour this rubbish, the publishers will continue to print it and fill their coffers to overflowing from it."

"I see."

Elizabeth waited several moments before she quietly added, "But did *you* not buy one of these pamphlets yourself, sir?"

The duke turned to his wife. "What is it you are teaching these girls, Margaret?"

"The child makes a valid point, Alaric."

"Valid?" The duke exhaled, looking again to his eldest daughter. "Yes, my dear child, I did purchase the

pamphlet," he paused, searching for a suitable explanation, "but only so that I might educate you and your sisters on what is proper and improper reading material." He plucked a book of poetry from Matilda who was reading over her bowl of breakfast porridge beside him. Mattie shrieked at the unexpected assault while the duke waved her book through the air like a war banner.

"This," the duke said, his voice gaining as he swept the book outward for all to see, "this is proper reading material for genteel young ladies. Pretty words to create pretty thoughts. *This,*" he went on, taking up the objectionable pamphlet, "is improper reading material, filled with nonsensical words that breed nothing but nonsensical thoughts." He walked to the hearth and flung the booklet into the embers, then turned to frown at his children behind him. "You would do well to remember that. All of you."

The dutiful chorus sang out again, "Yes, Papa."

At the opposite end of the table, however, Elizabeth was staring at her father in stony silence. She watched him return to his chair and retreat behind his newspaper once again, effectively putting an end to any further commentary. She wanted desperately to counter, but as her mother had always told her, "a wise woman must choose the most opportune time and place for such debate." The Drayton breakfast table when her father was in a foul mood to begin with was not the most propitious choice. So Elizabeth held her tongue and waited the handful of minutes until the clock in the hall outside the parlor struck nine, echoing in the lingering silence of the breakfast room.

"May I be excused from the table, please, Father?" she asked, setting her napkin onto the table before her.

The duke looked at her. "What are your plans for the day, daughter?"

Elizabeth did not hesitate in her response. "I thought to give some time this morning to my sampler work and letter writing before Mother and I are to go off to the modiste in Corbridge for a fitting."

The duke beamed his approval. "Splendid. You've been working very hard on that sampler, Bess. It must be quite good. Will we ever see it?"

Elizabeth eyed Isabella a second time, exchanging another private glance. "When it is finished, Papa. Not a moment before."

The duke grinned at his wife. "Our Bess is quite the perfectionist, Margaret. Just like her papa." He waved a hand. "Off with you then, child. Make good use of the morning's light."

Elizabeth pushed back from the table. "Thank you, sir. I intend to."

Moments later, Elizabeth was twisting the key in the lock on her bedchamber door to ensure that she wouldn't be disturbed. She turned to face the room. Mullioned windows were opened onto the bright morning sunlight, spilling past the pale damask draperies to glow like amber in the freshly polished wall paneling. A wardrobe, carved in elegant rosewood, stood in the far corner, filled with countless gowns of satin and silk. Her dressing table was lined with bottles of scent that had come from as far away as the Orient. A Savonnerie carpet stretched across the floor and hangings of elegant brocade draped her poster bed, a bed whose mattress was stuffed with the finest goose down in all England. She had but to pull a bell and an army of servants would come running;

she'd been born to a life of privilege, yes, but that privilege came at a cost.

Elizabeth crossed the room to where a small willow basket lay tucked upon a cushioned window seat. She removed from it the scrap of linen she had stretched across a wooden tambour frame, plucking the needle from where it was stuck at the fabric's edge. She studied the canvas thoughtfully before poking the needle through, drawing the colored thread its length and repeating it for a single perfect stitch. There, she thought as she held the piece out and admired the result in the light. After all, she had told her father she intended to work at her sampler. . . .

Elizabeth left the window and her needlework, and lowered herself into the chair behind her writing desk. She sat for several moments, her chin at rest in the palm of her hand, staring out onto the ornamental knot garden that stretched to the apple orchard below her windows.

Even at this early hour, it had all the makings of a perfect summer day. The duchess's roses were in bloom, spicing the air on the breeze gently rustling through the treetops. A chorus of birdsong trilled in perfect accompaniment as Caroline began her practice at the spinet in the drawing room below. Horses, their dark coats gleaming in the sunlight, grazed peacefully on lush green pastures in the distance. Elizabeth, however, scarcely noticed it at all. The serenity, the music, the beauty of the day, none of it reached her. It was her father's indignant words at the breakfast table that morning that echoed through her head instead.

Preposterous . . .

Idiocy . . .

Equality! A woman to a man? Have you ever heard of such nonsense?

Much as she loved her father, admired and respected his goodness and genuine love for his wife and daughters, there were times when he could be simply antediluvian. It was as if he'd woken that morning several centuries too late for breakfast. Why? she thought for what wasn't the first, second, or even the twentieth time, why had he afforded her and her sisters all the benefits of the best education their station in life offered, only to refuse to allow them to use it? Was it merely to have something to boast of with his cronies over brandy, like the agility of his hunter or the cleverness of his favorite retriever?

Yet even as she wondered this, Elizabeth already knew the answer. While her ability to translate texts into various languages or calculate a ledger column effortlessly in her head might be *novel* and *unique,* the world in which she lived was still primarily governed by men—

—and they liked it that way.

But that didn't mean she had to like it, too.

Fitting the small silver key she kept hidden on a chain around her neck into the side lock on her desk, Elizabeth sprang a false bottom concealed beneath the center desk drawer. She removed a small sheaf of foolscap tucked away inside, skimming through several sheets until she came upon the one she sought, reading its title to herself in the muted sunlight.

A Letter in Favor of Woman's Equality to Man . . . by a Lady of Quality.

Elizabeth smiled. It had been one of her better efforts.

She had suspected it from the moment she had submitted it to London for print. Her father's reaction that morning, and the fuss it was apparently creating in town, only confirmed it.

Setting the papers aside, Elizabeth took up a copy of *The Female Spectator* from inside the desk drawer. Unlike the one that had been tossed into the fire in the breakfast parlor that morning, this one was dated nearly two years earlier and had been read and reread so many times that its edges had grown worn and ragged. It had been a happy summer morning, quite like the present one, when Elizabeth had chanced upon the publication sitting at the circulating library in Corbridge. The title had caught her attention, but its candid subject matter soon had her enthralled.

The objection that I have heard made by some men that learning would make us too assuming, is weak and unjust in itself, because there is nothing would so much cure us of those vanities we are accused of, as knowledge. . . .

At long last, she'd thought, a journal written by women who weren't afraid to speak the beliefs that so many had kept suppressed for generations. Elizabeth had purchased a copy of the pamphlet and had read it from cover to cover, sitting down later to write a letter of commendation to its editor, Miss Eliza Heywood, a novelist and playwright of some repute, sadly famous more for having deserted an abusive husband than for her talent with the written word.

What followed was a correspondence that developed into a friendship between two like-minded women who had come from utterly different walks of life. Finally Elizabeth knew a kinship, a confirmation of the thoughts and opinions she had grown to have during her upbringing. And then one day had come the invitation for Elizabeth to contribute her own writing to the publication, anonymously, of course, since a scandal unlike any other would surely have ensued if it were ever discovered that the daughter of one of England's most respected dukes had authored such ideals.

In the beginning, Elizabeth had only intended to write one commentary, a simple examination of the disservice being done in keeping women from pursuing the same fields of study as men. Why? she had wondered through her pen, was it generally believed that a woman's intellect was better served by the choosing of hair ribands or the placement of a stitch upon a needlework sampler than in the study of philosophy or history? That one discourse had continued into two, and then, before she knew it, more, until Elizabeth was writing an ongoing dialogue, a "Letter From A Lady of Quality" for each successive publication.

And so Elizabeth drew a fresh sheet of foolscap from her desk and prepared to compose her next letter for publication, thinking for a moment before dipping her quill into the inkwell as she replayed the scene from the breakfast parlor that morning in her head.

What are your plans for the day, daughter?

Elizabeth began to write in her careful, elegant hand:

A Letter From A Lady Of Quality Opposed To The Keeping Of Young Women At Their Needles . . .

Chapter Two

One month later . . .

A murky mist hovered about the crumbling remains of Hadrian's Wall as the Sudeleigh traveling coach rolled sluggishly along the rugged Northumbrian road. Overcast skies blocked out any trace of sunlight overhead and the wind didn't so much as stir the tall moor grass, making it appear as if they were swimming in the breath of the slumbering dragon long fabled to have been hiding in the surrounding desolate, heather-clad hills.

Inside the coach were Elizabeth and Isabella; guarding the outside were two of the duke's most trusted men-at-arms—bulky expanses of muscle and brawn named Titus and Manfred. Of course, there was the coachman, Higgins, as well, but he didn't pose any real threat, being barely five feet tall and weighing all of ten stone with his boots on. They'd taken to the road late that morning, stopping once to rest the horses while they enjoyed a picnic lunch of bread, ham, cheese, and tart apples from the

Drayton orchard that the duchess had sent along. Now almost dusk, they were nearing England's northern border, where they would spend the night at a roadside inn. If all went as planned, by this same hour on the morrow, they would have reached their destination, the home of their widowed aunt, Idonia.

And then Elizabeth's punishment would officially begin.

"I cannot believe this is happening," she muttered. She had leaned her head against the coolness of the window pane and her breath fogged the glass when she spoke.

"You must have known Father would discover the truth about those letters eventually, Bess," Isabella said from the opposite seat. "It was only a matter of time."

They were nearly the same words her father had spoken several days earlier when he'd summoned Elizabeth to his study unexpectedly.

"Deceived! Ridiculed! And by my own daughter!"

The clamor of his anger alone had set the bottles in the inkwell upon his desktop to rattling. "You've done some outlandish things in the past, Elizabeth Regina, but this? How could you have done *this?* And even worse, how could you think I'd not have found out?"

Deep down inside, as she'd sat there facing her father more angry than she'd ever seen him before, Elizabeth had to admit there had been a small part of her that had wanted to be found out.

While she might, on occasion, spark a bit of conversational debate around the breakfast table, in the letters she'd written for *The Female Spectator,* she had expressed ideals even she had not dared to speak out loud.

She told herself she had been speaking for every woman who had ever lived a life of quiet acceptance, for every young girl whose spirit had been stifled beneath the cloak of ignorance. She'd wanted so badly to make a difference, yet now, reflecting back, it wasn't any of those things that lingered with her. Elizabeth could only see the look that had been in her mother's eyes as the duchess sat quietly in the corner chair while the duke had raged that morning. It was a look that seemed to say, "You cannot change the world, my daughter. And you should have known better than to try."

The duke had railed at Elizabeth for nearly an hour that morning, cataloguing every one of her shortcomings before he'd finally dropped into his chair, facing her with a furious scowl.

"Now I just have to decide what to do with you," he'd said with a shake of his periwigged head. "A shame you're too old to send off to a convent."

At that, the duchess had interjected. "Alaric, really!"

"Well, she is, Margaret. I should have done that eight years ago when she first pulled that exploit at Kensington, disgracing us in front of the queen as she did. I should have known then that it would come to something like this one day."

The duke sighed, twisting the errant end of his snowy white cravat as he pondered his predicament. Finally, he'd said, "Well, it may be too late now to change the mistakes of the past, but I can do the next best thing." Then he'd looked at Elizabeth. "I've made up my mind. You're going to Idonia's."

Aunt Idonia, whose idea of occupying herself was to rearrange her stockings in order of color, starting with white and working her way through the entire color spectrum to black.

Elizabeth had blanched at the suggestion. "Father, please . . ."

But the duke had simply shaken his head. "Do not even attempt to convince me otherwise. My mind is made up. I can only hope that a few weeks—or months if that is what it takes—in the north will help you see the folly of your actions."

Elizabeth had opened her mouth to protest, but the duke had held up a silencing hand. "I am doing this for your own good, Bess. At the very least let us hope this visit will expel these rebellious thoughts from your head once and for all. But don't fret overmuch. I'm not such a total beast as to send you off to my sister without reinforcements. Misery loves company, or so they say. I'll allow Isabella to go along with you. If you can convince her to do it, that is."

Elizabeth shifted her gaze from the coach window to where her sister sat across from her, head bent gracefully over a book of Shakespearean sonnets.

At times, it was a wonder that they could be sisters at all. All one had to do was look at her to see that Isabella Anne Eleanor Drayton had been born of a different world altogether, one in which faeries frolicked among a sea of bluebells and springtime never ended. Two years younger than Elizabeth, she had hair the color and softness of black silk that fell in loose waves over elegant shoulders. Her skin was pale as the finest ivory, her eyes the deep, deep blue of twilight.

In contrast to Elizabeth's fire and rebellion, Isabella was the image of everything that was soft and at peace with the world. She had the soul of an artist—not just seeing, but breathing in the world around her. When she moved, it was with the elegance of a swan. When she spoke, her voice carried a lilt just like a song. Isabella never challenged authority. She was utterly and maddeningly accepting of the ways of the world. At times, Elizabeth envied that quality in her almost as much as she found fault with it. Yet despite their differences, from the day she had been born, Isabella had been Elizabeth's closest confidante; she had in fact known about her sister's writing from the beginning, had even warned her against it while keeping her secret faithfully.

"He'll soon calm down," Elizabeth said not a little hopefully. "Father has been upset with me before and he always forgives me. Remember my season in London, when I wore breeches to the queen's masquerade ball? Father's anger that night was more fierce than a storm. It blew and it raged and it thundered, but it just as quickly passed, too."

Isabella looked up from her sonnets in disbelief. "How can you honestly say that, Bess, when it was nearly eight years ago, and he hasn't allowed you to return to London since?"

Elizabeth shrugged. "What care I for mincing bucks in powdered wigs and face paint? Father still forgave me that episode just as he'll forgive me this. I'm sure of it. Oh, I'll have to suffer through a fortnight or so at Aunt Idonia's, no doubt ready to yank out every hair on my head by the time we're through, but afterward, I shall be allowed to return home dutifully sorry. I'll even finish that damnable sampler, if that is what it takes. But in the end, all will be well, Bella. You will see."

Having convinced herself of it, Elizabeth turned her attention back to the scene outside the window, glancing at the fast-darkening sky. *Hmm,* she thought, *I wonder if it will rain.*

"I'm afraid it isn't as simple as that this time, Bess."

Elizabeth looked to her sister. Isabella's expression had turned suddenly grim.

"There is something you should know."

"What? What is it? Is something wrong, Bella? Are you unwell?"

"No, nothing like that . . ." Isabella looked at her, her eyes threatening tears, struggling, Elizabeth could see, as if uncertain of what to say. Finally, she burst out, "Oh, Bess, we are not going to visit Aunt Idonia, not at all. That was only a ruse to get you to agree to leave Drayton Hall willingly. Papa knew if you were aware of where we were going—where we are really going, I mean—you'd never agree to it and they'd have to carry you kicking and screaming out of the house."

Elizabeth suddenly remembered her father's comment about the convent. Surely he wasn't serious.

"Isabella . . . if we aren't going to Aunt Idonia's, then where exactly are we going?"

Isabella blinked.

"Bella, you must tell me."

"Oh, Bess, we are on our way to the estate of one of father's associates, a Lord Purfoyle, in Scotland."

Scotland?

Elizabeth was stunned. "Why on earth would Papa send us to Scotland? And why to Lord Purfoyle? We've scarcely acquainted with the man—I believe we met just once when he came to tea. I didn't even know he had a daughter our age. . . ."

"He hasn't. I mean, I guess he could have a daughter, but that's not why Father is sending us—is sending *you* to Lord Purfoyle's estate." Isabella hesitated. "Oh, how in heaven am I supposed to explain this? It is so atrocious. I'll simply have to just say it. Bess, Father means for you to wed Lord Purfoyle."

"Wed him?" Elizabeth felt all the color drain from her face. "But the man is as old as . . . as our father!"

"He's not quite so old as that, but Papa knew it would be your reaction, which is why he misled you into thinking we were going to Aunt Idonia's. Father holds Lord Purfoyle in great esteem and he reasons that a man of his maturity—"

"You mean a man of his *age,* Bella."

"A man of his experience," she went on, "will be a better husband to you than a younger man. Father will not be around forever. Think of it. He has already lost a number of his closest associates to death. He worries about your future, about all of our futures should something happen to him. The title, the estates, we will lose everything."

Isabella's words took Elizabeth aback. Her father had always been so vital, so timeless in her eyes. Her hero. Her protector. She had never once thought of him in such a way.

"Oh, Bess, I'm so sorry. But Papa said if I told you of this before we were out of England, he would make *me* wed Lord Purfoyle in your stead!"

Elizabeth's heart knotted inside her chest. She felt as if she'd just been betrayed in the worst of all ways, and by her own father, a man who, despite their differences of opinion on some matters, she had still always respected and adored. And Bella, too . . . what of her? She had known all along and yet had said nothing.

"How could you have kept this from me, Bell? Even with Father's threats, why did you not tell me before now?"

Before Isabella could answer, there came a sudden deafening crack from outside the coach. Isabella gasped. The carriage lurched forward, then tilted perilously sideways, sending Elizabeth tumbling headfirst from her seat amid a jumble of silk petticoats and lace ruffles. She bumped her head against something hard, then struggled to right herself. A moment later, the coach ground to a sudden, bone-jarring halt.

And then, silence.

Pulling herself upright, Elizabeth reached for the limp bundle that was her sister, her breath catching in her throat. "Bella? Are you hurt?"

"No," came a muffled reply from beneath a cloud of petticoats. "Just a bit disconcerted is all. Whatever happened?"

"I don't know." Elizabeth called out to the coachman as she pushed back the lopsided brim of her straw bergère. "Higgins, are you there? Why have we run off the road?"

"'Twere a sheep standin' in the middle of the road, my lady. I had to turn us off the road to keep from hitting him, but it looks like we've gotten stuck now. Might've broken a wheel, too."

"Oh, goodness!" said Isabella, lifting her head to peer out the window. "You didn't hit him, did you, Higgins?"

"Who?"

"The sheep, poor thing . . ."

"Bother the sheep, Isabella! We could have all been killed!"

"But he does not realize that, Elizabeth. . . ."

"Oh, he's a'right, Lady Isabella. Still standing in the very same spot."

Elizabeth glanced out the window to where, indeed, a shag-haired sheep stood watching them from the middle of the roadway. When he saw her glaring at him, he bleated.

Entertaining thoughts of mutton stew and leg of lamb, Elizabeth reached for the latch on the door. Outside, the back wheels of the carriage were hopelessly mired in what appeared to be a substantial stretch of bog. Higgins was on the ground, standing a space away and scratching his balding head beneath his hat.

"Do you think you can repair it?" she asked him.

"Aye, if I can get to it to fix it, that is. It looks mightily stuck."

The duke's two men-at-arms, Manfred and Titus, circled around from the other side of the lopsided coach. "We best get you ladies out of there and see what we can do to push the coach free."

But when Manfred took the first step toward the coach, he immediately plunged ankle deep in the mire. He moved to pull his foot free, slipping clean out of his boot instead, his toes wiggling through the hole in his stocking.

"Gaw, it's like molasses, it is," he said struggling to get his foot back inside his boot. He twisted his bulk, stretching back awkwardly, lost his balance and fell face first with a howl, flailing as he went over like a tree. When he gained his feet several moments later, the front of him—his hands, his face, his paunchy girth—was hopelessly covered with mud.

Titus was laughing behind him. "Didn't you know ye're supposed to take your coat *off* before you lay it down for the ladies to walk upon?"

Manfred delivered his comrade a lethal glare as he removed his handkerchief from his pocket and wiped at the mud dripping off his face. "I think I'll be steadier if I were t' carry you on me back, my lady, 'stead of in me arms. D'you think you can wrap your arms 'round me neck?"

"I believe so, yes."

Elizabeth reached for the doorway of the coach and pulled herself to stand at the edge, reaching out for where the man had doubled over and was waiting.

It was just as she was bent over Manfred's back, her feet dangling behind her in a most indelicate piggyback pose, that she heard an unexpected and unfamiliar voice coming from behind them.

"*Och,* but you English lassies do have a peculiar way of showing a fancy for the lads, you do."

Manfred turned about—with Elizabeth still draped over his shoulders—to see a stranger who had come unnoticed upon the scene.

He was dressed in Highland fashion, in a belted plaid that left his legs exposed beneath a loose flowing cambric shirt that he hadn't bothered to tie at the neck. His hair was as dark as soot and hung below his neck, tied in a queue beneath a Scottish blue bonnet decorated with a sprig of heather. He carried a broadsword at his side and a peculiar studded shield strapped to his back. It made him look downright primordial. His cocksure grin, however, and his obvious amusement at their situation touched a raw nerve with Elizabeth.

"I suppose you have a better idea?" she said, mustering as much dignity as she could while trying not to think of how ridiculous she must look hanging as she was over Manfred's backside.

"Aye, I do." He glanced at Manfred then, ignoring her altogether. "Put the lass back in the coach, man. You can wash yourself off in yon burn."

As Manfred helped Elizabeth back to the coach, the Scotsman kneeled, untying the leather laces on his peculiar-looking shoes. He removed them along with his tartan hose, then, without another word, proceeded to walk into the mire, sloshing and oozing his way to the coach in his bare feet. In one sudden motion, he swept Elizabeth from the step and into his arms, cradling her effortlessly before him. His eyes, a deep, dark blue, laughed at her above a cocked grin.

"In need of a lift, lass?"

Elizabeth frowned. "In England, sir, it is customary for a gentleman to ask a lady's permission before laying hands upon her person."

"*Och*, but you're no' in England any more, lassie. And I'm *sair*tainly no gentleman. This is the land o' the Scotsman, and there isna a thing genteel about a Scot."

"Truer words were never said," she remarked to the mud creeping up his hairy legs.

The man continued to stare at her. It was disconcerting, those blue eyes looking at her as if he could see straight to the deepest reaches of her mind. His mouth had settled into a straight line, but somehow she believed he was mocking her.

"I'll no' have it said a Scot, any Scot, ever took a lass who wasna willing." He grinned again. "Even if it is out of a bog. You want me to put you down then?"

Elizabeth glanced down to the sludge that surrounded them, from which a sour smell had begun to rise in the summer heat. "No, please, do not."

"I didna think so."

The man turned and trudged through the bog to drier land, more dropping her than setting her down before him. He didn't immediately move away, and stood so close she could see the flecks of gray that made his eyes so darkly blue. They were peculiar, those eyes, somehow making it impossible for her to tear her gaze away.

He said, "I'll just fetch the other lassie now."

Only when he turned to retrieve Isabella did Elizabeth realize her heart was pounding. Putting it off as the result of the mishap in the coach, she took a deep breath and focused on the arrangement of her skirts while he carried her sister from the coach, setting her right beside Elizabeth.

"Have you ever seen such a man?" Isabella whispered as the stranger set about helping Manfred and Titus to push the coach free of the bog. "He carried me as if I weighed no more than a feather."

Elizabeth crossed her arms, rubbing them as if taken by a chill. *But was it a chill—or was it him?*

"He is far too forward."

"He was just trying to be helpful."

"More likely he was just trying to sneak a hand

against your bodice, Bella. If Father were here, he would have—"

An idea struck Elizabeth—*boom!*—like a lightning bolt, an idea of such ingenuity, such cleverness, she could scarcely believe how brilliant she was.

Three quarters of an hour later, when the carriage was free and the wheel had been repaired, Elizabeth walked over to the stranger, a much different Elizabeth than the one she'd been before.

"I wish to thank you, sir, for your kind assistance." She offered him her gloved hand. "I shudder to think what we might have done had you not happened by when you did."

The Highlander looked at her curiously, as if seeing her for the first time.

"Pleased to have been of help, my lady."

He didn't move to take her hand. Instead he turned, taking up his shoes and hose as he readied to leave.

Leave? But he couldn't leave. Just yet.

Elizabeth followed him. "I, uh, neglected to ask your name. I should like to know to whom we owe our debt of gratitude."

The man looked at her but didn't stop walking. "Douglas Dubh MacKinnon fro' the Isle of Skye."

Douglas Dubh? What in the world sort of name was that?

He stopped for a moment at the burn to wash the bog mud from his feet and legs. As he bent to cup the water in his large hands, running his fingers down the length of his calves, Elizabeth found herself staring at the way the muscles in his legs pulled and flexed beneath the hem of his plaid. There was power in those legs. *Male* power.

The popinjays in London could pad their stockings with cork in earnest and never achieve legs that looked like *that*.

When she looked up again, Elizabeth realized the Highlander was staring at her—as she was staring at him.

Her cheeks went awash. My God, she thought, I am actually blushing.

"I am La—" she corrected herself, "I am Elizabeth Drayton. The other lady with me is my sister, Isabella Drayton. We are traveling to the home of our aunt in the north and were waylaid by that sheep over th—"

Elizabeth pointed to the road, but the damnable beast had vanished.

"In any case, we are indebted to you for your kindness, Mr. MacKinnon."

Elizabeth held out her hand to him. The Highlander glanced at her a moment, then bowed, ignoring her outstretched hand once again. "A pleasure, my lady."

He turned then and started to walk away. "Good day to you and your sister. Godspeed on your journey."

He hadn't made it more than a couple of yards before Elizabeth called to him. "Mr. MacKinnon, aren't you going to put your hose and shoes back on?"

He didn't stop. "Aye, after my feet have dried."

"But, uh, may I ask where you are headed?"

"I'm to an inn not far from here called The Reiver's Rest."

She followed him. "The Reiver's Rest, you say? Why, we are going to the very same inn."

It was an excellent lie, clearly delivered and brilliant.

Although from the way he was looking at her, she wondered if somehow he knew that it was . . . a lie, that is.

"It looks as if it might rain," she said quickly. "In fact, I'm quite certain I just felt a drop hit my nose." She turned her face to the clouds, then nodded. "Yes, indeed, there is another. Please, sir, allow us to offer you a ride to the inn. It is the least we can do in exchange for your kindness."

The Highlander eyed the clouds, hesitating as if considering her offer. "That really isna necessary, my lady."

"But I must insist." Elizabeth rewarded him with her sweetest smile, the one that never failed to get her what she wanted.

And it didn't fail this time, either.

"If you're certain . . ."

"Absolutely, and do sit inside with Isabella and me so we can chat along the way. This is my first time to Scotland, and I would love to hear simply everything about it."

Elizabeth waited.

Finally the Highlander nodded once and turned for the coach.

As MacKinnon ducked his head and slid onto the opposite seat, Isabella grabbed the lace cuff of Elizabeth's sleeve and gave it a warning tug. She whispered, "What in the name of all that is sacred are you doing?"

Elizabeth cast her sister a sidelong glance. "Nothing yet. But if I have my wish, this Highlander might just prove himself very useful in the next several hours."

Chapter Three

Douglas warily eyed the two beauties across from him inside the coach, wondering not for the first time what had possessed him to accept the invitation to join them.

Had he run completely daft? Little more than an hour before, he had been free and alone, quietly making his way home and thinking of little more than the haggis and warm bannocks Eithne was sure to have made ready for his return. He'd spotted the stranded carriage sitting atilt off the road. He'd stopped to offer his help. And now, somehow, suddenly, he found himself in a closed carriage with two unwedded young ladies, one with hair the color of midnight, who hadn't spoken above two words since his arrival—and the other, the fire-headed one, who had yet to shut up.

Even a blind man could see the situation spelled trouble.

Sisters, he recalled the one saying, yet with just his first look at them, he could see they were as different as was the night from the day. The dark one was timid, properly reserved, unwilling even to meet his eye as she glanced quickly out the window when the carriage started forward with a lurch. The other one, however, neither shrank nor flinched from his look, nor did she so much as take a breath while talking. As she babbled on and on, she looked at him boldly through eyes that were hazel in color, touched curiously with gray. She snooped, she pried, asking inquisitive questions, all while taking in every inch of him just as keenly as he was taking in every inch of her.

And then, perhaps in an afterthought of maidenly modesty, she finally glanced away, making at arranging her already tidy skirts more neatly about her. Douglas took the opportunity to study her more closely.

She was a beauty, no question about that. In fact the first thing he noticed—the first thing anyone would notice about her—was the stunning red-gold of her hair. It fairly gleamed and she wore it dressed simply, pulled back from her face to fall freely down her back, tucked beneath the brim of her straw hat. Douglas found himself wondering how it would shine in the sunlight, that hair, if it would feel like burnished silk against his touch. Thankfully she hadn't powdered it as was the current fashion in the south. That, Douglas thought, would have been a crime.

Given the fineness of her gown, a dark wine-red silk, she no doubt came from a background of affluence. The dress itself was cut low and fitted tightly to her narrow waist over full skirts and striped quilted petticoats. She wore a sheer white fichu tucked about her neck and shoulders, but it did little to hide the fullness of the breasts underneath, breasts that were very nice, indeed.

She was merely a lass, he told himself, a lovely one, aye, and he'd not seen one like her in too long a time. Perhaps never. Still, she was trouble. She was English and she was refined. And she was an innocent, of that he was certain, for she could have no earthly idea of the thoughts she was tempting with just the tilt of her head. That only meant Douglas needed to get as far from her as he possibly could. And he would, as soon as they stopped at the inn. Once he was away from the carriage, he reasoned, away from her, he'd not give her a second thought.

Then she moved, just slightly, leaning toward him, and her scent, mysterious and herbal, nearly sent him to his knees. In that moment, Douglas knew this was no *mere* lass at all.

"So, Mr. MacKinnon," she said with a flash of white smile. "What can you tell us about yourself?"

Douglas shrugged. "Naught to tell," he replied, focusing on the passing landscape out the window, determined to be as tight-lipped as possible. "I'm but a simple Scotsman on his way home."

"On Skye, I believe you said earlier."

"Aye, my lady."

He didn't say more.

"What is it that brings you here, so far from home, then, sir?" Her eyes sparked. "Some sort of clandestine intrigue, perhaps?"

Douglas looked at her, his eyes searching hers across the shadows of the coach. For a single moment he wondered if their meeting on that lone country road could have been more than pure coincidence. No, that wasn't possible. He'd only just left London a week before and had told no one else his route. He was simply letting his uneasiness get to him. This slip of a lass could have no idea of what he'd been about in London.

"Och, no, milady," he said, thickening his brogue. "Just a simple drover, I am. Gone to have a look at the cattle market in the south."

Douglas would have thought his response would put her off. What possible interest could a lady of fashion and refinement like her have in a common Scottish cattle drover? Curiously, however, she pressed on.

"A drover, you say? Like the outlaw Rob Roy? How fascinating. You must have some exciting tales to tell . . ."

She really was quite good, he had to admit. She kept up the conversation for the better part of the next hour, making it seem as if cattle drover was no less remarkable an occupation than circumnavigator. By the time they pulled into the courtyard of The Reiver's Rest, night had fallen and she had practiced nearly every feminine wile Douglas had ever heard of, and even some he hadn't. Despite his best efforts to both bore and ignore her, she'd worked, and then worked more in attempt to charm him.

Which left him with one very disquieting thought:

Why?

Why would this well-to-do, not to mention lovely English lass work so very hard and so very long simply to catch the eye of a poor Scottish farmer? She certainly must have her pick of any number of fine English lads more suitable to her background. Why then did she seem so interested in him?

Whatever her reasons, they couldn't be good. So when they finally stopped before the door of the inn, Douglas couldn't get out of the carriage fast enough.

He bowed his head to the two ladies after helping them down from the carriage. "My ladies, it has been a pleasure."

He turned then, ready to depart, but that voice, that same sweet voice that had just filled the past hour called, "Mr. MacKinnon, I—*we* would be most remiss if we didn't at least offer you a meal for your trouble."

"Oh, that isna necessary, my lady," he said. "I will—"

"Nonsense. You must be starving." She linked an arm through his before he could open his mouth to refuse. "Surely a strong, healthy man like yourself must have quite an appetite, especially after working so hard to help us with our carriage. You simply must allow us to get you some supper." She smiled up at him and blinked beneath the brim of her hat. "I insist upon it."

Douglas decided that the lass must be quite used to insisting upon any number of things. More out of curiosity than anything else, he allowed himself to be led toward the front door of the thatched-roof inn.

Inside, the beamed ceiling was low, so low that it nearly grazed Douglas's head as he ducked through the doorway. A lazy veil of smoke from both the stone hearth in the corner and the clay pipes of the patrons huddled about the tables hovered just above their heads. Every pair of eyes in the place turned upon them when they came in, no doubt wondering what a shabby character like himself could be doing in the company of two finely dressed young ladies. But after a moment or two, the others returned their attentions to their tankards and pipes, and Douglas found an empty table in the far corner.

He seated the ladies, then made for the taproom, where he sought out the proprietor of the place, a man named Turnbull whom Douglas knew well.

"What're you aboot, MacKinnon?" said the older man. He rubbed his beard-grizzled chin slowly as he narrowed his eyes on the two ladies across the room. "Two lasses you 'ave, and my guess is they're Sassenach lasses, too. I'll no' be having any skullduggery 'neath my roof. This is no' a house of ill repute."

Douglas scowled. "Dinna be jumpin' to conclusions, Turnbull. They were stranded. Their carriage had broken a wheel and I helped to set it to rights is all. Now they're just wanting to buy my supper for it. So be a good man and fetch us a few bowls of your wife's mutton stew. I'll eat it quickly and be off to my bed afore you know it."

The innkeeper eyed Douglas skeptically. "Jus' you make certain when you're aff to tha' bed, you're alone in it, MacKinnon. There's Sassenach patrols all aboot these parts since the Jacobites were routed up at Culloden just lookin' for a reason to take another Scot's life. Ye're a good mon, MacKinnon. I'd hate to see you be a *dead* good mon."

Across the room, Isabella eyed the other patrons of the inn with dismay. She'd never seen such a motley assortment of humanity in her life, and she sat at the edge of her chair, feet planted tightly together beneath her, refusing even to remove her cloak.

Elizabeth, however, quickly made herself comfortable, removing her hat, peeling off her gloves, and shrugging away her woolen cloak as she took in every-thing around them like a child on a first visit to the fair.

"Bess, if Father even suspected we were in a place like this, alone with a man we've scarcely met, he would—he would run positively mad!"

Elizabeth arched a brow. "Oh, and how is it any dif-ferent than his having sent me into Scotland with a mind to marry me off to a man I've scarcely met? 'Tis a sim-ple matter of which stranger appeals more, Bella, and for the moment, I'm choosing the Highlander."

Isabella could not honestly disagree. Still she sat for-ward, taking her sister's hand. "I know you're angry, and it is deplorable what Father did. I know in his heart he had his own good intentions, and I know though he might threaten it, he would not ever make you do some-thing you truly didn't wish to do. But really, Bess,"—she glanced about at the dimly lit taproom, at the shadowy figures hunched over their respective tankards of ale—"do you honestly think this is wise?"

Elizabeth was oblivious to her sister's question. The dirt, the stench, the underlying threat of danger fasci-nated her in a way she couldn't even begin to describe. All her life she had been waiting for something like this to happen—some dark, precarious adventure that would take her places she'd never before seen. And now that it had, her heart drummed excitedly in her chest, and her spirits took wing. It was as if she'd been living her life until then inside one of her mother's glass-panelled dis-play cases, where she kept the porcelain figurines she was so fond of collecting. Only this particular little fig-urine had just escaped.

"Bess, are you listening to me?"

But Elizabeth scarcely heard her sister. She was far too mesmerized by the vast amount of bosom being displayed by the serving girl who had just come to greet them. It was a remarkable bosom, really. She simply couldn't grasp how a girl could be trussed up in such a fashion while serving numerous tankards of ale and not fall out of her gown.

"What'll ye like?" the girl asked, tucking her tray against her hip and pushing a straggling wisp of brown hair from her eyes, eyes that drank in every detail of the two ladies' fine gowns.

Elizabeth rubbed her arms. "Have you anything that will warm us? The weather has taken a chill turn tonight. I swear I can feel it all the way to my bones."

The girl smiled, displaying her lack of one front tooth. Rather than make her look unattractive, it gave her an appealingly mischievous quality. "*Och,* but a wee dram o' the *uisge-beatha* will chase away yer chill, my lady."

"*Oosh-ke vah?*" Elizabeth attempted to repeat.

"Aye, 'tis the 'water of life,' it is. Will warm yer belly up right quick."

It certainly wasn't something the ladies in her mother's parlor had ever sampled. "That sounds perfect, I—"

"Effie, I think tea would be more suitable for the lady," MacKinnon interrupted.

"Tea? Why can I not have this *uisge-beatha*?"

He looked at her. "'Tis potent, is all. A man's brew."

A man's brew? Elizabeth turned to the bosomy serving girl. "Miss Effie, have you yourself ever partaken of this *uisge-beatha*?"

"Oh, indeed, my lady. All m' life. In fact my da used

to rub it on my gums when I were a wee bairn cutting teeth. And my grannam is nearly ninety and swears by it to cure her cough. 'Tis nothing like it to chase away whatever it is that ails you."

Elizabeth glanced across the table at Douglas as if to say, *So much for your man's brew* . . .

He simply shrugged. "So then 'tis simply a drink more suited to a Scot than a Sassenach."

That had done it. There was no earthly way she was *not* going to drink the stuff now.

"A dram of this *uisge-beatha*, if you please, Effie." She glanced at the mule-headed MacKinnon and smiled. "In fact, why don't you make that two drams?"

"Oh, no, thank you, Bess," Isabella cut in, "I think I shall prefer the tea instead."

Elizabeth looked at her sister. "I wasn't ordering for you, Bella."

"Oh." And then she repeated a moment later on a nod of realization, "Oooh . . ."

The trio sat in silence around the small table and waited for Effie to return. When she did, it was with three wooden bowls of steaming stew, a pot of tea for Isabella, and two of the tiniest glasses Elizabeth had ever before seen. Effie uncorked a bottle and set it on the table between Douglas and Elizabeth, giving them each a glass.

"Goodness, this will hardly hold more than a splash," Elizabeth said as she watched MacKinnon carefully pour them each their allotted thimbleful of the brownish-looking water. Elizabeth took up her glass and gave it a quick sniff, saying, "You needn't put down that bottle yet, MacKinnon. This will need refilling in but a moment."

And with that, she took up the glass, tipped it to her lips, and swallowed down the whole of it.

A moment later, she thought sure she had just swallowed a poison worthy of Lucretia Borgia or something the head housekeeper at Drayton Hall, Mrs. Burnaby, would only use to clean the worst of the chamber pots. Her eyes watered, her throat burned, and her stomach felt as if it had been shot through with a flaming arrow. And one look across the table at the Scotsman told Elizabeth he knew exactly what she was experiencing. In fact, from that crooked smirk and those laughing blue eyes, she could see he was fully enjoying her efforts to suppress the almost overpowering urge to cough.

In the back of her head, a tiny voice whispered, *Well, after all, he did say it was potent. . . .*

Blackguard.

Elizabeth blinked back her watering eyes, swallowed against the scorching in her throat, put on a pleasant face, and even managed to pull a smile.

The Scotsman only grinned the wider, damn him. "Are you ready for your other dram now, my lady?"

"Oh, indeed, sir." Elizabeth wasn't about to concede to the smug Scotsman.

There came no cataclysm with the second dram. In fact, Elizabeth no longer felt or tasted much of anything at all. Her insides had taken on a comfortable warmth, as if the fire from the hearth had alighted in her belly, so much so that she loosened the fichu from around her neck and tossed it heedlessly upon the table. Her cheeks felt marvelously hot. Her head felt as if it had ascended to the clouds.

It wasn't until after the third dram, however, that the room began to spin.

Some time later, after a sparse few bites of stew and another dram or two of the drink, Isabella's usually soft voice suddenly hissed and echoed to Elizabeth's drumming ears.

"Bess, I think I should like to retire . . . *now.*"

"Be my guest." Elizabeth hiccuped. She blinked, wondering when Isabella had managed to acquire a twin.

"Don't you think you should retire, too, Elizabeth? Remember Lord Purf—" She stopped herself, then said, "We've a long ride north tomorrow, and it would be best to get an early start."

Elizabeth grimaced at the reminder of where her father was sending her. *Lord Purfoyle.* It was like a sudden dousing in ice water, that name. "Pah! All the more reason I shouldn't retire all night. Will you deny me this last little bit of freedom, Bella? After all, it was you who didn't tell me the truth of our little journey to the north until it was too late . . ."

The sisters exchanged a private look and then Elizabeth waved her hand as if shooing away a nonexistent fly. "Go off with you, Isabella Anne Drayton. Mr. MacKinnon and I will finish off our last drams of *uisgebeatha.* Then I promise you I'll hie right off to bed like the dutiful little—"

Thankfully, Douglas saw it coming. He caught her before her head hit the table.

"Oh, my God!" Isabella cried. "Is she d-dead?"

"Nae, lass, but she'll likely wish she was when she awakes on the morrow."

Douglas had no other choice but to pick her up. He couldn't believe what she'd drunk. Stubborn little idiot.

"Why isn't she moving, then?"

"She's sleeping is all, miss. And will likely have no memory of any of this in the morn. Just lead the way, and I'll help you get her to her room so she can sleep the drink off."

Thankfully, their table was near the stairs leading up to the inn's bedchambers. While most everyone else's attention was taken up elsewhere in the taproom, Douglas quickly lugged Elizabeth up the narrow flight of stairs, pitying her the headache she was certain to wake to even as he thought it would serve her right. After all, he had tried to warn her.

She mumbled something when he laid her upon the bed, something that sounded like "smug Scot," then flopped onto her back with her arms flung outward. In moments, she was softly snoring.

"She'll be fine come the morn," Douglas said to a clearly distressed Isabella, who was wringing her hands beside him. "You'd best leave her till then."

The lady nodded. "Thank you, Mr. MacKinnon. It looks as if we owe you another debt of gratitude. It seems you've come to our rescue not once, but twice today."

Douglas smiled at her, genuinely sorry for the distress her sister was causing her, then bowed his head before leaving the room. Rather than retire to his own bed, he decided to return to the taproom first to settle his bill with Turnbull. If there were patrols in the area, as the innkeeper had said, it would be best for him to be off before the dawn.

He met with the innkeeper, then exchanged a quarter hour's conversation with a couple of the other patrons before heading for his room. He was on the second stair when he spotted the small lady's shoe lying abandoned where it must have fallen from her foot when he'd carried her upstairs. The same dark wine color as her gown, the glass beads sewn upon it glimmered in the low light from the fire. It was a pretty thing with a high heel and pointed toes—brazen, just like its mistress.

Douglas stopped outside the closed door to her chamber and knocked softly. There came no answer. He was just about to leave the shoe sitting on the floor outside the door when he heard a muffled voice beckoning from inside.

Quietly, Douglas turned the knob. "Excuse me, Miss Isabella, but I found—"

"Isabella isn't here."

In the light from the sconce in the hallway behind him, Douglas could see Elizabeth sitting on the edge of the bed, clearly fully awake. In fact, her gown was gone, abandoned to a pool of rumpled wine silk on the floor, and her hair was unbound, hanging around her shoulders.

She wore a chemise—and nothing else.

Douglas was stunned, both by the vision of her and by the mere fact that she wasn't still lying unconscious on the bed. He'd seen fully grown men who wouldn't have awakened that quickly after the sousing she'd taken, let alone have the faculties to undress without doing themselves a serious harm.

"I . . . Your shoe must have fallen off on your way up the stairs. I was just returning it."

The lass stared at him in the candlelight. She cocked her head to one side and said, "Indeed? Just like the prince come to find the fair Cinderella?"

She laughed at her jest, a sulky sound. Douglas simply stared at her, trying to ignore the fact that the room had just grown several degrees warmer despite the fact that there was no fire in the hearth to have made it so.

But there was a fire in her eyes as she continued to stare at him, the sort of fire that made his belly instinctively tighten.

He said the only thing that sprang to mind. "In Scotland we call that fairytale *Rashin-Coatie*."

She said nothing, just continued to stare at him.

Douglas took two steps into the room, placing the shoe upon the foot of the bed. "I'll just be on my way then. . . ."

"A moment, if you please, Mr. MacKinnon."

Douglas eyed her, waiting for her to go on.

"I should like to speak with you directly if you don't mind, about a proposition I should like to make to you."

Now what was all this about? "A proposition, my lady?"

"Yes, sir. A business proposition. I should like to employ you, Mr. MacKinnon."

"Employ me?"

"Yes. It would only be for a short while. You see, I should like you to be my betrothed."

Betrothed? Of all the things she could have said to him—hundreds, thousands of things, really—this was the very *last* thing Douglas would have ever guessed.

Surely he had heard her wrong. Surely he was dreaming this whole thing. Surely the whisky was making his head think fantastical thoughts.

"I beg your pardon? Did you just say 'betrothed'?"

"Yes. As I said, it would only be for a short while. You wouldn't, of course, really, truly marry me, but would just *pretend* that we were to wed. I promise you would be handsomely rewarded for your effort."

She was speaking of money, he knew, but somehow Douglas found his gaze straying to where the ribbon drawstring of her chemise trailed downward between the curve of her breasts. He pulled his gaze away.

"You've had too much to drink, lass. You dinna know what you're saying."

"No, sir," she answered quite seriously. "I know precisely what I am proposing to you."

"But you dinna even know me. I am a stranger to you. Why in the name of heaven would you want me to do this?"

Elizabeth simply stared at him and the motivation behind her proposal hit him in the next moment like a ton of stone. His clothing, his speech, his grubby appearance . . . what she saw when she looked at him was an uneducated, impoverished, backward Scottish farmer. In other words, she wanted to buy him, to be her diversion for whatever reason for a time, as easily, as thoughtlessly as she would buy a new pair of stockings. She no doubt expected he should be on his knees thanking the heavens for this inimitable bounty. And when she was through with him, when he no longer held any appeal, like those stockings, she would toss him aside just as easily.

Anger, as fierce and sharp as a broadsword, sliced through him. "I dinna think so."

"*What?* You are refusing me?"

Douglas seriously doubted she had ever been refused anything in her life. Until now. "Yes, I am."

"I am offering to make you a rich man, Mr. MacKinnon. All you have to do is give the pretense of wanting to wed me. It wouldn't even be for all that long. All you need to do is come with me to my home and meet my fa—" she corrected, "meet the rest of my family, announce our betrothal, then you may continue on your way to Skye a much richer man."

So that was it. She wanted him to meet her family. Her father in particular. He recalled the conversation with her sister in the taproom. Something about a Lord Purf-something and their journey north. She must have a wealthy da whom she sought to devastate for wanting her to wed and settle down with a respectable nobleman. So instead she would bring him home the most distasteful example she could find for a husband. A farmer . . . even worse than that, a *Scottish* farmer.

Douglas didn't even know the man, but already he pitied him.

"Surely there must be some nice, young, Sassenach laddie you can find to play your game, lass. I'm not the man for the job. Good luck to you."

Douglas started to leave.

"Mr. MacKinnon, please . . ." Her voice grew softer. "Don't go. Wait a moment. There is something else you can have, too, if you'll agree to my request."

Surely she didn't mean . . .

She left the bed and crossed the room like a brisk

wind, placing herself between him and the door. The light from the hall behind her set her hair aglow, made the sparse bit of chemise she wore seem all the more insignificant. Without the heels of her shoes, she stood only to his chin. It made her seem fragile to him somehow, more vulnerable. That same herbal scent he'd spent an hour swimming in inside the coach drifted across his face, spiced by the slight scent of the whisky she'd drunk. For a moment, neither of them moved, or spoke a word. Her lips had parted. It would be so easy to kiss her, he thought. All he had to do was close his eyes and . . .

And then she shoved her hand forward between them and opened her fist, revealing a rather large jeweled ring.

"This heirloom came to my family a gift from Queen Elizabeth herself. As you can see, it is engraved with her initial, and it opens to reveal a cameo portrait of her father, King Henry, and her mother, Anne Boleyn. It has been in my family for generations and was given to me when I was born. It is the most precious thing in the world to me. As to its monetary worth, it is priceless. And it will be yours. If you will agree to my proposition."

Douglas felt his body tense, growing as rigid as a pikestaff. Struggling to hold his anger in check, he thought of how many times, a lifetime really, he had stood back watching as his family, his clan, and his country yielded to the desires of the English. His father, and his grandfather before him, had lost everything they'd had fighting for the rights of his countrymen. He himself had spent nearly the whole of his life paying court to the English king from Hanover in an effort to secure the lands his family had held since nearly the be-

ginning of time, lands the Crown had confiscated after
the last rebellion in 1719, when his father had come out
to fight for the Old Pretender, James. All his life Douglas
had been fighting, fighting to preserve the ancient pride
and distinction that stretched all the way back to the first
MacKinnon, Fingon, great-grandson of the great Scottish king Kenneth MacAlpine. And now this spoiled
Sassenach lassie stood before him smelling like a summer's breeze and tossing her fiery hair, thinking she
could buy his honor for the price of some family bauble?

"My answer is the same, miss. *No*. Now take yourself
off to bed, afore you get yourself into more trouble than
you can possibly manage."

Douglas watched the expression on her face grow
dim, shadowed, as she realized she could not sway him.
Without a word, she walked around him and returned to
the bed, sliding atop the mattress to retreat beneath the
bedcovers. Douglas turned to leave, wishing he'd never
stopped to help the coach earlier that day. He'd only
thought to offer his assistance, but this was going quite a
step further than he'd ever intended.

He was nearly out the door when her voice, suddenly,
unexpectedly quiet, beckoned him back.

"Please, don't go."

Douglas stopped at the door even as he told himself to
continue through and keep walking until the image of
her eyes, her mouth, the sound of her voice, vanished
from his memory.

Reluctantly, however, he turned. "What is it now,
lass?"

"It is . . . very dark in this room." Her voice had softened to a trembling whisper. "Please stay. For a little while. I . . . don't much like . . . the dark."

"I can fetch Miss Isabella for you, if you—"

"No!" She shook her head. "No, please do not. She would think I am being childish."

The way she spoke, the way she looked at him in that sparse flicker of light coming in from the corridor stirred something deep inside Douglas he'd never felt before. He knew pride when he saw it, and he also knew fear. She didn't want her younger sister to see that she was frightened of the dark. Even admitting it to him was a trial for her. This wasn't a lady who easily admitted to weakness. He had realized this when she'd so recklessly drunk, and continued to drink, the whisky earlier that evening, even though he knew she had probably never before tasted anything stronger than a watered-down claret.

Her eyes pleaded with him in the near darkness not to leave her alone. Though his every sense told him he should go, Douglas found himself turning, crossing the room to sit on the edge of the bed beside her.

"I'm not going anywhere, lass."

He told himself he would stay only until she fell asleep.

What he hadn't counted on was falling asleep himself.

Chapter Four

Douglas awoke on the singular thought that somehow during the night, whilst he'd been asleep, and without him even being aware of it, someone had clubbed him over the head with a cudgel.

Repeatedly.

Any movement, just the effort of opening his eyes to face the light of dawn through the small curtained window set above the bed caused him to suffer a teeth-clenching jolt. It seemed suddenly every noise—the lads working in the stables outside, muffled voices coming from the downstairs taproom, the simple closing of a door down the hall—all of it took on a thunderous magnitude.

Why the devil had he drunk so damned much whisky?

He'd not woken to a morning like this since he'd been a lad of fourteen, the day after he and his younger brother, Iain, had stolen their way into their uncle's underground distillery. They'd been two green boys who'd wanted to play at being men, and Douglas had learned then that while the drink of his ancestors went down quite smoothly, it came up with a violence that could make a grown man—or a fourteen-year-old lad—weep out loud.

He'd spent two days afterward hanging over a chamber pot, and Douglas had sworn never to do such a thing again. From then on, the only whisky he took would be in toasting—at weddings, clan celebrations, the birth of a new bairn. And he had stood by that promise for seventeen years—until a hazel-eyed hoyden had issued him a challenge, a challenge that now left him wondering if his head had somehow gotten itself wedged between two boulders during the course of the night.

Douglas shifted on the mattress, seeking the soft solace of a pillow to place over his thrumming head. He would have groaned if that small effort wouldn't alone have caused him more agony than it was worth. So he burrowed under the bedcovers instead, like a mollusk in the sand. It was then, and only then, that Douglas realized he wasn't in fact alone on the bed.

A curtain of silken hair fell softly against his shoulder, hair that when his vision finally cleared, revealed its color of burnished gold. He knew that hair, knew the lass it belonged to, too. She was the same lass whose slender arm was apparently hooked around his waist—his very naked waist—with her hand splayed very closely to his groin.

Like an early morning mist burning off with the coming of dawn, the memory of the night before slowly came clear. He remembered how he had brought the fallen shoe to her room, how she had begged him not to leave because of the dark. From where he now found himself, he had apparently done just that. He hadn't left, even though he'd intended to the moment she fell asleep. All he could think was that he must have somehow dozed off himself.

It had been the whisky, yes, that was it, and the fatigue of having traversed the north of England on foot throughout most of the previous day. He had been so intent on getting home to Skye, he hadn't realized how very tired he'd obviously been. When she'd called him into the room, he'd been lulled by the darkness, the sound of her voice, the whisper of her soft breath. Any ordinary man would have been unable to resist. But that still left one question remaining:

What the devil had happened to his clothes?

Just the awareness of where he was, how he was dressed (or rather undressed), and with whom, made Douglas's groin grow hard. No hope for it. His belly tightened as he thought of how close her fingers were to him, how soft her skin felt against his, how sweet her hair smelled as it draped against his shoulder. He looked down at her in the pink light of dawn, watching her as she slept. Her brow was furrowed and her mouth frowned as if in dreams she struggled against some foe. Instinctively Douglas reached to gently smooth the troubled crease away.

A part of him wanted nothing more than to just stay there in the warmth of that bed, listening to the soft cadence of her breathing as the dawn sun crept higher in the morning sky. The saner part of him, however, realized the utter danger of his situation. He had to find his clothes and get out of that room as quickly as possible.

Unfortunately, that part of him didn't react quite as promptly as it should have.

"Elizabeth, I'm sure you'd love nothing better than to sleep the day away, but we cannot—"

A scream loud enough to shatter glass ripped across the room. It deafened him just as surely as the stark light pouring in through the open door was blinding his eyes. Douglas grabbed the nearest pillow and buried his head beneath it.

"Elizabeth Regina Gloriana Drayton, what in the name of God have you *done?*"

The sound of her sister's shrill voice wrenched Elizabeth immediately awake.

"Good God, Bella, why must you harass me at this unholy hour?"

She groaned against the pain in her head and burrowed into the warmth of her pillow. Until her pillow moved and she realized it wasn't a pillow at all.

Elizabeth shot up.

"What are you . . . ? Who are you . . . ? I beg your . . . What do you think you are doing in my bed? You must get out—immediately!"

She was wearing a chemise, nothing else. One sleeve had slipped down, baring her shoulder. Aghast, she grabbed for the pillow that covered his head, only to freeze when her hand glanced his leg. His very *naked* leg.

"Y-You're not wearing anything underneath these blankets."

"No, I'm not."

When next she looked down, it was the face of the Scotsman from the day before staring at her through those damnable blue eyes. He didn't, however, move to get out.

"How the devil did you get in here?"

"You invited me in, lass."

"I did no such thing. You're lying."

"When I was returning your shoe last night . . ."

Elizabeth quieted, suddenly remembering what had happened the night before. In truth, she'd thought it had been a dream.

I'm not going anywhere, lass.

Just as she'd asked, he hadn't left her alone. He'd stayed with her all night, to keep watch against the shadows and that nameless, faceless demon that had plagued her almost all her life.

For as long as she could recall, Elizabeth had always hated the dark. She'd been probably all of six years of age when she and Bella had been playing in one of the many empty bedchambers in Drayton Hall's long unused east wing. A game of hide and seek, and an empty coffer trunk was all it had taken. Elizabeth had slipped inside, never realizing the latch on the outside could—and did—fix in place quite on its own. She'd been effectively trapped, but by the time she'd realized it, Bella had gotten distracted by some new game, as four-year-olds are wont to do, and had wandered away. It took her parents and the Drayton staff until the next morning to find her. By then, Elizabeth's voice had been hoarse for having screamed for help through the most terrifying night of her life. She'd felt quite certain that she was going to die.

The nightmares had begun soon after, waking her in a panic in the middle of the night. To combat them, Elizabeth would steal away to the library to read and avoid the darkness of her bedchamber. Finally, from sheer exhaustion, she would doze off, only to be discovered by her father the next morning curled up in his favorite armchair. He'd thought it an extraordinary interest in books, and it did indeed become that. He just never knew the true reason why it had begun. Elizabeth had told no one, not even Bella, partly for the weakness it implied, but mostly out of the fear that Bella would spend the rest of her life blaming herself for having left her sister behind that day.

Elizabeth said to Isabella, "Yes, he's right. I did invite him in."

Isabella stood in the open doorway, her face a mask of absolute horror. "Oh, Bess, how could you?"

Before Elizabeth could come up with any sensible response, Manfred and Titus arrived, with Turnbull, no doubt alerted by the sound of Bella's screams.

"What happened?" grunted Manfred, clearly out of breath from having come running.

"I think it's fairly evident what has happened here," Isabella said with a murderous glare to the Scotsman. "Mr. MacKinnon has ravished my sister."

Manfred sucked in his stomach.

Titus actually growled.

Behind them, the innkeeper was shaking his head in disbelief. "Och, but I warned you, MacKinnon."

"This is a mistake. Nothing happened. I would remember if I had ravished someone last night."

Isabella remained unmoved. "Your declaration doesn't carry much conviction, Mr. MacKinnon, in the face of the fact that you are lying in my sister's bed completely unclothed."

"Bella," Elizabeth said, "what he says is true. We were talking and we simply fell asleep. That is the whole of it. Nothing untoward happened—truly. I'm almost certain."

"*Almost* certain? Oh, that reassures me, Elizabeth. That is a feeble explanation, even for you. As for you, sir, I believed you a gentleman. How dare you take advantage of an innocent girl?"

"Innocent?"

"Yes, innocent!" She advanced into the room, hands fisted. "Do you mean to suggest that my sister was—had been—" She came to stand at the side of the bed, drew back her fist, and clouted him hard on the head.

"Isabella!"

"Don't you 'Isabella' me! Do you have any idea of the enormity of the blunder you have just made?"

"Bella . . ."

"Do you know who our father is, Mr. MacKinnon?"

"Bella, no. Don't . . ."

"I'll tell you who he is, sir. Our father is Alaric Henry Sinclair Fortunatus Drayton, the fifth Duke of Sudeleigh in Northumberland, and Elizabeth is the eldest of his children—and, I might add, his favorite."

"Bella, that isn't true."

"Oh, *shush,* Bess! We all know he worships you." Isabella railed at Douglas. "My father is a very powerful man. He'll have your head for this, you know." She glanced down at the bedcovers which had slipped to his waist. "As well as any other pertinent parts of you."

Sitting on the bed, Elizabeth could but stare, still hoping she was dreaming this whole horrible debacle. Who was this . . . this *virago* posing as her sister? Quiet, undemanding, *sweet* Isabella had never struck anyone or anything in her life. She'd never given her mare, Sugar, more than a soft nudge with her heel to urge her to go, and when Caro's mongrel puppy had once chewed through her favorite pair of dancing slippers, Bella had simply ruffled the dog's fur and scolded him as she would an infant.

But now . . . ? Elizabeth was utterly struck dumb at the sight of her sister as she paced the room, her skirts whisking against the floorboards as she alternately wrung her hands and waved her fist at the Scotsman.

"How are we going to explain this to Father?" Isabella said now, more to herself than anyone else in the room. The others simply stood watching her. And waiting. Finally she stopped, her face registering an idea. "I know what we will do."

Elizabeth blinked. "You do?"

"Yes. It's a bit on the absurd side, but I begin to think it is the only solution. Yes, it is. I'm certain of it." She turned. "You and Mr. MacKinnon will marry."

"Marry? Me to him? Bella, have you completely lost your senses?"

"Yes, Elizabeth, marry, and no, I haven't lost my senses. It shan't be difficult at all. We're in Scotland. We need no crying of the banns, no special license. Heavens, from what I understand, you can have it done by the local blacksmith before breakfast. And that is precisely what we will do, but we'll have it done after breakfast. You really must eat something. Then we'll return to Drayton Hall having done the necessary"—she looked hard at the Scotsman—"the *honorable* thing. I daresay Mr. Turnbull here can direct us to a local parson who will see to the job."

The innkeeper took his cue and hollered to the hall, "Effie, have the stable lad run and fetch Hamish Beaton here quick! And call for Mrs. Turnbull, too. We'll be needin' witnesses!"

"Thank you, sir."

Isabella started plucking Elizabeth's clothing from various resting places about the room. She had some trouble locating one of the white silk stockings, until she found it flung across the back of the wardrobe. She shook her head, hissing a curse at the stocking under her breath.

"Bess, it is time you get up and get dressed. You certainly cannot get yourself married in your underwear." She stopped at the edge of the bed, clutching Elizabeth's clothing, and frowned at Douglas. "Nor should you, sir, I suspect, wearing nothing at all."

"Pardon me, Miss Drayton," MacKinnon said calmly, as if discussing nothing more important than the weather, "but you seem to have overlooked one significant detail."

"I have?"

"Yes. You see, generally when two people wed, the bridegroom must agree to the thing."

Isabella's eyes burned. "*That,* Mr. MacKinnon, is no longer relevant." She scooped up Douglas's plaid from where it lay on the floor and tossed it at him, hitting him in the nose. "Let me just say you gave up the right to disagree when you compromised my sister. Serving maids and strumpets are one thing, sir. Ladies of noble breed-

ing are another. And before you try to tiptoe your way
out of this, let me just add that if you should refuse, sir,
besides being an entirely deplorable response to this entirely deplorable situation, one of your own making I remind you, I would be forced to ask our associates here,
Titus and Manfred, to use whatever means necessary to
gain your agreement, even if it means taking you before
the local magistrate and charging you with rape."

"Bella!"

On cue, the two behemoths stepped forward from the
doorway as one.

"Now, sir," Isabella finished, lifting her chin, "I suggest you get out of that bed immediately, get yourself
dressed, and prepare yourself to become a member of
our family."

Douglas's face set into stone, dark, unreadable stone.
His eyes were icy with rage.

There was no possible way for him to get out of this,
and he knew it. But he took his time in conceding. He remained on the bed, staring at Isabella.

She, in turn, stared straight back at him.

After a moment, he slid his legs over the side of the
bed. His feet hit the floor. He gripped the edge of the
bedcovers, ready to flip them back. He stared at Isabella
for one long moment, challenging her, and she lost her
nerve at the last second and turned to face the window.
Her bravado, so new to her, didn't stretch quite that far.

Behind him, however, Elizabeth refused to shy away,
and for it she got a thorough view of the lovely lean muscles in his bare backside as he stood and deftly wrapped
the plaid around his waist to cover himself. She knew
she should be embarrassed to her toes. She'd *looked* at

him, and kept on looking. As he stood, she retreated to the shadows afforded by the bed hangings to hide her interest. Before he left, Douglas turned once to look at Elizabeth, and that look was icier than the coldest Northumbrian wind.

"I will see you belowstairs, madam. Or should I call you 'wife'?"

"Outside, if you please, Mr. MacKinnon," said Isabella, and gave him a shove. "It is bad luck, you know, for the groom to see the bride before the wedding . . . despite the fact that he spent the night before seeing far more of her than he ought."

MacKinnon headed for the door, his expression akin to murder.

He stopped before leaving, though, turning back.

"What is it now, sir?" Isabella asked impatiently.

But he didn't answer her. Eyes locked on Elizabeth, he crossed the room instead. When he reached for the bedcovers beside her, she froze, but he only flipped them back, uncovering the white sheet underneath.

"It is as I thought," was all he said, then turned to leave once again.

When he'd finally gone, tailed by Manfred and Titus, who no doubt sought to make sure he didn't flee, Isabella closed the door. She stood a moment, her back to the room, her head bowed forward as if summoning up the courage to see this thing through. Finally she turned, strode to the bed, and yanked Elizabeth up by her arm.

"Bella!"

"This goes beyond anything I could ever have imagined, Elizabeth, even from you." As she talked, Isabella wrapped the width of Elizabeth's corset around her waist, threading the laces through with the expertise of a weaver. "You'll be lucky if Father doesn't lock you up in that convent for the rest of your life after this."

She tugged hard on the laces, pulling Elizabeth back and causing whatever breath she had in her lungs to "whoosh" out in a rush. Elizabeth braced herself with the bedpost as Isabella tugged on.

"Isabella, really, this is not necessary, all this upset, this hasty marriage."

"Oh, yes, it is necessary, Elizabeth. It is absolutely necessary." Isabella tied off the corset with a knot, then sank onto the bed. Suddenly she no longer looked the part of the enraged hoyden who had been issuing orders. Instead she looked pale and frightened and very, very worried.

"Oh, Bess, what on earth happened in here last night? When I left you, you were deeply asleep. I couldn't even rouse you to undress you. I shouldn't have left. I should have stayed with you. Then none of this would be happening right now."

They were the same words four-year-old Isabella had sobbed when they'd discovered Elizabeth locked inside that trunk.

"Bella, please don't cry."

"Surely he didn't take you unwillingly, Bess. I know he's a Scot and a bit rough around the edges, but no ravisher of women would have stopped to help us as he did on the road yesterday. And I know you. You would never allow a man to do that to you and live to see the light of the next morn, even if you were downright sotted. So how, Bess, how did this ever happen?"

Elizabeth lowered herself onto the mattress beside

her, taking her sister's hand in hers. "Honestly, Bella, I don't remember anything. We were talking and then it is as if my memory has been blotted out." She puzzled over it a moment, then said, "I knew that *uisge-beatha* didn't taste right. How on earth could something be intended to taste that terrible? It must have been spoiled. Do you not think so, Bella? Bella?"

But Isabella wasn't listening. She was staring off at the bare floorboards. "It is all my fault. Father charged me with the task of keeping watch over you on this journey, and I have failed. We didn't even make it to Lord Purfoyle's, we barely made it out of England, and now I'm going to return you home little more than a day after we have left only to inform our Father that you ended up spending the night in bed with a strange Scotsman."

"But we don't even know what happened, *if* anything happened at all."

"That no longer matters." Isabella sighed. "The thing is something very well *could* have happened here last night. And as far as scandal goes, 'could have' is as good as 'did.' For once in your life, Bess, think of someone other than yourself. Think of what this will do to Father, to Mother. Think of the scandal this would cause if you simply returned home and tried to make nothing of it. Father would never forgive you. He'll forbid you from ever seeing Caro and Matilda, even Catherine, again for fear that you might inspire in them your same willfulness."

Elizabeth sagged against the bed board. The ache in her head had dulled to a slow drum and she felt as if she'd just been punched in the gut. She adored her little sisters. They were everything to her, especially Caro, sweet eight-year-old Caroline, who had always looked upon her eldest sister as her champion. She could never do anything to hurt them. Never.

"Father wouldn't do that."

"He would. He already said as much when he charged me with taking you to Lord Purfoyle. Oh, Bess, don't you see? Father would have no choice but to make you marry someone after this. Who would you rather it be? Lord Purfoyle, or Mr. MacKinnon?"

Elizabeth thought about it. "I'd sooner marry a goat than Lord Purfoyle."

"Well, at least Mr. MacKinnon isn't any goat." Isabella's voice softened. "You are doing the right thing, Elizabeth. Everything will work out. You'll see. We'll have a quick breakfast, get you married, and then head straight back to Drayton Hall. We should be able to make it there by supper if we make good time, and then, once we're home, Father can figure out what to do next." She finished dryly, "He might even make you a widow."

Elizabeth stared solemnly at her feet as the enormity of the situation finally began to sink in. Isabella was right. She had brought this on herself almost from the day she'd been born. All her life, Elizabeth had acted without thought for the consequences, mostly because having been born to the privilege and protection of the name of Drayton, daughter to a duke, the consequences had never been anything more than a stern reprimand. This time, however, the risk was considerably higher. Because now it had cost her her freedom.

The one thing she had vowed never to lose.

Chapter Five

Back in 1727, when Alaric Henry Sinclair Fortunatus Drayton succeeded to the dukedom of Sudeleigh, he inherited seven homes, over one hundred and twenty-five thousand acres of land, and a legion of servants to maintain it all. There was a townhouse in London on fashionable St. James's Street, a sizeable property in Surrey near the sea, as well as a handful of other holdings strewn all about the English countryside. Few, however, would disagree that the thirty-five thousand acres which comprised the Sudeleigh ducal estate was the very finest of them all.

It was a vast property thick with woodland of oak and pine, and rivers that threaded their way through verdant parkland and rugged countryside alike. Seeing to the estate's transformation after generations of neglect by former dukes had been the first project he had undertaken. On the advice of his friend and colleague, the Earl of Burlington, Alaric had hired famed garden architect

William Kent, sparing no expense in the creation of a landscape replete with Roman statuary, grottoes, and a "natural" fountain. Crowning it all was an extravagant tower folly set upon a picturesque hillock sloping down to a tranquil swan's pond and known as Drayton's Milepost because it stood exactly one mile from Drayton Hall.

It was there on that same hillock, at the foot of that tower, that the duke stood now, one hand holding the hilt of a sword he'd never used and the other at rest in the pocket of his waistcoat. His wife, Margaret, was seated beside him, her pale silk skirts elegantly arranged around the feet of a Queen Anne chair, while their three youngest daughters, Catherine, Matilda, and Caroline, circled their feet. In the distance behind them, rising from a forest that had once been hunted by kings, stood the smoky redbrick façade of the hall.

It was the close of what had been a near-perfect day. The birds were nattering in the trees and horses from the Sudeleigh stable grazed lazily on distant pastures in the ebbing sunlight. The duke and his family were dressed in their very finest for the sitting of the "official" portrait of the family of the fifth Duke of Sudeleigh.

For the occasion, the duke had engaged the services of famed portrait artist Allan Ramsay. It had taken some time and a good deal of persuasion, but Alaric had managed to convince the artist to fit a stop at Drayton into his already busy schedule. Unfortunately, the man had arrived only a few hours after two members of the family, Elizabeth and Isabella, had gone from home. And it was this fact the duchess had spent the past several hours bemoaning while they sat poised on that picturesque hillock.

"Alaric, I simply cannot believe you are having such a significant piece of family history done without the whole of our family in it."

The duke rolled his eyes beneath his cocked tricorne, muttering out of the side of his mouth so as to keep his expression as noble as possible. "I've told you already more times than I care to count, Margaret, there is nothing I can do about it. Mr. Ramsay is a very difficult man to engage. If only you knew the devil of a time I had getting him here at all. He only has a short amount of time to do the portrait now as he is on his way to London to paint a portrait of the king—the king, Margaret—George II, to celebrate his defeat of the Scottish insurrection. I rather doubt our cousin from Hanover would be pleased to be kept waiting whilst we call our daughters back."

"Then let Mr. Ramsay return when he is through with the king."

Good God, though he loved the woman deeply, at times he wanted to throttle her.

"Once he arrives in London, he'll without doubt be kept busy for months, even years afterward painting portraits of everybody else, too. If the king smiles upon Mr. Ramsay's work, as he likely will, every earl, duke, and marquess will flock to his studio for their own. So if we don't have him do the thing right now, while he can, we may never get it done at all. And so help me God, this family will have an Allan Ramsay portrait!"

The duke's voice had gained in volume throughout his diatribe until he'd nearly been shouting at the finish.

"Your grace," said the famed artist from behind the

shield of his canvas. "I must ask that you please hold still."

Alaric glared once at his wife, then nodded to the artist. "Yes, of course, Mr. Ramsay. So sorry. We won't distract you again. Will we, Margaret?"

The duchess, however, only managed to hold her tongue another thirty seconds.

"Can you not pay the man more to induce him to wait until we can at least summon the girls home from Scotland? It is your fault they aren't here to sit for the portrait in the first place, sending them off all in a huff as you did. What will people think, Alaric? They will look at this portrait for centuries to come and they will say, 'Oh, yes, it is indeed a lovely piece, but did not the duke have *five* daughters?' "

"That is quite enough, Margaret . . ."

The duchess simply frowned, knowing when she'd pushed her husband too far. She also knew that for as long as she lived, whenever she looked at the famous Allan Ramsay portrait of her family, she would only think of how ashamed she was for having allowed Alaric to send the girls off as he had.

She had never seen Alaric as furious as he had been when he'd learned of Elizabeth's involvement with that notorious publication, *The Female Spectator.* While Margaret agreed that Elizabeth had indeed gone too far, deep down she knew her daughter's intentions had been good. Her method of following them, however, was just a bit too scandalous for the daughter of a duke.

If only she had defended Elizabeth more strongly against her husband's anger, perhaps she could have prevented him from sending her off to Scotland, and especially into the hands of that toad Purfoyle.

What could Alaric have been thinking? The man would make Elizabeth the very worst of husbands, he with his corpulent belly and even more corpulent opinion of himself. Elizabeth deserved a man who would treat her with respect, who would admire her for her intelligence, who would honor and esteem her, and love her with as much passion and commitment as she showed for everything she did in life. Elizabeth deserved no less.

And despite all his thunder and fury, the duchess knew Alaric would never force his daughter to wed a man she didn't love. He was just trying to give Elizabeth a scare. Margaret knew her husband loved Elizabeth, loved all their daughters with an adoration not demonstrated by many of his peers.

Elizabeth, in particular, had always held a special place in her father's heart. And it was for that reason Margaret had allowed him to send her off as he had, thinking that the time away would cool Alaric's temper and make him realize just how much he missed her.

Margaret, for one, couldn't wait for them to get back.

"Papa," said Caro from where she sat on the ground at her parents' feet, breaking the duchess from her thoughts, "is that a carriage approaching on the drive?"

"A carriage? At this late hour?"

The duchess craned her neck to see, but—drat it all!—she was sitting in such a way, her backbone straight, her chin held high as duchesses were apparently meant to do, as to make the view of the drive all but impossible.

"Were you expecting anyone, Alaric?" She noticed the little one squirming. "Caro, dear, do sit still for Mr. Ramsay."

"But it looks like *our* carriage, Mother."

"Our carriage?" The duke turned. "But that is impossible. Elizabeth and Isabella took the carriage and they couldn't possibly have made it all the way to Purfoyle's estate and back so quickly. . . ."

The look on his face already suggested the dread at what so swift a return might indicate.

"But it is our carriage!" squealed Catherine. "Oh, Mother, now Bess and Bella can be in the portrait, too!"

The younger Draytons all leapt to their feet at once, scattering in three directions as they abandoned the portrait poses it had taken nearly an hour to arrange. In moments, they were racing down the hillside, voices squealing, their wide dress panniers joggling about like the cook's beef gelatin.

"Girls, wait!" the duchess called. "Come back! Your coiffures! They will be ruined!"

"Where the devil are you all going?" the duke bellowed. "Get back here this instant! We are supposed to be sitting for the portrait!"

It was of no use. They were gone, all three of them, bounding off like bunnies to greet whoever rode inside the advancing carriage.

The duchess smiled an apology to Mr. Ramsay, who was standing with his brush poised inches from the canvas. "Do forgive us, Mr. Ramsay. It seems our eldest daughters have just returned unexpectedly from their trip to Scotland. Perhaps we can continue the portrait again in the morning?" She turned to leave, anxious herself to see her daughters, but hesitated. "I wonder, sir, would it be too late for you to add the figures of our other two daughters to the portrait?"

"Margaret . . ."

By the time the carriage achieved the front circle drive, the little ones were there to greet it, gasping against the tight lacings of their stays from their run. The duchess skipped along behind to join them a few minutes later, her own sides stitching, just as the Sudeleigh footman came forward to open the carriage door.

"Bella! Bess!"

The duchess was at once thrilled, and then alarmed at the unexpected return of her two eldest daughters. She couldn't help but wonder what had gone wrong. Had Elizabeth learned the truth of their journey and refused to go through with it? Or, God forbid, had one of the girls taken ill?

It was Isabella who emerged first from the carriage and was immediately encircled by her sisters. Her face looked anxious. *Oh, dear,* thought the duchess, *something* was *the matter.*

Margaret turned to see that Alaric had finally made his way down the hillside to join them. His face was set in stone as he stood back, crossing his arms over his chest. Anyone else might have thought him angry, but five-and-twenty years of sleeping in the same bed with a man made a wife see through such a façade. Alaric was just as worried as she that something might have happened to their daughters.

Isabella exchanged hugs with her sisters before extricating herself to greet her waiting parents.

"Mother. Father."

The duchess took her hands. "Isabella, my dear, how are you? Is . . . is everything all right?"

"Yes, Mother, but—"

Margaret's attention drifted to the open door of the coach, where Elizabeth was just then emerging. No outward signs of injury, she noted with relief. But what of illness? Elizabeth did look a bit pale. . . .

"Mother . . ."

"Oh, Elizabeth, is everything all right? You look peaked. Did something happen on the road to Scotland?"

"In a manner of speaking, yes, something did happen. Something quite unexpected."

"I knew it. I knew there was a reason you had come back so soon. I—"

It was then Margaret realized that a third person was emerging from inside the coach—a very male, very Scottish third person. She stood back and watched in bewilderment as the figure of a man stepped out.

Her first thought was to wonder how all three of them had fit inside the coach. He was tall, fierce-looking, and stood proudly as every pair of eyes immediately fixed upon him. He wore a tartan plaid thrown carelessly over a coarse linen shirt that was open at the neck. His dark hair was tied behind him and his eyes, she noticed, missed nothing as he assessed his new surroundings.

He was a man. He was a Scot. And quite a magnificent one at that.

"Girls," Margaret finally managed, "I see you've brought us home a guest."

"Yes, that is what I had started to say," Elizabeth said. "Father, Mother, Katie, Mattie, and Caro . . . I'd like you all to meet Douglas Dubh MacKinnon. He is from the Isle of Skye. . . ."

The duchess immediately offered her hand in greeting. "Mr. MacKinnon, a pleasure to meet—"

". . . and he is my husband."

The last thing the duchess heard before she fainted was the unmistakable sound of her husband's bellow.

Caroline Drayton was quite an adept one at slipping her slight, eight-year-old body into the most inconspicuous of places. If it wasn't inside the cellar storage cabinets to sneak one of Cook's biscuits, it was in the back of her sister Matilda's wardrobe, or under the housekeeper, Mrs. Burnaby's, bed.

It was a particularly useful talent to have when one wanted to know what was going on in one's own family but was considered too young to learn of it firsthand. From her bedchamber on the second floor, Caroline could slip out the window and make her way undetected across a network of intersecting gables all the way to the main section of the house. From there, she could access any number of places—the parlor where her mother liked to sew, or even the downstairs kitchen where she had once spied on the footman, Harry, kissing Meg, the housemaid. Caro didn't quite understand why he'd felt it necessary to put his hand under her skirts, but whatever his reasons, Meg must not have minded too much. Instead of pushing him away, she had only moaned just like her sister Catherine sometimes did when she ate her favorite strawberry dessert, the one with all the custard poured on top. From that day on, Caroline had always wondered if Harry's kisses perhaps tasted like strawberries and custard.

For this day, however, Caroline chose the window that opened onto the upper corridor, right outside the door to her father's study. Experience had taught her that once everyone came inside from the carriage drive, and once her mother recovered from her swoon, this would be the place for the discussion that was certain to follow. It was the room where all the important things were discussed, and Caro had discovered that she could learn a great many things simply by climbing inside the huge Chinese urn that stood in the far corner by the window, as long as she removed her dress panniers and all but one of her petticoats, that is.

She had just managed to do just that, dipping her slippered feet inside, when she heard the others approaching in the hall. Any moment now, the door would burst open and the particulars of just how Bess had come to be married to that Scottish man with the strange name would be revealed. Caroline couldn't wait to hear it.

She bent her knees and wiggled her bottom just right, ducking her head down beneath the rim of the urn just as the door across the room came open and everybody surged inside.

"Very well. The little ones have been sent to their rooms," she heard her mother say. "Now we will all take a seat and discuss this situation calmly."

If Caro could have seen through the side of the urn, she knew she would have seen the duchess looking at her father when she said this.

"Calmly? Are you out of your mind, woman? Your

daughter has just told us she is married! And to a complete stranger! Even worse than that, to a *Scot!*"

"Alaric, keep your voice down. The windows are open. He'll hear you."

"Oh, he's down in the reception hall, no doubt scrutinizing the china vases with a mind to what he can pilfer. They're all thieves, you know. Reivers the lot of them!"

"Father, that's not true," Elizabeth said. "He wouldn't do that. He's not a reiver. He's a drover."

"Is that supposed to make me feel any better about the fact that he is now my son-in-law? What I want to know, Elizabeth Regina Drayton, is wherever did you get such a dim-witted idea in your head as to wed the man?"

"She got the idea from me, Father. In fact, I made her do it."

Bella?

"It seemed the best way, the only way to sort out the situation. Elizabeth had . . ." She hesitated. "Elizabeth took ill at the inn last night. Something she'd eaten . . . or rather something she drank."

"Elizabeth," said the duchess, instantly concerned. "Are you feeling unwell?"

"No, Mother, I'm fine. Well, except for a slight headache . . ."

The duke interrupted, "What the devil did you drink?"

"It was something called *uisge-beatha.* It was a chilly night and the serving girl said it would warm us, but it must have been spoiled. It didn't taste right, not at all."

"*Whisky?* You besotted yourself with *whisky*?"

"Apparently so, Father, but you'll be relieved to know I didn't like it. Not at all. It made my head feel odd, as if it were no longer attached to my body, and my stomach became most upset. Afterward, I went straight to bed and stayed there until morning."

"That still doesn't explain why you have returned here claiming to be married to a Scot when you should be on your way to Lord Purfoyle's estate."

"Because when I awoke in the morning, *he* was in bed beside me."

"He? You mean this Scot? Are you . . ." Her father drew an audible breath. "Are you telling me you slept with the man?"

The duke broke something then, something that sounded as if it was made of glass and probably cost a lot of money. Inside the vase, Caroline had to cover her mouth with her hand.

"I was delirious!" Elizabeth shouted. "I didn't know what I was doing. I don't even remember asking him to come to my bed."

"*What!* Dear God, Margaret, take out my dueling pistol and shoot me right now."

"Alaric!"

"Honestly, Father, I don't think anything happened anyway. We both just fell asleep."

"Oh, yes. Right. And I'm the King of England."

The duchess broke in. "Alaric, your face is turning as red as a pomegranate. You will sit down now and calm yourself before we hear anything further."

"Good God," the duke croaked, "is there more?"

Caroline listened as her father took several slow, deep breaths. No one else in the room said a word.

Finally Isabella spoke. "Father, Elizabeth had no way of knowing that what she was drinking would cause her to lose all sense and reason like that. She had never partaken of such strong spirits before."

"And with good reason. How much of this whisky did Elizabeth actually partake?"

"Oh, only two or three . . ." Elizabeth answered.

"Seven," Isabella corrected.

"Seven . . . seven what? Sips?"

"Drams," answered Isabella.

"Drams! Good God in heaven, Elizabeth, 'tis enough to lay a grown man flat . . . which is, obviously, precisely what it did to you, as well, it would seem, as the bloody Scot."

He said those words—"bloody Scot"—as if they tasted unpleasant.

"So you now see, Father," Isabella said, "why having Elizabeth and Mr. MacKinnon wed was the only solution."

The duke sighed. "In the face of those circumstances, Isabella, I believe you did the only thing you could have thought to do. I myself would have had the man strung up from the nearest gibbet, but you're a lady and such thoughts do not occur to you. There you have it. The question now is what to do about it."

"I've thought about that, Father," Elizabeth said. "And I think I have come up with a sensible resolution, one that will solve all the problems at once."

"Oh, you have, have you?"

"Indeed. We can have the marriage annulled."

"Annulled?" The duke was yelling again. "Have you lost your mind?"

"Why is that so unthinkable? Marriages have been annulled before. I'm not even certain we actually are married. That 'parson' was the inn's groomsman."

"You were in Scotland?" asked the duke.

"Yes."

"There were witnesses to this agreement?"

"Yes."

"Then you are indeed as married as if the Archbishop of Canterbury had performed the ceremony himself."

She knew it wasn't possible, but Caroline would have sworn she could hear Elizabeth frown.

"Well, if it is that effortless for someone to get married, then it must be just as effortless to get unmarried. So we'll do just that, agree not to be married and be done with it. You all can stand as witnesses. Then Mr. Mac-Kinnon can return to his island and I can stay here and we can forget any of this ever happened." She paused, then added, "Of course, under the circumstances, Lord Purfoyle wouldn't likely wish to continue his suit."

"Oh, and that would just devastate you, wouldn't it?" The duke chuckled, but it was far from a happy sound. "I always knew you were a shrewd one, but even I couldn't have thought you'd come up with such an elaborate plan to ensure you'd never have to get married. At least to a proper husband, that is."

"You think I planned this?" Her outrage sounded genuine.

"But Father," said Isabella, "I am the one who insisted they get married."

"Then you were in on it, too."

"Alaric!"

"I wouldn't doubt it, Margaret. I wouldn't doubt that all my daughters are scheming against me. Isabella probably knew all along about those ridiculous articles she was writing for that damnable magazine, too."

"It wasn't my place to tell you, Father."

"Ha! You see?"

"Bella," Elizabeth cut in, "you mean it wasn't you? I thought you had to be the one who told Father . . ."

"It was Mrs. Burnaby who told me."

"The housekeeper?" Elizabeth and Isabella answered in unison.

"Yes, only after one of the maids found a sheet of foolscap with one of those articles written on it when she was cleaning. You should have been a little more careful in disposing of your early drafts. They brought it to me and I recognized your handwriting, Elizabeth."

As they continued talking, Caroline, still hunched inside the urn, tried desperately to make sense of all she'd just heard so she could be sure to have the details right when she repeated it all for Mattie and Katie later on.

First, Father had sent Bess off with Bella to marry some man named Lord Purfoyle, but Bess and Bella had returned home with that handsome Scotsman, Douglas Dubh MacKinnon, whom Bess had married instead after she drank some terrible thing called whisky or *uisge-beatha* and woke up with him in her bed. But what was wrong with that? Caroline wondered. She sometimes slept with her dog, Agamemnon, and no one was trying to make her marry him. And just what sort of name was *Dubh* anyway? Had Bess already been in love with the *bloody* Scot? Was that why Father had sent her away? No one had ever told Caro what Bess had done. They'd all just shaken their heads and *tsked* as if telling her might make her want to do it as well.

"Call the bloody Scot in here," said the duke then, breaking the little girl from her jumble of thoughts. "The rest of you may leave. I wish to speak with the man alone."

"Alone?" Elizabeth said. "But why, Father?"

"That, Elizabeth Regina, is my business. Now for once in your life, just listen to me, and go."

Chapter Six

"His grace's study is here, sir."

Douglas spoke not a word, simply nodded his thanks to the young housemaid who'd delivered him to the closed door down a corridor that had seemed to stretch a mile. He waited while she bobbed a nervous curtsy and then turned, tripping off down the hall. No doubt she would spend the rest of the night telling the other servants how she'd had to walk beside the barbarous Scot whom Lady Elizabeth had brought home—as if he were a vagrant, or a stray dog.

When she'd vanished around the corner, after one last glance at him, Douglas raised his hand and knocked.

"Come in."

The room on the other side was bright and smelled of history, books, and money. Arcaded bookcases lined the walls, set off by tall windows with rich draperies that fell from the ceiling to the floor under intricate plasterwork archways. Life-sized portraits in gilded frames painted by artists the likes of Van Dyck and Nicholas Hilliard hung over walls paneled in a rich, polished oak. A huge marble mantel towered at one end. Across the stretch of Turkish carpeting, sitting behind an immense mahogany desk, sat the venerable Duke of Sudeleigh.

Douglas's first look at the man when they'd arrived out on the carriage drive earlier fit every notion his countrymen had ever held of the Sassenach nobility. Richly dressed, powdered, and bedecked in fancy clothes, the man had obviously never worked ·a day's labor in his life.

Once inside the house, however, that opinion was only confirmed.

Every spare bit of space was occupied by knick-knackery of some sort. If a man's worth was determined simply by the size and number of his possessions, then Sudeleigh must undoubtedly be very valuable indeed. Every convenience but awaited his wish, and if one wasn't at the ready, there was a bell board attached to the wall behind his desk by which he could summon a servant from any room in the house. Still, despite all this extravagance and wealth, there was a light behind the duke's eyes, a flicker of something other than bland privilege, that immediately cast him as a force to be reckoned with.

Douglas came into the room, stood in the middle of the carpet, and stared at the man. "You asked to see me, your grace."

He purposely spoke with a heavier brogue than was his custom, rolling the R in "grace" for added effect.

"Mr. MacKinnon is it?"

Douglas simply nodded.

The duke motioned him to a chair, a dainty, finely carved little piece that looked ridiculous beneath his bulk. Douglas stretched his long legs out in front of him.

"My daughters have explained the circumstances of your, ah, sudden presence in our lives, at least their account of it. I have summoned you here now in hopes of hearing your side of the story."

"I fear I can tell you little more than they, your grace. I simply stopped to assist the ladies with a broken carriage wheel. Afterward, they offered me a ride to the inn. I'd been walking a long way and I'd lost a goodly amount of daylight in helping with their coach, so I accepted their offer. When we arrived at the inn, I made to take my leave, but the eldest one . . ."

"Elizabeth," the duke grumbled. *"Your wife."*

"Aye. She insisted I should have a bit o' supper for my trouble. Insisted on paying for it, too."

The duke simply nodded and waited for him to go on. His expression, however, was growing more dour by the second.

"We were in the taproom and it was a bit of a cold night. Lady Elizabeth asked for a dram o' *uisgebeatha* . . ."

"Whisky! You gave my daughter whisky to drink?"

"I didna give her anything, your grace. I tried to warn her against it, even, but she wouldn't listen. She was very determined."

The duke expelled an audible breath. He obviously knew his daughter well. "Go on."

"I could see she was partaking too much of the drink." Douglas leveled the duke a stare. "I'm afraid she fell into a bit of a swoon."

"A stupor is more likely." The duke's mouth grew strained above his laced cravat.

"The other one, Lady Isabella, became alarmed. She thought her sister could be mortally affected, but I assured her she would be all right come the morn. I helped to carry her up to her room and then I left, but when I went back down to the taproom, I found Lady Elizabeth's shoe lying on the stairs. It must have fallen when we carried her up from the taproom. So I thought to return it to her."

"Just like bloody Cinderella," the duke grumbled.

Douglas looked at the man. "That's precisely what she said, as well."

"That still doesn't explain how it is you came to be in her bed, sir."

Douglas nodded. "When I brought the shoe to her room, she was awake."

"Elizabeth? After all that whisky?"

"Aye, I was just as startled as you are, your grace. She asked me to come in. She seemed a wee bit skittish of being alone."

"It's the dark. She's afraid of it. Has been nearly all her life, although she'd never dare admit it." Sudeleigh shook his head. "It has been ever since she was a child and got herself locked in a trunk while playing hide-and-go-seek with her sister. Even now I find her in this room late into the night, curled up in that chair by the fire after having fallen asleep while reading."

Douglas glanced behind him to the overstuffed chair the duke had indicated. An image of Lady Elizabeth as a child came to his mind, hair the color of fire, that stubborn chin, tucked up against the cushions of the chair. It tugged at him, the vulnerability of it.

He turned back to the duke. "I could see she was in a bit of a state, so I stayed, thinking to leave as soon as she fell asleep. Tha's the last thing I remember before waking the next morn in bed. In *her* bed. When Lady Isabella found us, she of course assumed the worst." Douglas leveled the duke a stare. "I didna touch your daughter, your grace. I swear upon it. But if I didna agree to wed her, Lady Isabella would have had me thrown in the gaol. As your grace is undoubtedly aware, these are perilous times in Scotland. If the English authorities there thought I had wronged an Englishwoman . . ."

The duke sighed, nodding. "The king's son, the Duke of Cumberland, has spared nothing in his retaliation against the Jacobites for the rebellion. I have little doubt you would have been killed."

The duke sat in his chair for several moments, obviously chewing over the tale. He drummed his fingers against the desktop, his eyes fixed on the feather quill sitting aslant in his inkwell. The clock on the wall behind him ticked off several minutes. A door closed somewhere out in the hall. After a time, he got up from the desk and walked across the room, stopping at the near window to peer out at the grounds. He didn't say a word. Douglas simply sat, waiting for the man to come to terms with this most unexpected and unwanted turn of events.

Finally, the duke turned. "She wants me to arrange for an annulment, you know."

Douglas looked at him, saying nothing.

"It would take an Act of Parliament, or maybe even a

royal decree, but I have the king's ear and I would be willing to attempt it. For her. I would do anything for my daughter, and she knows this. What I need to know now is how much you would want to agree to that."

Douglas looked at him, not sure he understood. "How much, your grace?"

"Money, MacKinnon. Name your price. How much will it cost me to secure your agreement to an annulment? It does help matters quite a bit if both the bride *and* the bridegroom want out of the thing."

Sudeleigh had left the window as he talked, circling the room to his chair. He took up his quill and started to scribble something out, a bank draft, all but waiting for Douglas to furnish the amount.

Douglas felt his jaw tighten. "I dinna want your money, your grace."

The duke looked taken aback. "If you're thinking to get more from a dowry than what I will pay outright, you're in for a sorry bit of disappointment. There is a stipulation that any dowry will be forfeit if my daughters should marry against my wishes. Come now, man, surely there must be something else. Everybody wants *something*. Look around you, Mr. MacKinnon. You can see I'm a very wealthy man. Any shrewd man would take advantage of such a situation."

Douglas's voice lowered to nearly a growl. "I'm not such a man."

The duke quietly replaced his quill in its holder. "So if not money, then something else perhaps? Artwork? Land?"

Standing his full six feet and three across the other side of the desk, Douglas stared down at the man. Always the Sassenach thought he could buy a Scotsman's honor. It was as if it was beyond their comprehension that some things were simply out of reach of their pocketbooks. As he stood there, anger stewing, a thought occurred to Douglas, a way to effectively turn the tide in his favor.

What price, he wondered, would a Sassenach place on his own honor?

"Very well, your grace. I would ask your sponsorship."

"I beg your pardon? Did you just say you wanted my *sponsorship?*"

"Aye." Douglas lowered himself into the chair again, leaning fully against its spindly arms as he contemplated his inspiration.

"You've the king's ear, you say? Well, for me the man has been all but deaf. I've spent the past several months in London seeking an audience with King George in order to plead for the return of my family's lands, lands that were confiscated by the Crown after the last Jacobite rebellion."

"So you are a Jacobite?" He might as well have said he was Lucifer.

"I didna say that. My father, however, was a Jacobite and came out for the Old Pretender both in the '15 and again in '19. Because of his part in the rebellions, he lost my family's home to the Crown. But my father is dead now, died in France where he'd been in exile for nearly these thirty years past, and those lands are by rights now mine. I've worked nearly all my life to see them restored. Archibald Campbell assured me that if I didna come out for the Bonnie Prince this time, I would be certain to receive them back."

"Campbell? You are acquainted with the Duke of Argyll?"

"It was his grace who recommended I go to London to seek an audience with the king. I did, but I was left waiting for days, then weeks."

The duke looked at him. "It would seem to me that Argyll sought more to distance you from the Highlands, MacKinnon, and prevent your taking the side of the Young Pretender."

Douglas frowned. The same idea had occurred to him. He hadn't at all liked being made into such a pawn. He went on, "When I heard tell of the Jacobites' final defeat, I expected then the king would grant me an audience so I could finally present my petition. But still he would not see me, and so I waited more, until I received word calling me back to Skye." Douglas braced himself against his deepest emotions as he said, "I'm told my brother had been killed at Culloden."

For the briefest of moments, Sudeleigh appeared genuinely moved. He shook his head. "I am sorry." Then he sat with his hands folded before him, priming himself for his next words. "So, in exchange for my daughter's freedom, you seek my intervention with the king?"

Douglas inclined his head. "You asked me to name my price, your grace. This is mine."

The duke sat back.

Douglas simply waited.

Finally, the duke spoke. "Mr. MacKinnon, I—"

He paused, his attention suddenly focused on a rather large urn that stood in the far corner of the room. He got up from his desk and crossed the carpet to it. Then he looked inside.

"Caroline Henrietta Drayton! What do you think you are doing in there?"

A tiny voice replied from inside the urn. "Please, Papa, don't be cross. I just wanted to know what was happening. You never tell me anything . . ."

The duke took a deep breath, then let it out. "Well, so now you do. Now get yourself out of there before I—"

"But I can't, Papa," she sobbed. "I'm . . . I'm stuck!"

In the next moment, the child began to wail, a plaintive sound that echoed inside the massive urn. The duke reached a hand inside to try to free her, but the more he struggled, the louder she wailed, no doubt squirming her way more thoroughly into a knot as she did.

Soon, the duke was shouting. The child was screaming, and Douglas sat back and simply watched. The door across the room burst open and the rest of the family, alarmed by the clamor, came charging inside. In moments it was pandemonium.

One of the daughters, Douglas couldn't remember her name, went to the bell board and began tugging on them—*ding, ding, ding*—one after the other, jerking them all in hopes of summoning help.

A small spaniel came scampering into the room and began to bark and prance and yowl about everyone's feet.

Someone shouted, "Agamemnon!"

Another burst out, "She's turning quite blue!"

Unable to stand the chaos any longer, Douglas got up, took his pistol from his waistband, and strode across the room.

"Father! That Scottish man is going to shoot Caro! Stop him!"

They all turned and screamed as one. Douglas stood back, lifted his hand, and smashed the butt of his pistol against the side of the urn, cracking it open like an egg.

The little girl tumbled out, her face nearly purple from crying. She ran straight into her mother's waiting arms, collapsing against the duchess's skirts in a sobbing, terrified ball of child.

Everyone else fell silent, staring at Douglas in utter disbelief.

Until the duke roared a moment later, "Are you out of your mind, man? That was a Ming. A one of a kind! And it cost me a bloody fortune!"

"Actually, your grace," Douglas said calmly, eying the broken pieces of the urn, "it was Japanese. Imari, I believe. A nice piece, aye, but not nearly as valuable as a Ming."

"Alaric," said the duchess as she smoothed a hand over Caroline's curls to calm her, "the man just saved your daughter's life. I should think a show of gratitude would be more appropriate than screaming at him."

The duke was staring at Douglas, dumbfounded. Finally, he said, "Yes, right. My apologies, MacKinnon. Thank you for reacting so quickly."

Douglas ignored him. He turned instead toward the duchess and squatted down beside where she held Caroline tightly in her arms. "Are you all right now, lassie?"

Caroline pulled her tear-streaked face away from her mother's neck to look at him, sniffed, blinked twice, then nodded.

He smiled at her and touched a fingertip under her

chin. "What were you thinking then? Were you trying to become a marmalade in your da's big jam jar there?"

The lass smiled at him. A collective wave of relief passed over the room, and eight-year-old Caroline Henrietta Phillipa Drayton silently vowed that funny name or not, she would love the bloody Scot for the rest of her life.

Douglas heard voices coming from inside the formal drawing room as he made his way down the hallway.

It had been nearly two hours since his meeting with the duke and the subsequent rescue of his daughter, two hours during which Douglas had walked the periphery and intersecting pathways of the duke's knot garden, and then, because he didn't have anything else to do, had walked them all again.

He hadn't seen Elizabeth since the incident in the study with the urn. When peace had been restored and the broken porcelain had been swept away, she'd followed her sisters from the room without giving him a backward glance. Douglas told himself to be glad of her indifference, that whenever she was near, trouble wasn't far behind. The less he saw of her then, the better.

Several times, however, while he'd been walking in the garden, a small part of him almost seemed to sense her presence on the gentle waft of the breeze, as if she were there but somehow hidden from view. Once, he even thought he'd caught a glimpse of her passing by a window, but decided it was probably nothing more than the flutter of a curtain, a shift of the light.

As for her father, Sudeleigh had also retreated after their meeting and had yet to give Douglas an answer to the proposal he'd made. After he'd freed the wee lassie from the urn, the man had said simply he needed time to consider it more closely and had holed himself up behind the closed door of his study ever since.

If there was one thing Douglas didn't have, it was time. He was needed at home, had been gone from there too long, and with or without the duke's blessing, married or no, he had every intention of resuming his journey home on the morrow.

As he neared the drawing room door, Douglas happened to catch a glimpse of himself in the hall pier glass. He was unshaven, his clothing rumpled from two days' wear, and his shoes looked as if they'd just walked all the way from London, which indeed they had. It was no wonder they all looked on him as they had. He looked every bit the shabby, impoverished, *barbaric* Scot they believed him to be. But then, when he'd set out from London a handful of days before, he'd never expected he'd find himself calling at the home of the Duke of Sudeleigh. Nor had he expected to end up the man's son-in-law, either.

Only the duke and another gentleman, whose back was to Douglas, were present in the drawing room when he arrived. Douglas hesitated in the doorway, taking in their rich coats, tailored knee breeches, and polished shoes. Absently he ran a hand back through his hair to neaten it.

"Ah, MacKinnon, there you are," said Sudeleigh. "Allow me to introduce you to—"

"Douglas! Good God, is that you?"

"Allan," Douglas answered, genuinely taken aback at

the sight of a familiar face in such an unfamiliar surrounding.

It had been probably a dozen years or more since the
two had seen each other, but there was no mistaking that
square jaw and dimpled chin, the shrewd dark eyes that
caught every detail, sign of the true artist himself. The
two men shook hands warmly. "This is unexpected,"
Douglas said.

"I should say it is."

"You are acquainted with Mr. MacKinnon, Ramsay?"
asked the duke.

"Aye, your grace. We were at university together."

"University?" The man looked incredulous, as if the
artist had just told him they'd once met on the face of the
moon.

"As a matter of fact, your grace," said the artist,
"Douglas's uncle, the MacKinnon chief, was the subject
of one of my first skilled portraits. I traveled all the way
to Skye just to paint him. A great man he is, Iain Dubh
MacKinnon." Ramsay looked at Douglas. "How do
things fare at Dunakin?"

"Not well, I'm afraid. I've just learned we lost young
Iain at Culloden."

Ramsay's expression dimmed. "'Tis a terrible loss.
So young. But try, if you can, to take heart in his passing. Your brother was a warrior in every sense of the
word and left this world in the way he would have
wanted. Fighting."

"Aye, what you say is true." Noticing the duke's interest, Douglas quickly turned the conversation away
from his family. "So how fares your da? Still living in
that goose pie of a house in Edinburgh?"

"Aye, that he is. Still calls it that, too. In fact it is known across town now as Auld Ramsay's Goose Pie."

"Och, no. You canna be serious. It was meant as a jest when I called it that."

"Aye, Douglas, but you know my da. Says 'tis the best name he's heard yet to describe it. So the name just stuck."

The three men chatted quietly over the next quarter hour, filling the time with commonplace topics, the weather, hunting, even card play. At precisely the stroke of eight, the ladies came into the room to join them.

From the moment they arrived, resplendent in silks and lace, Douglas forgot all about the duke and their discussion earlier that day. As soon as he saw them, as soon as he saw *her,* he was captivated.

Elizabeth wore her hair up, with thick glossy curls gracing her neck, a neck adorned by a single strand of pearls the same creamy color as her skin. Her gown, cut low over her breasts, was a smoky blue satin edged in golden lace that glimmered beneath the candlelight whenever she moved. She was exquisite, a vision, indeed, like an apparition who could tempt a man with just the arch of her brow or a single crook of her finger. And all the while he was standing there watching her, marveling at her, yes, even desiring her, it never even occurred to Douglas, not once, that this same bewitching woman was his wife.

"Supper is now served, your grace," said a footman who'd just come into the room. Douglas had been so intent on Elizabeth, he hadn't noticed the man's arrival.

"Indeed," said the duchess, "then we shall all move on into the dining room."

The duke, however, called Douglas back, motioning for the duchess to go on with the others. "We'll join you in just a moment, pet."

When they were alone, Sudeleigh turned to face Douglas. The expression on his face was grave, purposeful. He'd apparently reached his decision in the matter of this marriage.

"Your grace."

"A question, if you please, sir, before I make my answer to your proposal."

Douglas inclined his head. "Aye."

"Why did you conceal from me the fact that you were of the Scottish nobility? Mr. Ramsay made mention of your estate, Dunakin. That would make you the Earl of Dunakin?"

"The title was forfeit with the land. I hid nothing, your grace. You simply saw what you wanted to see. A poor, uneducated *bloody* Scot who had seized the opportunity to wed a duke's daughter."

The duke's face colored only slightly at having been overheard earlier that day.

"Few farmers can tell the difference between a Ming vase and a Japanese imitation," he said. "Apparently few dukes can either." Sudeleigh smirked at himself. "I don't suppose you've told my daughter the truth of your identity."

"Like her father, your grace, Lady Elizabeth saw only what she wanted to see. I saw no reason to tell her otherwise."

The duke stared at him for a long moment. Finally he said, "Mr. MacKinnon, as I'm sure you must be aware, if I were to seek the annulment of your marriage to my daughter, it would produce a scandal of unfathomable proportion in London."

"I cannot see that anyone would care."

"I would care a great deal, as it could have an effect on my position at Court. Obviously I am reluctant to arouse such a stew of gossip, but at the same time, I am also a father who loves his daughter, and thus does not wish her to live a life of unhappiness."

Douglas merely nodded.

"I'm sure you are aware that my daughter has a tendency to be . . ." He hesitated, searching for the right words. "A bit headstrong."

Douglas saw no reason to affirm the obvious.

"She was our first, and I have been too indulgent with her, I admit. She has never had to learn what it is to face the consequences of her deeds. I come to think, however, after this most recent affair, that she is badly in need of a lesson. I would like to propose a counter-offer, if you will, to your proposal. I will grant you my sponsorship in the petition for the return of your lands *and* your earldom, and I will guarantee you an audience with the king, in exchange for your cooperation in an annulment—only after you take my daughter with you back to Skye and live with her there for the space of two months."

Douglas's mouth dropped open. "You canna be serious."

"Oh, but I am. I believe there is a term for such a thing in Scotland. What is it called? Handfasting? Well, consider this to be like a handfasting. . . ."

"Your Grace—"

"Allow me to finish, MacKinnon. As part of the bargain, I do not wish for you to reveal the truth of your circumstances to Elizabeth. She got herself wed to a man she believes is but a poor Scottish farmer. She must therefore see what it is to be a poor Scottish farmer's wife."

Douglas frowned. "Such a deception does not sit easily with me."

"MacKinnon, regardless of my other imperfections, which my wife would tell you are many, I do believe in the sanctity of marriage. I cannot in good conscience seek to annul what the good Lord has brought together, whatever his reasons, without giving it a sporting chance. I also cannot allow my daughter to continue to skirt responsibility for what she does. If, after two months, the two of you still wish this marriage dissolved, and if you give me your word as a gentleman that there has been no consummation of the marriage, I will petition the Crown myself for an annulment, regardless of the scandal or damage it might do to my name at Court. Otherwise, if you refuse my request and do not take Elizabeth with you back to Skye, I will have you brought before the courts, the *English* courts, on charges of deserting your wife. And as for your lands . . ." Sudeleigh played his final card. "I understand His Majesty is considering deeding those estates formerly held by the Jacobites to his loyal *Sassenach* subjects, in hopes of preventing a further insurrection by the Young Pretender."

Douglas's vision blurred. "Bastard! This is absolute blackmail!"

"That, sir, is what your people term it. I prefer to call it a simple bargaining maneuver. Be that as it may,

MacKinnon, these are my stipulations. The choice, and its outcome, are entirely yours."

Douglas felt as if his insides had just turned to solid stone.

Why had he stayed when she'd asked him to that night? Why hadn't he listened to his better sense and gone, regardless of her fear, regardless of her pleading with him to stay? He could be halfway to Skye by now, untroubled . . . and unmarried. If only she hadn't looked at him with those bewitching hazel eyes, eyes that somehow reached to his very soul.

Both he and the duke knew well that Douglas had no choice in the matter. He needed the annulment just as much as she did. But more than that, he wanted his lands, and he would do just about anything to get them back.

Even if it meant he had to play at being a husband for a couple of months.

"It is agreed, your grace."

Having won, the duke quietly nodded.

As the Scotsman turned and strode from the room, his effort to contain his rage was evident in his very stride. Standing behind him, the duke couldn't help but smile. For he had seen the way MacKinnon had looked at his daughter when she came into the room, how he hadn't been able to take his eyes from her. He knew well that look. He knew well what it meant. It was the same look he himself had had for his own Margaret that night at the opera, the first time he'd seen her after his return from the Continent nearly a quarter century before.

It was the look of desire—undeniable, unavoidable, unintended desire.

And *that* was the finest kind of desire of them all.

Chapter Seven

The duke waited until the last of the supper's six courses had been served before making his announcement.

"You want me to do *what?*"

Elizabeth nearly choked on a spoonful of her lemon syllabub. Always her favorite sweet, the spiced cream went quickly sour in her mouth. As she chased it down with a small sip of mint tea, she could only hope that she hadn't heard him right.

She prayed that Caroline might have coughed, or Agamemnon had barked, or the clock in the hall had been chiming nine o'clock, anything to explain why she'd *thought* she'd heard those most impossible words.

But if she'd been mistaken, if her father hadn't just said that, then why had everyone else sitting around the table suddenly fallen so silent, unless . . .

Oh, God. She had heard him right.

Not for a single moment during the ride home from Scotland and in the hours since they'd returned had Elizabeth even once considered the possibility that her father would want her to stay married to the Scot. The Duke of Sudeleigh, after all, was a sensible man.

Well, most of the time, anyway.

"Surely you're not saying you mean for me to *stay* married to him, that you mean for me to *live* with him? No, Father, you couldn't have said those things. For if you had, that would only mean you haven't considered even one of the surely ten thousand and twenty-three reasons why we"—she looked at the Scotsman and decided she really didn't wish to speak of them as one— "why Mr. MacKinnon and I cannot possibly spend eternity together, beginning with the fact that we are complete and utter strangers and have absolutely nothing in common with one another. This is not what I expected of you. Not at all."

"Is that so?" The duke crossed his arms. "Then tell me, just what did you expect me to do when you returned home with this bit of news, Elizabeth?"

She faltered. "I . . . I expected you would write a letter, or send for your solicitor, or do whatever else it might take to terminate this . . . this matrimonial pretense!

"I don't even know how I allowed Isabella to convince me to do it in the first place. All I can think is that it must have been the effects of that wretched whisky. It befuddled me, but you have no such excuse. I mean really, Father, what can you possibly be thinking?"

The duke looked at her across the length of that crowded supper table.

"What I am thinking, Elizabeth Regina, is that I'm a man who believes there is a reason behind everything that happens. And whatever it is—be it the work of the Lord, the saints, or even the spirit of your dead grandmother—there is a reason why you came to be the wife of Mr. MacKinnon."

"This was Isabella's doing, Father, not the Lord's, certainly not Grandmother Minna's. Grandmother would never approve of something so unconventional as this."

"Unconventional as it may be," the duke said, "I cannot in good conscience seek to put a marriage—any marriage—asunder precipitately. The bond of matrimony is a sacred thing. Did I not wed your dear mother even though I was a young man and had never before laid eyes upon her? At the time, I did not wish to marry anyone, much less a girl of thirteen, but I did so out of respect for the wishes of my parents"—he looked at his duchess—"and it was the best decision I have ever made."

Elizabeth frowned. This was getting nowhere. She tried another approach. "So, fine, then I'll stay married to him for the two months if that is what you wish. But why must you send me all the way to Skye as well?"

"Because your husband is needed there, and as his wife, it is your duty to go with him."

Husband . . .

Wife . . .

Duty.

The words sent a distasteful shudder weaving down her backside.

Elizabeth scarcely realized her father was still talking, until he said, "So I have discussed the matter thoroughly with Mr. MacKinnon, and together we have determined upon this compromise."

Together?

She turned on the Scotsman. "And did either of you ever once consider that perhaps *I* might like to be included in this discussion? Particularly as it does pertain to me, and to the rest of my life, did you not think I should have some say about what I think is best?"

The duke stood his ground. "That is precisely what got you into this entanglement in the first place, Elizabeth, thinking you knew what was best. Which is precisely why I am not inviting your commentary now. This has already been decided for you. You will travel with Mr. MacKinnon to his homestead on Skye, and will live with him as his wife for the next two months. And that is my final word on the matter."

He was serious, truly, horribly, serious. This was not some hideous jest. Or a nightmare she might hope to wake from. This was *real*.

The beginnings of a severe headache pressed sharply against Elizabeth's forehead, causing her to wrinkle her brow. What had happened to her father? Why was he refusing to see how ridiculous this was? Why wasn't he listening to her?

In the face of his obvious pigheadedness, Elizabeth did the only thing she could think of. She turned to the duchess.

"Mother . . ."

Her grace, bless her shoe buckles, came immediately to her daughter's defense. "Alaric, I cannot help but agree that Elizabeth would be ill suited to life as a farmer's wife." She quickly added, "I mean no offense, Mr. MacKinnon."

The Scotsman merely shrugged. "No offense is taken, your grace."

Elizabeth turned to him. "Do you mean to say you honestly agree with this . . . this absurd stipulation?"

He nodded over a sip of wine. "Aye, lass, I do."

"But you didn't even wish to get married. If you will recall, you were forced to do it."

"Aye, but I find I've had a change of heart, lass."

"What?"

"Aye." He looked at her. "After speaking with your da, I've opted to give you a go."

"*You*'ve opted to give *me* a go?" Elizabeth's vision blurred. "How dare y—!"

She drew up, narrowed her eyes, and prepared to launch into a storm of invective—until a realization suddenly and clearly dawned on her.

"Of course. You saw this house and everything in it and thought you'd just stepped into a fortune, didn't you?" She looked to her father. "Can you not see what he is about, Father? No doubt he assumes the longer he stands fast, the more you'll pay just to be rid of him."

But the duke didn't seem concerned, not at all. "Truth be told, Elizabeth, at first I offered Mr. MacKinnon any sum he chose to agree to the annulment, but he refused it."

"Of course he refused it. He's a cattle drover! He knows what it is to bargain for the most lucrative price. You're a duke, and I'm your oldest daughter, so he must realize you would give him anything he wanted to—"

"Actually, I tend to believe he would have agreed to the annulment for nothing."

Nothing? Then why didn't he?

Something wasn't right, and when the two men exchanged a private glance, Elizabeth knew there was something about the matter she wasn't being told.

She lifted her chin. "And if I should refuse to go with him?"

The duke's expression sobered. "I thought this might be your response, Elizabeth, so I have come up with a compromise for you."

"Compromise?" This brought Elizabeth forward in her chair. "What sort of compromise?"

The duke leveled her a stare. "If you will give me your word that you will try, really try to make the best of this marriage for the next two months, and if you still wish for the annulment afterward, I will petition the Crown myself for it. Furthermore, I will settle on you an annuity that will allow you to live comfortably for the duration of your life. I will never again beleaguer you with prospective husbands or make any attempt to influence you to marry. You may live here at Drayton Hall, or you may even take up residence at one of the other properties, if you so desire. They most of them stand empty as it is. The choice is up to you."

Elizabeth could only stare at her father, dumbfounded. "Even the house in London?"

"Yes, Elizabeth," the duke said calmly. "Even the house in London."

London.

All her life, Elizabeth had dreamed of living a life of her own in that wonderful, extraordinary city among the noise and the people and the hundreds of millions of *things* that simply awaited her pleasure—the theatre, the museums, the menagerie in the Tower. She could dress however she liked, even if it wasn't considered "fashionable," and eat porridge for supper if the mood struck her. She would surround herself with a circle of acquaintances from every walk of life—writers, scientists, politicians, even royalty. She would hold soirees where they would have intelligent discussion about literature and other topics of the day amongst both men and women together. And she would write, *oh,* would she write. . . .

The duchess spoke up then, breaking Elizabeth from her grand imaginings.

"Alaric, do you realize what it is you are saying?"

"Yes, Margaret, I do. Believe me when I say I have given this quite a lot of thought. From the time she was a little girl, Elizabeth has always told us she has no wish to marry. To this day, she has never wavered in that wish. I simply want her to see what it is she is refusing before she resigns herself to a life of solitude. So I am just choosing to delay a bit before seeking an annulment. The damage is done. They are already wed and there will be a scandal no matter what comes of it. So we might as well take advantage of the opportunity that has presented itself. Trial marriages have been done in Scotland for centuries. Whether she wants to believe it or not, I do want Elizabeth's happiness, and if this is what it takes, and she will agree to spend the two months on Skye as I am asking, then I am willing to make this compromise." He took up his glass of wine and swallowed a sip. "Granted, of course, that at the end of these two months, the marriage has not been consummated."

There was silence from around the table as everyone considered the duke's most unconventional proposal.

Finally, it was the littlest one who spoke first.

"Father?"

"Yes, Caroline?"

"What does that word mean?"

"Which word, my dear?"

"Um . . . that word you said. *Consummate.*"

The duke looked across the table at his wife. "Margaret, why is the child not yet in bed?"

"I thought, after the ordeal she went through earlier today with the vase, that she could . . ." At the duke's deepening frown, the duchess gave it up and called for a maid to come and take charge of her daughter.

Caroline, of course, immediately protested.

"But Mama, I haven't yet finished my syllabub!"

"You've had more than enough, Caroline, dear. Your father is right. After-supper conversation is not appropriate for young girls. It is time for all you little ones to go off to bed now. Good night, sweetings."

"*Ohh,*" chorused the younger three Draytons.

While her sisters gave their mother sulky parting kisses, Elizabeth sat at the other end of the table, chewing over her father's offer.

Two months alone with the Scotsman.

In exchange she would receive a lifetime of freedom, to do what she wanted, when she wanted.

Could she survive it?

Elizabeth smiled.

It would be the easiest thing she had ever done.

"Good night, Bess."

Elizabeth looked up to see that Caroline had finished circling the table and was standing before her now, arms open, waiting. The sight of her small face immediately made the troubles she faced melt away into the background.

When Elizabeth had heard Caroline's screams earlier that evening, and had seen her tiny body knotted so tightly inside that urn, she had known, truly known, how terrible a thing fear could be. She'd been paralyzed by it, unable to think what they should do to free her. But she hadn't had to think. She hadn't had to do a thing. It had been MacKinnon who had known, who had acted without hesitation and without a care for whether the vase he shattered were a priceless treasure or a clever copy.

Elizabeth realized then she had never thanked him for it.

"Sweet dreams, puss," she said and kissed Caroline on the tip of her nose. "Off with you now."

But when she reached the door, where her nursemaid awaited, Caroline paused a moment, then turned slowly to make her way back across the room.

"Good night to you, too, Mr. Dubh."

Elizabeth watched as the Scotsman smiled warmly at her sister, not in the way adults generally did, but with genuine, heartfelt affection.

"Good night there, wee lassie," he said tucking a finger underneath her chin. "Now you hie yourself off to your dreams and no more trying to be a pretty marmalade in a jam jar, aye?"

Caroline smiled. "Thank you again for saving me today, sir. I shall never forget it."

She reached up then, wrapping her tiny arms tightly around his great neck. And then Caroline did the unimaginable. She kissed the man on the tip of his cragged nose, just as Elizabeth had always done to her, whispering to him in a voice that only Elizabeth could hear.

"And if Bess decides not to be married to you anymore, don't be sad. When I grow up, I will marry you."

The Scotsman grinned and kissed Caroline on the nose in return. "I'll be certain to remember that, lassie."

It was well into the early hours of morning when Douglas finally resigned himself to the fact that he was not going to achieve sleep with any success. He'd spent several hours since supper lying in the bed he'd been given for the night, staring at the pattern of light cast by the moon across the decorative plasterwork ceiling. The fire in the hearth was nearly spent. The rest of the family had long since retired, and he hadn't heard a servant walking in the hall in over an hour. Any moment and the clock ticking against the wall was going to strike the unholy hour of two.

When it did, Douglas finally got up and headed off for a quiet walk through the house.

This restlessness he felt was really nothing new to him; it was a feeling he had known since he'd been a lad. When he was home at Dunakin and unable to sleep, he would often climb the tower stairs to the castle ramparts, looking out over the sleepy waters of Loch Alsh. He would think about his father living far away in France, outlawed from his homeland for standing by what he'd believed in. His hands would rest on the same mortar and pitted sandstone that had protected the MacKinnons for over five centuries, and he would draw comfort from the wisdom, the honor of his ancestors who had stood on those same ramparts before him, the sons of kings, warriors, men of honor.

With the wind whipping sharp across his face, stung red by the salt of the sea, Douglas would look out across the churning waters of Kyleakin to the cottage lights that dimmed and flickered along the Scottish mainland. If there were a mist, it would turn the moon into a fat milky pearl, hovering in an ocean of shimmering haze, and he would let it embrace him, that mist, like a smoky mantle.

But he was far away from his home now and Douglas moved without a sound along the thick carpet, winding his way past doors and along curving stairwells that daren't give the slightest creak beneath his weight. He stopped for a time in a long picture gallery, lit blue by the moon beaming in through a wall of windows on one side. Portraits of Draytons past stared down at him from paneled walls, Tudor personages predominating, some he recognized, some he did not. There was a good portrait of King Henry the Eighth in all his massive glory, staring out regally from behind that podgy bearded face with the bland air of someone born to royalty. Lords and ladies, knights and princes, they stood as a testament to the generations past. There was a portrait of what must have been one of the earlier dukes of Sudeleigh, dressed in the style of the previous century and looking a great deal like the present duke. Children posed with hounds. Ladies looked serene and noble. And at the very end of the gallery, framed in gilt, a single portrait hung alone.

At first glance, Douglas thought it might be a portrait of Lady Elizabeth, for she had the same red-gold hair, the same slender face, and those keen hazel eyes. She sat holding a book, her hair hanging free about her shoulders. But as he took a closer look, noting the details of the costume, he realized this wasn't a portrait of Lady Elizabeth at all. Instead it was the young princess, Elizabeth, daughter of Henry, painted when she'd been a young lass, long before she'd ever become Virgin Queen of England.

The resemblance was uncanny, and Douglas stared at the portrait a while, comparing the two feature-for-feature. It was as he turned to leave that Douglas noticed the ring on the slender finger of the portrait's subject, the same ring Elizabeth had offered to give him the previous night at the inn, if he would agree to pose as her betrothed.

Now, some four-and-twenty hours later, they were wed.

As he left the gallery, Douglas spotted a door slightly open down the hall. He recognized it as the duke's study, and wondered if perhaps he might find a book inside to help him relax. But when he pushed the door open, he found himself stopping to gaze at the sight that met him on the other side.

She was sitting in an armchair, asleep in the light of the fire, wearing a white nightgown that buttoned to her neck, making her look more vulnerable somehow. Douglas entered the room on silent feet, stopping just beside the chair. A book lay open in her hands. He reached for it and as he knelt staring down at her in the flickering hearthlight, he found himself studying her face for what was really the first time, the sweep of lashes, the pale, tiny-veined lids, a nose that wasn't pert or quaint or even delicate, but slender and straight.

He looked at her mouth for a very long time. He couldn't help himself. And suddenly, his own mouth longed to taste it, to feel the fullness of her lips move against his.

Lulled by the embrace of the fire, by the pull and promise of her kiss, Douglas found himself lowering his head to hers.

The moment they touched, mouth to mouth, the fire snapped in the hearth, shooting sparks every which way.

She jerked awake and stared at him in the firelight. Her breath, warm and startled, fanned against his face. He straightened over her slowly, watching her blink, her brow furrowing in confusion. Douglas didn't say a word, just held himself still and stared at her in the glow of the fire.

A few moments later, her eyes drifted closed once again.

Taking up a blanket folded over a nearby chair, Douglas draped it gently over her. She sighed and curled into it. He tossed another log upon the fire, and then lowered himself into the chair across from her, crossing his legs to sit and watch her sleep in the firelight.

Chapter Eight

"Bess, please, just talk to Father. He loves you. He will listen to you. I know you can make him reconsider this . . . this unreasonable proposal."

The sisters were standing together in Elizabeth's bed-chamber, surrounded by a scattering of stockings, gowns, and slippers. It was late afternoon. The sunlight outside was just beginning to gray. Elizabeth pulled another gown from inside her wardrobe, giving it a quick glance before she tossed it with the others already heaped across the bed.

She stood back for a moment and studied the burgeoning pile of lace and satin and silk.

What exactly, she wondered, did one wear to stay at a farm on a remote Scottish island? She quickly cast aside the pastel yellow silk with the Belgian lace edging, then turned toward her fretting sister.

"Bella, I have already told you I don't wish Father to reconsider. Unreasonable proposal or no, I want to go to

Skye. Can you not see? All I have to do is get through these next two months and then I will be free, free to do as I please, when I please. I need never fear having to live under the thumb of a domineering husband. I need never again listen to Father lament my spinsterhood as if it were some strange new disease one of my sisters might catch. I can live my life in total independence just as I have always dreamed."

But Isabella just stared at her, stared at her for some time, her face screwed up with anxiety until she finally blurted out, "But you don't understand. This isn't the way it was supposed to happen!"

Supposed to happen . . . ?

"Bella, what do you mean?"

Isabella turned away and crossed the room to stand before the window with her arms folded tightly over her chest. She had her back to the room, quiet, still. After a moment, Elizabeth could see her shoulders trembling.

Was she crying?

"Bell? Bella, what is wrong? I don't understand what you mean. What was supposed to happen?"

Isabella turned to face her. All of her emotions—confusion, reluctance, dread—fluttered across her face like falling autumn leaves. "Oh, Bess, don't you see? This is all my fault!"

"Your fault?"

"Yes. I'm the one who made you do this. I felt so badly for not telling you the truth about our trip to Lord Purfoyle's estate. If only I had told you as soon as I knew of it, then maybe we wouldn't have ended up on that road right when that sheep was standing in the middle of it, but Father said if I told you . . . and well, after I found you that morning, I thought that if you married Mr. MacKinnon, it would do away with any threat of Lord Purfoyle completely. Which it has. And that's good. But now this. I knew Father would be angry, but I never expected . . . I never even dreamed he would demand that you stay married. He's a Scottish farmer! You're the daughter of a duke! I was certain Father would demand an annulment and then it would no longer matter. But instead it is such a mess."

Elizabeth took her sister by the arms. "Bella, stop. Please don't blame yourself for this. I'm the one who drank all that whisky. I'm the one who ended up with him in my bed. And in the end, I'm the one who vowed to be his wife in that taproom."

"Yes . . . but now how will you ever find the right man? The one you are truly destined to be with?"

Elizabeth shook her head. "Isabella, there is no right man for me. I've always known that. I'm not like you. I don't believe there is always one special woman for one special man destined to run across one another in some crowded ballroom, who will know the moment their eyes meet that they were meant to spend their lives together. It just isn't logical to me."

Bella lifted her head, looking at her sister as if she were suddenly looking upon the face of a stranger. "How can you say that, Elizabeth? What of love? Of passion?"

"Sweet Bella. Love and passion, swiftly beating hearts and tender romance, they are the things of novels and poetry to me. I know you believe in them, believe without doubt that you will one day find your Prince Charming, and I love that in you, that unflinching faith in the idea, truly I do. But just as it is so much a part of you, that faith, it just isn't in my nature to spend my days dreaming about a knight errant on a white horse or wishing for pretty words whispered in the moonlight. I'm simply not made in that way."

Bella wasn't to be convinced. "You only think that because you have never once considered it any other way. What of children, Bess? I've seen you with Caro, how you are with her, have been with her since the day she was born. You love her so much. Do you never wish to be a mother yourself? To know what it is to give life to a child of your own body?"

A child. Elizabeth hesitated. For the first time in her life she felt something, like the flutter of a bird's wing, deep, deep inside her. It lasted only for a moment, then it was gone.

"I won't need to have any children of my own, Bella, when I can be the eccentric aunt to all the many you're going to have—when you find your Prince Charming, of course. Then I shall spend my days indulging their every whim and spoiling their supper with sweetmeats every chance I get."

But Bella was still frowning. "I shall miss you terribly, you know. As will the others. Caroline is beside herself about it. She's hidden herself away beneath her bed and refuses to come out. And Mattie is quite certain you'll be snatched away by faeries in the middle of the night. Catherine simply takes out her displeasure on the spinet, pounding on the keys till I swear I can hear them begging her to stop."

Elizabeth took her sister's hands and squeezed them tightly. "And I shall miss you all, too. But really, two months isn't so long, and just think of what a grand adventure I will have to tell you when I return." She put on a smile. "Now help me finish in here so I can be on my way and then home all the sooner."

Bella nodded reluctantly and then contented herself with folding Elizabeth's chemises, packing them neatly inside one of her traveling trunks while Elizabeth took to the wardrobe with renewed vigor. She picked through her bonnets and shoes, shifts and stockings, tossing them at the open lid of the trunk, while others were left behind. The work of it kept her hands busy; she only wished it would have kept her thoughts occupied, too, so she wouldn't have to think about the weeks to come.

Much as she'd like Bella and everyone else to believe she was assured of the challenge she faced, the fact of the matter was she was terrified to her toes.

All her life she had stood fast in her desire for a life independent of the captivity of marriage. After all, she had been named for the Virgin Queen of England, the unflappable Elizabeth, who had needed no man to show her how to rule an entire kingdom. But just like the bird who teeters at the edge of its nest readying to take flight for the very first time, Elizabeth found a small part of her clinging to the security she had always known at home.

What would it be like, she wondered, living in a land as foreign to her as the Far East, a land that was peopled by raiders and rebels, whose children were taught war cries instead of nursery rhymes? Would they look on her as an enemy? Would she ever see her home, her family, again? Would some kelpie come and snatch her away while she lay in her bed at night?

Elizabeth was so lost in her jumble of thoughts, she never noticed that Isabella had come to stand beside her.

"Elizabeth, what of Father's condition—that you not consummate your marriage?"

"What of it?"

"Do you really think you can hold fast to it?"

"Isabella Anne!"

Isabella instantly blushed. "Well, I cannot help but be the slightest bit curious about it . . . about what it would be like to . . ."

"To fornicate with a man?"

"Bess! Must you always be so forthright?"

"What would you prefer I call it? 'Basketmaking' like the ladies in mother's tea circle?"

Isabella had to giggle at that, remembering how they'd sat one summer's afternoon while her mother and her small society of friends, dressed in their finest gowns, had discussed the intricacies of "basketmaking" all the while thinking the girls none the wiser.

"You cannot deny Mr. MacKinnon is a very handsome man."

Elizabeth looked at her. "Handsome? I suppose he is, in a rugged, utterly primitive sort of way."

"He is quite tall."

"Lumbering," Elizabeth countered. "Like a tree."

"And his face," Isabella went on, "is very strong. Almost as if it were cut from solid stone."

"The man rebels against the idea of a razor. He is forever unkempt. His hair is too long, and he always wears it tied back in that ridiculous string of leather with bits of it falling about his forehead. In fact, now that I think of it, he *is* quite a barbarian."

Isabella, however, was of another mind, one where knights and damsels dwelled in shining castles that stood high in the clouds. She scarcely heard her sister's comments. "His eyes are like iced steel, so blue they can just melt you with their stare. And his mouth, full, firm, uncompromising . . ."

But they can turn to tenderness with just the touch of a kiss . . .

The thought came unbidden.

"Elizabeth, are you feeling all right? Your face . . . it looks suddenly flushed."

Elizabeth pressed a hand against her cheek, disgusted to feel it warm beneath her fingers. She turned away. "From the way you rattle on, it should have been your bed he slept in, not mine. I would swear you are half smitten with the man. Now, enough of this silliness. The day grows late and I've packing to finish. Where is that footman? We called for him some time ago to come and fetch these trunks and he—"

She yanked her bedroom door wide, stopping when she found the way blocked on the other side.

"What are you doing here?"

MacKinnon stood in the doorway, filling it, his face dark and impassive. His eyes, the same ones Isabella had just been extolling in poetry, looked at her hard. They never once left hers.

"I came to fetch your trunks."

Elizabeth felt her arms go to gooseflesh beneath his stare. "We have footmen to see to that, Mr. MacKinnon." It was all she could think of to say.

"And I've arms that are just as able to do the job, my lady." He pushed past her and walked into her room without waiting for any invitation. The place seemed to shrink with just the arrival of him.

Elizabeth was suddenly very conscious of the mess they'd made in packing and started retrieving some of the scattered things from the floor. "I'm not quite finished packing. Perhaps if you—"

"Is that one there ready to go?" He motioned toward a trunk that stood nearest the door.

"Yes, but you'd better wait for the footman. It really is quite heavy—"

He lifted the trunk in one swift sweep, hoisting it upon his broad shoulder. He balanced the heavy case seemingly without effort, and headed for the door. "I'll be back for the other."

Elizabeth merely stood and watched him go. She had no other choice.

When he was gone, Isabella came across the room to stand beside her. "Did you see that, the way he lifted that trunk as if it weighed nothing? It would have taken two of our footmen to carry that."

Elizabeth didn't say anything.

She couldn't.

It was taking every effort for her to keep her mouth from falling open.

They were leaving at dawn the following morning, traveling on horseback since a carriage, even a small gig pulled by one, wouldn't be able to travel any further than Fort William into the Highlands.

At supper the night before, Douglas had convinced the duke that they would be safer on land since the waters on Scotland's western coast were heavily patrolled by English cutters on the lookout for the fugitive Prince Charles. He assured him he could steer them through safely using little known drover's paths and hunter's trails far away from the main roads. Elizabeth's trunks with her clothing, books, and other personal belongings, however, would be too much of a hindrance for them to bring along. So her things would have to be sent separately by boat, meeting them when they arrived on Skye nearly a fortnight hence.

At precisely six o'clock, wearing her best riding habit and smart cocked hat, Elizabeth strode out the front door of Drayton Hall, pulling on her gloves. The morning had broken only a half hour before to a sky laden with low-scudding clouds and the threat of coming rain. The heaviness of the air, however, only matched the heaviness of the mood as the Draytons assembled en masse to bid Elizabeth farewell.

Elizabeth embraced her younger sisters, first Catherine and Matilda, reminding them to write to her every day while she was away. Caro, who had been coaxed out from under her bed only moments before, clasped her pudgy arms around Elizabeth's voluminous skirts and begged for the umpteenth time to go with her. In order to convince her to let go, Elizabeth had to remind her of how difficult the journey would be and that they didn't have lemon syllabub in Scotland. She promised she would be back with lots of stories to tell her and would send her youngest sister a present when she got there.

After disentangling herself from Caro, Elizabeth turned to Bella, who managed to smile at Elizabeth even with tears glistening in her eyes.

"What shall I do without you here?" Isabella whispered against her cheek as she hugged her tightly. "We shall all of us waste away from boredom without having you here to yell at Father over breakfast about Socrates or the state of things in the Colonies."

"Then you shall just have to yell at him in my stead, Bella." She looked at her sister seriously. "I am counting on you to see to things here for me while I'm away. Someone has to help Caroline with her ciphering. And Mattie, you must make certain she practices her penmanship each day. She's developing quite a lovely hand. Oh, and Father always forgets to take time away for his afternoon walk in the garden. It keeps his temper calm and that makes Mother a much happier woman. Will you do that for me?"

Fighting hard against her emotions, Isabella nodded.

The duchess embraced Elizabeth next, squeezing her more tightly than she'd ever done before. "Be careful, my dearest," she whispered. "Scotland is a vastly different place than England." She pressed a small pouch that felt heavy with coin into Elizabeth's gloved hand. "Just in case you should need it . . ."

Elizabeth nodded her thanks before finally turning to face her father.

He stood at the end of a sniffling assembly of females, trying very hard to appear austere and ducal. His cravat was knotted neatly, his wig powdered and trim, but as he took her by the shoulders, pulling her against him to plant a kiss on her cheek, she heard his breath hitch just a little. "I will come in two months' time, Elizabeth, to hear your decision. Whatever it may be."

Elizabeth nodded, swallowing against a lump in her throat. Despite their disagreement, she would truly miss him.

"Yes, Father," was all she could manage before she

broke away, squaring her shoulders as she moved down the steps to the drive where her horse—and her husband—awaited.

Since they were going to ride, MacKinnon had abandoned his plaid in favor of a pair of tartan trews, a Scottish sort of breeches, closely cut, that covered both feet and legs, which he wore beneath his dark-colored coat. His bonnet of blue sat atilt his forehead as he merely sat his horse, watching the farewells through eyes that were hooded and vague.

"Take care of my daughter, MacKinnon."

"Aye, your grace," was all he said.

Then, with the help of the mounting block that had stood before the Drayton house for centuries, Elizabeth hoisted herself onto the sidesaddle. She arranged her skirts around her and took up the reins from the stable boy, before turning her mount to steal a final glimpse of her family as they stood atop the steps.

The image of them burned itself into her memory. Elizabeth blinked against the sting of tears. How she would miss them.

With a click of her tongue and a nudge of her heel, she started off down the drive, ready to embark on the most significant two months of her life.

Chapter Nine

Douglas glanced once at Elizabeth as they crossed the rushing waters of the burn, and with it, the border into Scotland.

They had been riding for hours, crossing bleak marshland tufted with reedy grass where only the hardiest of sheep would graze. The sun, what there was of it, hovered high above them, lost in a sky that was as colorless, as barren as a blank artist's canvas, without so much as the dark fleck of a bird in flight to smear it. Now and again they would pass the ruins of the ancient pele towers that had once defended the border marches against lawless bands of reivers. They were now naught but empty crumbling shells whose stone walls sometimes seemed to echo, whenever the wind blew just right, with the clang of steel on steel and the thunder of marauding hooves.

Nearer the border, moorland had finally given over to mosses and lush valleys, with forests so thick with pine and oak that at times all but the smallest traces of daylight were blotted out.

Instead of circling the woods, Douglas went through them, on an old reiver's trail known by very few, steering their course clear of the main northbound roads in order to avoid the patrols that were certain to be guarding the border. As such they hadn't seen another soul since they had skirted that last tiny village some distance back.

Elizabeth had said very little during their journey, answering his few attempts at conversation with a "yes" or a "no," sometimes just a shake of her head. She sat stiffly in the saddle, even all these hours later, staring ahead in stony silence at the neverending stretch of distance. Douglas had only known her a few days, but it was long enough to know that this silence of hers wasn't a good thing. This was a woman who always had something to say, and the fact that she didn't now—and hadn't for some time—was starting to become cause for concern.

Douglas pulled his horse to a halt, then turned in the saddle to face her. They were on a narrow path only wide enough for a single rider.

"Your cook packed us some food and we've made good time so far. Would you care to stop for a wee bit to stretch your legs and have a bite to eat?"

Elizabeth glanced at him negligently, then nodded. Nothing more.

Frowning, Douglas led them through the trees to a small clearing where the burn rippled softly over moss-skimmed rocks thick with gorse and tufts of marram grass. Heather bloomed in brilliant splashes of red, fuchsia, and white, and the sun had finally broken through, glistening on the damp fir branches like faerie teardrops.

Douglas watched Elizabeth dismount, then take a moment to accustom her legs to standing again after all the time she'd spent riding. Amazingly, she still looked as neat and trim as she had when they had departed with her hair tucked up beneath a smart hat, and a snowy cravat knotted primly beneath her chin. The tip of her nose, he noticed then, had a nice touch of color to it from the wind.

Without a word, Elizabeth led her mount to a patch of sweet forest grass to graze, removed her gloves and knelt beside the burn, dipping her fingers in the cold water to ease their stiffness.

"Are you going to be silent like this all the way to Skye then?" he finally said, hunkering down a space away to cup the water in his hands for a drink. It slid against the dryness of his throat, cool and bracing and good, so good in fact that he cupped some more and ran his hands back through his hair, over his face, relishing the sweet, wet chill of it.

Douglas stood and gave his head a shake to dry it, dashing droplets everywhere. He took a deep breath, filling his lungs with the brisk of the air. It felt good to be back, back on this land, sweet Alba, land of the Gael, kingdom of the mist and the thistle. He closed his eyes, threw back his head, and yelled from sheer unadulterated joy.

When next he looked, Elizabeth was staring at him as if he'd just crawled out from beneath a rock.

"You should try it," he said. "It's glorious. Go on, open your arms wide and give out a good wail."

But she simply gazed at him blankly, as if he wasn't really there.

"It will be a very long journey indeed, lass, if we cannot at least pass the time with some conversation."

"I haven't anything to say."

"Somehow I find that difficult to believe."

She stared at him, and Douglas noticed for the first time the way her brow creased deeply right in the middle between her eyes when she frowned.

"Actually, it's just that I haven't anything to say *to you*, Mr. MacKinnon."

Douglas quirked a small smile. "So do you mean to say you'll not be speaking at all while we're together? Not even to hear the sound of your own voice? Because two months is a dreadful long time for a person to hold their tongue." He added, "Particularly when that person is a woman."

He watched as she straightened and shook her hands dry. Her backbone went as straight as a bayonet, her voice cut as sharply as its blade.

"Sometimes, Mr. MacKinnon, holding one's tongue can be a blessing to the others in company." She added, "You should consider that the next time you feel the urge to bay at the moon."

Now that's more like it, Douglas thought with satisfaction.

But he wasn't finished with her. Oh, no. Not yet.

He straightened and followed her as she made her way back to the horses. "Perhaps it would help matters for you, make you more at ease in speaking with me, if we did away with the formalities. Besides, it wouldn't do for the wife of a Scotsman to be calling him anything other than his given name. Which is Douglas." He grinned. "In case you've forgotten."

"I am well aware of your name, sir."

"Och, but there you go again. Not 'sir,' or 'Mr. Mac-Kinnon,' but Douglas. Of course, if you'd prefer it, I suppose you could call me 'Sweetheart' or 'Hinny' instead . . ."

"Douglas will be sufficient," she said, giving him her back.

"Fine. Well, then, glad we have that settled . . . *Bessie*."

She whirled on him. "My name is Elizabeth."

"Aye, that it is. But it's a somewhat complicated name, particularly for a Scottish barbarian like myself to remember."

They were her words, overheard when she'd been talking to her sister. From the look that came over her face, an appealing rush of color to her cheeks, she realized it as well.

"If you cannot call me by my given name, I would rather you call me nothing at all then."

"*Nothing-at-all-then?*" He rubbed his bearded chin. "Oh, I dinna think I like the sound of that one at all. Bessie it is, then."

"Not if you expect me to answer you."

As Elizabeth started rummaging through the saddle panniers, Douglas sat back against the trunk of a fat oak, folded his arms and crossed his legs before him to watch her. She took out a round of dark bread, some cheese, an apple, and a skin of wine.

He closed his eyes and tilted his face to the sky. "I'll

take mine here in the shade where its cool and the ground is soft."

He couldn't see her, but he knew she was staring at him. "You'll take your what?"

"My food, Bessie. Just some bread and the apple. Maybe a little wine. You can serve me here."

"Serve you?"

"Aye." He stretched his arms contentedly. "'Tis a wife's duty, after all, to serve the man. And you are my wife, even if it is just for two months." He opened one eye then. "So serve me."

It was a good thing Douglas's reflexes were sharp. More by instinct than for any other reason, he raised his hand just as the apple sailed straight for his head. It slapped into the palm of his hand and he closed his fingers over it. Grinning, he took a bite of it. "Many thanks, Bessie."

Elizabeth stared at him, watching as he closed his eyes, and chewed the apple with such relish that the juice ended up dribbling down his chin.

Uncivilized . . . dunder-headed . . . clod!

She wanted to clout him. She wanted to push him into the river and dance on his head, only he wouldn't drown. No, the water was too shallow, damn it. And his head was too hard. It would be a waste of both her time and her effort.

She tossed the food back inside the panniers and turned, her skirts swishing as she stalked away.

"Lost your appetite then, Bessie?"

She refused to give him the satisfaction of a response. But just as soon as she was out of eyeshot, Elizabeth kicked at a rock, wincing when it proved far more inflexible than the toe of her half boot. Limping slightly now, she found a stray twig that proved much more amenable than the rock. She unleashed her frustration on it, snapping it in two, then in four for good measure.

Bessie . . .

He made her sound like a bloody cow! She might as well hang a bell around her neck and stick a bucket under her belly. Try as she might to come up with some ridiculous and laughable name for him, she could think of nothing. Nothing at all. Douglas was simply that. *Douglas.*

It was sometime later when Elizabeth finally realized she had no idea how far she'd walked. Nothing looked familiar and there wasn't any sign of Douglas or the horses anywhere behind her. The sun was starting to darken behind a new cover of clouds, but she wasn't too worried. She would have the trees to shelter her if it started to rain and he certainly couldn't go any further without her. It would serve him right for calling her that horrible name. So she sat down atop a large boulder to wait, searching for more reasons to make it his fault.

After a while, her irritation began to melt as she let the serenity of her surroundings embrace her. She closed her eyes and a soft breeze rushed through the reeds along the riverbank, filling the air with the fragrance of pine and heather and rushing water. Her shoulders loosened and the tightness knotting in the back of her neck began to ease as deep in her mind's eye, she began to picture a house. It would be made of pale sandstone with a fanlight over the front door and tall narrow windows that faced onto a busy street, gleaming windows that winked in the morning sunlight like diamonds. In the back, behind a high wall, she would have a garden, her own private Eden with an ivy-shaded bench where she could sit and read for hours in the summer sunlight with the mingling scents of honeysuckle and jessamine, lilac and lavender all around her. The address would be fashionable, but still tucked away from the fray of the city, near the park so she could ride in the mornings before anyone else but the costermongers were about.

It was her house.

She wondered what it would be like, living on her own, accountable to no one. She wondered at the fascinating things she would see and do, the intriguing people she would meet. She wondered if she would take a lover . . . and then she wondered why she should not.

She was so lost in thought, so caught up in her plans, she never heard the sounds of approach coming from behind her—until a gravelly voice suddenly pulled her, jerking her back to the present.

"Well, wha' 'ave we 'ere, Brodie? By the looks o' it, she's a wee faerie sprite me mither used to tell me stories 'bout when I were a laddie."

Elizabeth spun around, searching the trees.

"Nae, she be no faerie, Murdoch. She looks more like a fine Sassenach lassie sitting all alone 'ere in the woods jus' waitin' for us to come upon her and show her wha' a true Scotsman can give her."

Elizabeth turned just as two men slipped from behind the cover of the trees not a handful of yards away.

How had she not heard them?

They wore plaids dyed in muted shades of green and brown, making them nearly indistinguishable against the trees. Their faces were grimy, their hair hung long, stringy beneath their tattered bonnets of blue. They didn't wear coats, only masses of plaid thrown over bony shoulders and ruddy linen shirts that were torn and stained. They each carried a rusty sword and pistol strapped to their sides. And as they drew nearer, Elizabeth realized that the rust on their swords was not rust at all. It was something else that looked very much like dried blood.

The sun seemed to darken. Even the birds had grown suddenly quiet in the trees. Elizabeth's heartbeat raced, thudding against her chest, even as she told herself to remain calm, not to show her fear.

Something told her if she showed how terrified she truly was, she was done for.

"Good afternoon, gentlemen," she said in the calmest, most pleasant voice she could muster. She cleared her throat and attempted a smile. "Thank you for the offer of your company, but I was just going on my way. This is a lovely spot, and I have enjoyed it, but the day grows short and I am due to meet my husband."

The security of that word—*husband*—gave Elizabeth the strength to slowly rise from the rock she'd been sitting on and start to move away.

"But *sair*tainly you can stay a wee bit *lang*er, lassie."

Elizabeth shook her head. "Oh, I'm afraid I really cannot. You see I promised my husband I would only be a minute, and I fear it's been much longer even than that. Good day to you both."

Elizabeth turned and started away. She decided against weaving a path through the woods and instead took to the open ground that ran alongside the burn. It would be better for her if she suddenly needed to run.

Unfortunately, where she stood, the burn was too wide, its waters rushing too strongly for her to distance herself from them by taking to the other side. With the weight of her skirts, she wouldn't make it halfway across, so instead she put a firm grip on her skirts and picked her way swiftly along the rocks that littered the water's edge.

It hadn't seemed such a distance in coming there, but now the empty woods stretched in front of her with no end in sight. Where was Douglas? Where were the horses? She wasn't even sure she was heading in the right direction. She glanced back once when she heard the sound of footsteps and was alarmed to see that the men were trailing her. They were grinning and they did not run, but rather matched their stride to hers so that no matter how she tried, she couldn't put any further distance between them.

Elizabeth stopped suddenly and turned to face them.

"Truly, gentlemen, I do appreciate the offer of an escort, but I can make it very well on my own. Please do not trouble yourselves on my account. It really isn't necessary."

"But we wouldna be proper gentlemen, now would we, if we were to let a fine lassie like yerself wander off alone? There be brigands and the like hiding in these woods. You ne'er know what sort o' mischief might befall you."

His companion, Brodie or Murdoch, she knew not one from the other, chuckled. "Aye, brigands. And out here, in the thick of beyond, there's no' a soul who could hear you scream. . . ."

He took a step toward her. Elizabeth didn't hesitate. She turned, grabbed up her skirts, and ran for her life.

Behind her, the men whooped, sending up a cheer as they took to the hunt with the eagerness of predators. Elizabeth focused on the line of trees ahead, willing herself to reach them, hoping she could lose them in the thick of the forest, refusing to give in to the fear that was threatening to overtake her.

She reached a clearing where the ground flattened out and she tore across it, fighting for every breath against the lacings of her stays. Her hat tumbled to her feet. Her hair was soon falling from its pins down her back. The two men only laughed behind her, easily closing the distance between them.

When one of them grabbed her elbow, Elizabeth screamed. She was pulled to the ground, twigs and rocks digging into her backside as he captured her beneath his weight.

"Now where're you off t' in such a hurry, eh, lass?"

She opened her mouth to scream but he smothered it with his hand. She was breathing hard through her nose. His face was inches from hers, smelling of everything foul and vile. Close to him now, she could see an angry scar that slashed its way across one cheek, ending at his ear. Elizabeth's vision blurred and she struggled against him, flailing as he reached for her skirts, grappling with the layers of petticoats underneath as he tried to yank them up.

Elizabeth managed to free her arm and ripped at his face with her nails, tearing at his eyes, his ears. He yelled and hit her in the jaw, stunning her for a moment before she clouted him once on the side of the head. He shouted to his friend and in the next moment, her arms were being jerked above her head, stretched and held there.

She'd never felt so afraid in her life. The sunlight began to fade. Somewhere in the back of her mind she realized she was going to faint. She couldn't breathe. She couldn't see. All she could do was smell his stench, feel him pressing her hard into the ground as he fumbled with his clothing, trying to free himself.

She couldn't faint. She couldn't give up. She had to do something—anything—but give up, but before she could think of what that something was, the weight of him was gone and she was suddenly free.

A single pistol shot sounded, sending the birds from the trees in a panic. Elizabeth lifted her head and through the tangle of her hair, she saw Douglas standing not two yards away, looking down at the motionless body of the brute who had been assaulting her. His eyes were cold with rage. The barrel of his pistol was still smoking.

Then he turned on the other man.

"We . . . we were just having us a bit o' fun with the lass! We didna hurt her. Not badly anyway. Wha's your trouble, man? She's only a bloody Sassenach!"

Douglas grabbed the man by his throat and lifted him until his feet were dangling and his breath was clogged in his neck. He lifted the pistol, placing the nose of it against the man's nostril. It didn't seem to occur to him, or to the man quavering in his grip, that he'd already spent his shot. When Douglas spoke, his voice was as hard and cold as the steel blade of a sword.

"That *bloody Sassenach,* you worthless piece of filth, is my wife. If you wish to see the break of another day, I suggest you run from here as fast as your scrawny legs will carry you. Don't stop running until you are bent and vomiting. And if you ever treat another woman with such disrespect, I will hunt you down wherever you run and I will kill you."

Douglas threw the man away from him, sending him sprawling not six inches from the lifeless body of his friend. He scrambled to his feet and ran across the clearing, disappearing through the trees in seconds.

Douglas walked over to where Elizabeth now stood, her arms wrapped around herself, trying to stop her body from trembling.

"Did he harm you, lass?"

She shook her head, still staring at the dead man and what remained of his face.

The moment he saw a tear slip down her cheek, Douglas felt his own strength slip with it. With that tear came a loss of innocence that would stay with her forever. All her life, Elizabeth had lived within the safety of her station, daughter to the Duke of Sudeleigh, protected by the mantle of his power and his authority throughout the kingdom. But now that sense of safety had been destroyed.

He should have been there. He shouldn't have let her walk so far away from where they'd stopped. He should have followed her. He should have protected her. It was his duty as her husband, and in that he'd just failed. He couldn't stand it. He gathered Elizabeth into his arms and held her as she sagged against him and wept.

After some time, when her body felt weak and her tears would come no more, Elizabeth slowly lifted her head, to look up at him.

"This isn't England, Elizabeth," he said quietly. "You no longer have the protection of your father's name where everyone knows you. Scotland is a wild, untamed place. You cannot just go wandering off at will. I know you were angry, and, aye, I pushed you to it, but there are fugitive Jacobite soldiers crawling throughout these hills, men who haven't seen a woman in months and who would love to punish an unprotected English woman for their loss at Culloden. I'm sorry that I wasn't here when they came upon you. It will never happen again. You have my word."

Elizabeth scarcely heard what he said, but just the gentle sound of his voice offered her comfort, soothing her fears, wrapping her in its warmth.

Douglas had saved her life.

He had killed for her.

He had slain the dragon.

And just like the fairytales passed down through the ages, when the danger was over, and peace had been restored once again to the land, the damsel always did the same thing, right before the words *happily ever after* ever were written.

She rewarded her knight with a kiss.

And Elizabeth did the same.

It was her first kiss.

And quite simply, it took her breath away.

Chapter Ten

"How dare you?"

How dare I?

Douglas reeled as Elizabeth flattened her hands, the same hands that had, moments before, been fisted tightly in the linen of his shirt, and pushed him away from her hard.

She said nothing, just stared at him through eyes dim and defensive. But she didn't need to say a word for Douglas to know what she was thinking. Her thoughts were written clearly on her face. The daughter to one of England's most wealthy and powerful dukes had just joined her mouth to that of a poor, simple Scottish farmer. No doubt she was wondering if she'd just completely lost her mind.

"Have you just completely lost your mind?"

He blinked once, twice. "Have *I* lost *my* mind?" he echoed. "What the devil did I do?"

"You kissed me!"

Douglas shook his head. "I think you know better than that, lass."

Elizabeth took a step back, then another, seeking to put as much distance as she could between them. "Well . . . it was nothing. A blind impulse, that's all. A purely emotional reaction to a distressing situation. I was in danger, and you saved me. Naturally I would want to show you my gratitude."

"I see."

"And that was all that kiss was. Gratitude." She was blathering now. "Besides, I have always wondered what it would be like to kiss a man. It is one of those experiences everybody should have at least once. Like walking barefoot on the shore or . . . or tasting whisky." *Or, dear God, why had she just said that?* "So I tried it, and that was that. A kiss. Nothing more. Nothing more than a touch of lips really." A touch of lips and mouths and breaths that had melted her bones inside her body . . .

Elizabeth shook her head as if by doing so she could shake the memory of the past minutes right out of her head. How could she have done that? How could she have kissed him of all people? He was her husband, for heaven's sake, the one person she should *not* be kissing.

She looked at him. And waited. Douglas simply stared at her, damn him, saying nothing. She needed to do something—anything—to end this awkward stretch of time and so she turned and walked the two yards away to where her hat had fallen in the heather. Her fingers trembled slightly as she clasped the cocked corner of it and pushed it onto her head, shielding her face.

"Where are the horses?" she turned and asked for want of anything better to say.

Douglas simply looked at her. "Over there, beyond the trees."

"Well, we'd best be going if we're to make it much farther before nightfall."

"Aye."

But he wasn't moving to join her as she walked away. Instead he bent and started picking up some rocks from the bank of the burn, a half dozen or more, tossing them into a small pile on the shore.

"What are you doing? I thought we were leaving."

"I've to bury the man first."

"Bury him?"

Elizabeth glanced at the motionless heap crumpled on the ground. How odd that in the wake of the kiss they'd shared, she'd almost forgotten that a man lay dead at her feet. "But you shot him. You had to shoot him."

"I do not take any satisfaction in his killing, lass. It was a necessary thing to put a stop to a terrible deed. But out of respect for his clan and the sanctity of a life lost, I must give him a proper burial. 'Tis the Scots way."

Elizabeth stood, watching Douglas as he stooped to pick up another rock, then two.

Nearly an hour later he had buried the body beneath a heap of hastily gathered stones, a cairn to which Douglas fixed a scrap of the man's plaid by way of a marker. When he was finished, he stood back, made a swift sign of the cross, and recited a prayer in Gaelic for the salvation of the soul of the dead man. The breeze blew; the trees rustled like the distant whispers of mourners around them. As the sun began to loll in the distant western sky, they mounted the horses and continued on their way.

Elizabeth was not unexpectedly quiet for some time afterward as they traversed hill and glen and long stretching pastures lined with drystone walls that seemed to go on forever.

"What are you thinking, lass?" Douglas finally asked.

Elizabeth took in a deep breath. "I was just thinking that I have never faced death in such a way before. I've never really faced death at all, other than my grandmother Minna, who died when I was seven—but then she was ninety and we had known it would soon happen. But this . . . this is different."

"It's a thing I am all too familiar with, the ugliness that is the hatred of man to man, clan to clan . . . Scot to Sassenach."

They rode a little further in silence. Douglas changed the subject. "Is there anything you'd like to know about Skye afore we get there? Have you any questions? Worries? Scotland is a very different place than what you are accustomed to."

"I've begun to realize that already." They continued along, the horses stepping with sure feet over the rough and rocky ground. Finally she asked, "Tell me what your home is like, where we are to live."

For the slightest moment, Douglas thought to tell her the truth, that he was not the simple farmer she believed him to be. He was a chieftain in the clan MacKinnon, nephew to the chief, and laird of his own castle, Dunakin, in name if not on paper.

But he couldn't. He knew this. He'd made a bargain with the duke, a bargain that would see his birthright restored.

So Douglas answered her in the only way he could.

"It is a croft, lass. Not grand like Drayton Hall, but it is warm in the winter and snug with everything a body needs to get by. It was built by my great-great-grandfather, a marriage house for his wife, and it sits nestled in a glen inland from the sea. The hills that surround it are carpeted in heather, and a burn runs behind it. The mist for which Skye was named greets you through the window most every morn and bids you good night at e'entide."

"It sounds nice." The love he had for his homeland had softened his voice, misted his eyes. "I have never asked you about your family. What is it you call them? Your clan?"

"Clan and kin are two very different sorts of family, lass. The MacKinnons can claim several thousand among the clan, but for my own kin there is only myself." Douglas hesitated. "My younger brother, Iain, I'm told, died at Culloden."

"You have no one else? No parents? No sisters?" Elizabeth couldn't imagine being without her own burgeoning family, the laughter, the loving spats.

"A MacKinnon is never truly without kith. My mother was Norah MacKinnon, lost when she delivered our only sister, also named Norah, from the womb. A fever took them both within days of one another. From the time I was three years old, I didna see my father. He was exiled to France after the Jacobite rebellion in '15."

"And he's never come back?"

"Aye, he did return to Scotland twice, but I was never taken to see him because it was too dangerous for him, the risk of his capture too great. I'm told he died earlier this year and is buried alone somewhere in France."

Elizabeth lowered her eyes. "I am sorry."

"There is nothing to be sorry for, lass. My father, and my brother, too, they both of them died fighting for what they believed in."

"They were Jacobites?"

"In every sense of the word."

"Those men who attacked me. They were Jacobites, too."

Douglas was ashamed of the behavior of his countrymen. "Aye, they were, but dinna liken their kind to that of my da. The Jacobites of the early rebellions were a different breed of men. My father, men like him, they knew what it was they fought for and followed the call of their Scottish honor. Those men today were . . ." He searched for the appropriate word. "They were the worst sort of man there is."

"Are you a Jacobite, too, Douglas?"

Douglas looked at her. How should he answer the question he had asked himself more times than he cared to count?

"I didna come out to fight with the Bonnie Prince when he raised his standard at Glenfinnan last year. Before anything else I am a Scotsman. My honor and duty will always be that of a Scotsman."

If she noticed that he hadn't truly answered her question, she didn't pursue it, and they had arrived at their stopping point for the night, a small inn tucked away on the outskirts of a tiny Lowland village. The whitewashed stone and thatched roof of the house known as The Shieling was owned by a husband and wife, she Scottish, he English. Because of this unique mix, Douglas knew there would be no questions, no suspicions cast upon the two travelers just arriving.

A woman greeted them when they entered the dimly lit taproom. "*Och,* well, if it isna Douglas Dubh MacKinnon come all the way fro' Skye to taste some o' my cooking." She had a tray hitched upon the crook of her ample hip, a wisp of soft brown hair falling over her eyes, and a smile as warm and as welcoming as the fire glowing in the stone hearth behind her. "'Tis been too long, it has, since you've come to stay with us, MacKinnon."

Douglas smiled at her. "You're looking fine, you are, Màiri Hetherington. Does that man o' yours, Tom, still treat you well then?"

"Aye, well enough, for if he didna treat me finely, you know I'd have clobbered him sound in the heid by now, I would."

Douglas laughed, a full, throaty sound that brought a shimmer to the blue of his eyes. Elizabeth couldn't help but notice that when he spoke amongst his countrymen, Douglas fell more easily into his native tongue, his words smoky with the dialect of the Gael.

"So will you and the lass be wantin' a room for the night then, MacKinnon?"

"Two rooms," Elizabeth replied before Douglas could open his mouth.

Màiri lifted a brow.

Douglas said, "Aye, two rooms if you have them, Màiri."

"I'm afraid we're a wee bit crowded for the night. All we've got left is the loft room." She looked at Elizabeth. "'Tis two rooms connected by a doorway on the topmost floor of the inn, lass. There's only one bed, but we'll bring in a cot for you to sleep in the side chamber if you'd like, Douglas."

"That'll do fine, Màiri. We'll take our supper in the rooms, too, if it widna be too much trouble for you."

"Och, you know 'tis no trouble a'tall, MacKinnon. We've colcannon and haggis in the kitchen with some fresh bannocks I've just taken off the fire. You know where the room is, so get you and the lass on up and I'll bring up your supper directly."

"Excuse me, Mrs. Hetherington," Elizabeth said then, stopping the Scotswoman in mid-stride. "Would it be too much trouble to have a bath brought up as well?"

Màiri glanced at Douglas. "A bath? We dinna . . ."

"Màiri, we've had a rough time of it traveling today and so if you'd do your best to see to the bath, I'd be most obliged."

Màiri smiled. "A bath it is, then."

She made off on bare feet, Elizabeth noticed, skirts swishing on the dirt floor strewn with fresh-smelling herbs and rushes. Douglas motioned to Elizabeth, leading her up a narrow stairwell tucked in the far corner of the taproom. It was very dark, and with no lantern to light their way, Elizabeth stumbled on the stairs, catching herself on Douglas's arm. At the very top, he opened a door onto a room that was tucked generously beneath the inn's thatching.

A small bench and two chairs were set before the stone hearth. Beyond that lay another room with a poster bed in one corner and a washstand in the other. Though sparsely furnished, the room looked clean and cozy and smelled of herbs. Having spent all day on horseback, Elizabeth would have slept in the barn if she'd had to.

Douglas knelt before the hearth to coax a fire. Within minutes the room was bathed in a faint red glow that flickered and danced across the whitewashed walls.

Màiri came in shortly after with a heaping tray steaming and smelling delicious.

"I've put the water on in the kitchen to heat for your bath, lass, and I've a lad gone to fetch the tub for ye. 'Twill take a short while, but you can take your supper and have some tea in the meantime. I brought you a cake of some heather and oatmeal soap to wash with, too."

"Thank you."

"Douglas," Màiri went on, "I'm afraid that scruffy terrier bitch of Tom's decided to deliver a litter of pups on the cot. She snipes at anyone who comes near them, too. But I've plenty o' blankets and woolens that you can lay on the rug in front of the fire for your bed."

"That'll do, Màiri."

When she'd gone, Douglas joined Elizabeth at the table before the fire.

Elizabeth eyed the tray of food. "What exactly is a haggis?"

Douglas took up a forkful of the stuff that resembled a crumbling sort of pudding. "I'll tell you, but only after you've taken a bite."

He offered the first bite to a wary Elizabeth. She took it and chewed slowly, tentatively, then swallowed. She nodded. "It is spicy and a bit grainy in texture, but really quite good. Tastes a bit like a sausage." She took up a second bite.

Douglas smiled. "I'm glad to know you like it, lass. Most Sassenachs think the haggis a vulgar dish, but it stands as a testament to the Scotsman's resourcefulness when times of want called for using not only the loin of the sheep to survive. To make it you just toss in a bit o' oatmeal with some—"

"No." Elizabeth gave him a small smile. "Don't tell me. I think this is probably one of those things better left unspoken."

The tub was brought up while they ate, a huge wooden thing Màiri no doubt used for washing the inn's laundry, and was filled with bucket after bucket of steaming water. When the lad had poured the last bucket, nodding and backing from the room, Elizabeth turned to where Douglas yet sat stretched out before the warmth of the fire.

"I, uh, should like to take my bath now."

Douglas had been so comfortable in her company over supper, he'd forgotten he should leave. He reminded himself that getting comfortable with her was a thing he couldn't do.

"Will an hour be long enough for you? We've a long day's journey again tomorrow, so we should retire early."

Elizabeth nodded. "An hour will be fine, thank you."

He was at the door, however, when she realized he couldn't leave just yet. "Douglas?"

"Aye?"

"I wondered . . . if I might beg your assistance before you go."

"What is it, lass?"

She felt her face grow flushed. How utterly humiliating. "My abigail, Dulcie, wouldn't travel to the Highlands with me. Apparently she didn't wish to give up the comforts of home, which in itself isn't really any problem. Dulcie is older and I don't really mind having to fend for myself. But she laced me into my things this morning—more specifically she laced me into my *corset*—and it seems she has employed her famous secret knot, one for which she alone knows the secret for loosening. Without the aid of eyes on the back of my head, I don't think I will be able to get the thing undone."

"I see."

Douglas stepped back into the room, closing the door behind him. "Well, then, I'd best see what I can do about that knot."

It never even occurred to her to call for Màiri. Elizabeth turned away, shielding her burning cheeks, and quickly unfastened the buttons on the front of her riding coat. She was nervous and her fingers shook, taking some effort, but she finally managed to get them all free. She slipped off her jacket, then the linen shirt she wore underneath. She undid the tapes of her skirts and let them drop to the floor before turning to face him once again.

Limned by the firelight, blushing before him, Douglas felt his throat tighten around his breath. She was the picture of loveliness, wearing naught but a thin linen chemise and white stockings that were gartered with small ribbons just above her knees. The corset she wanted him to remove circled her, bringing her waistline to nothing and the fullness of her breasts to a definite something.

Oh, good God.

She came to stand before him, sweeping the length of that red hair over one shoulder. Her neck and shoulders were pale above the strings that crisscrossed her back-side, soft as silk when he brushed her with his fingertips. He saw her shiver, saw the gooseflesh rise along the back of her neck, and was seized with the solitary won-der of what it would be like to cover that same spot of shivering skin with his mouth.

The room was growing hotter, and Douglas had a dif-ficult time concentrating his attention on the knot that lay nestled at the small of her back. He gave a string a tug, but it didn't budge. He tried another. He realized he needed to get closer and knelt behind her, to where his eyes were inches away from the rounded curve of her bottom, discreetly covered by only that thin scrap of linen chemise.

The awareness between them sparked like the fire in the hearth. He yanked on the strings, tried pulling at the knot, but it wouldn't yield. "Good God, woman, what sort of knot is this?"

" 'Tis some sort of trick to loosening it. But I've never actually done it myself."

Douglas struggled with it some more, becoming so in-tent on unraveling it, he never even realized that one of his hands had spanned her waist, his fingers resting on the flare of her hip.

But Elizabeth realized it. Oh, did she.

From the moment of her birth, the hands of others had cared for most every intimacy in her life. Dressing, bathing, even the combing of her own hair was some-thing which she was accustomed to having done by oth-ers. But this was the first time in her four-and-twenty years that she had ever been touched so familiarly by a man. Instead of troubling her or shocking her, however, it set her heartbeat to racing.

"Perhaps I should just call Màiri." The awareness between them had become so real, so tangible, it could have been a living, breathing thing.

"No, I think I've almost got it—oh, bloody hell!"

Before Elizabeth could turn to see what was happening, Douglas had unsheathed the small knife that he kept tucked inside his stocking and sliced through the stubborn lacings.

Her corset fell free.

Elizabeth turned around to face him, clad only in her thin summer chemise. Her cheeks were red and her eyes were wide. Douglas took in a slow breath and held it, staring at her mouth, the fullness of her bottom lip. He remembered how it had felt against his mouth when she had kissed him. He was seized by the almost uncontrollable need to taste her. He even took a step toward her, and when she didn't step away, he knew that if he did, if he kissed her right then, she would let him.

He also knew that he wouldn't stop at just a kiss.

Douglas stepped away.

"I'll be in the taproom while you have your bath, lass. I'll return in a hour."

Without a look back, Douglas turned and left the room, closing the door behind him.

He came back precisely an hour later.

Elizabeth, however, was still in the tub.

Chapter Eleven

Elizabeth stirred, opening bleary eyes onto a sluggish fire that lay smoldering in the hearth beside her. The room was splashed with shadows that rose and fell with the gentle flicker of the flames. Quiet surrounded her, and for the first few moments she felt quite as if she were floating.

She had no idea that she wasn't in her own chamber at home in Drayton Hall. At any moment she expected Caro or another of her sisters to come bursting through the door with some frightful dilemma for her to solve, like which gown Catherine should wear to the Sanderson ball or what color riband looked best with Matilda's hair. It wasn't until the room around her began to come into focus, the bare stone walls glowing pink in the light of the fire, the earthenware claret bottle that served as a vase for a cluster of wildflowers, that she remembered where she was, not at all at Drayton Hall, but at a remote inn somewhere north of the Scottish border.

Good God. She had fallen asleep in the bath.

The long hours of riding had obviously taken their toll on her. She couldn't remember how she'd even gotten to the room. She knew she had eaten but she couldn't for the life of her remember what it had been.

She remembered Douglas saying he would return in an hour, and realized she had no idea of just how much time had passed since he'd gone. It could have been moments. It could have been more. Judging from the chill temperature of the water, it had been quite a while.

She glanced quickly at the door. Had he locked it before he'd gone? Or could he walk in at any moment and find her there, still in the tub? In fact he could be climbing the stairs at that moment, heading even now for the door. Surely he would knock before coming in, warn her of his return. Wouldn't he?

The most likely answer to that question brought Elizabeth upright with a splash, had her dashing for the door to turn the key until she heard the click of the lock. Only then did she take another breath.

She turned and arched her neck sideways to ease the cramp that pinched there from having been slumped against the side of the tub. She watched the dance of the fire in the small stone hearth. She listened to the silence of the night. Her hair, which she'd washed with the floral soap Màiri had given her, hung in damp twisting strands down her shoulders and back. It dripped onto the floor beneath her. Standing before the hearth, she reached for the thick cloth she had been given to dry with, dried her arms and her hair, and wrapped the length of it around herself. The night air gave her gooseflesh despite the warmth of the fire. She was so tired, she could have sunk to the floor and stayed there till morning. All she wanted was to slip beneath the bedcovers, bury herself against the pillows, and sleep.

She turned for the bed and the nightclothes that awaited, with the thought to do just that—and promptly let out a shriek worthy of a banshee.

"What are you doing in here?"

Douglas lay in the shadows on the bed. His arms were linked behind his head and he was watching her in the soft hearth light. She couldn't see his expression. All she saw was his eyes.

"I was but waiting for you to finish at your bath."

"My—? Why didn't you alert me? Allow me time to cover myself? In case it has escaped your notice, I am undressed!"

At that he merely nodded. "Aye, lass, that you are."

Elizabeth flushed red at his words, and was suddenly very grateful for the darkness in the room. "You shouldn't be here. It isn't right."

"In case you've forgotten, lass, that rug you're dripping on is to be my bed for the night."

Elizabeth *had* forgotten, until just then when he'd mentioned it. She looked down at the water puddling at her feet, then looked at him. "But did you have to come in while I was bathing?"

"I came in while you were *sleeping*. 'Tis a very different thing. I knocked at the door. Twice. When you didn't answer, I thought you must have already gone off to bed. I knew you'd be spent after the day we'd had, and I didn't want to wake you, so I decided to come in. The room was dark, and it took a few minutes for me to see clearly. When I realized you were still in the tub, I thought it best just to sit and wait for you to awaken."

Elizabeth tightened her grip on the towel, but he simply shrugged, as if finding a naked woman was a commonplace occurrence. And perhaps it was. For him. But being a naked woman in front of anyone other than her maid, her sisters, or the pier glass in her bedchamber was not at all commonplace for Elizabeth.

"You should have turned immediately when you realized where I was and left the room."

"I told you I'd wait an hour, lass. And I did. Precisely an hour."

He was right. And she knew he was right, but just the thought of him standing there, *watching* her as she lay naked and asleep in the tub, was mortifying. It stripped her bare all over again. "And just how long had you stood there, seeing more of me than anyone else in my life ever has?" She held up a hand. "Don't tell me. I really don't wish to know."

She snatched her nightgown from the foot of the bed, all the while keeping a death grip on the towel wrapped around her. "A gentleman would have made his presence known," she muttered more to herself than him.

Douglas fixed his gaze to hers. "And as you are well aware, lass, I am no gentleman."

Elizabeth looked at him. She could think of absolutely nothing to say in response.

When she continued to stand there wrapped in the towel, clutching her nightgown and staring at him like a garden statue, Douglas said, "The night grows late, and we've another long day's ride ahead on the morrow. You best get to bed, lass."

"I can't do that."

"Why?"

"Because you're in it."

They stared at one another through a long moment. Douglas slid from the bed. He waited.

"Might I at least be given the courtesy of dressing in privacy?" It seemed ridiculous to say, given the fact that not five minutes earlier he had seen every inch of her, but she said it nonetheless.

"Take yourself in there." Douglas gestured toward the adjoining room. "I'll have the lads come to fetch the tub and the supper dishes away whilst you dress."

Elizabeth waited until Douglas had gone, then retreated through the adjacent doorway. She dried herself quickly, toweling her hair, and slipped on her nightrail, a heavy linen shift that buttoned to her chin and fell to her toes. She fastened each button, even the topmost one that felt too tight against her throat. She waited in the antechamber until after she was certain the tub had been removed before stepping back into the empty bedroom.

When Douglas returned almost a quarter hour later, Elizabeth was sitting in the chair before the fire. Her feet were tucked up beneath her as she pulled a comb through the tangles in her damp hair. It was a commonplace task, one performed every day by countless many, but somehow she managed to make it charming. Douglas found himself pausing in the doorway and feasting on the picture of her in the firelight.

It was the very contrast of her, having gone from the noble lady filled with hauteur and indignation, to a simple maid, that intrigued Douglas most. Feet bare, face scrubbed pink, no one would know that her father was one of the most powerful men in England. In fact, no one would even care. They would only care that she looked and smelled as soft as a summer morning.

"What is it?" Elizabeth asked when she noticed him standing there, gawking at her like a half-witted fool.

"I . . ." He hesitated. " 'Tis nothing."

Douglas left the doorway and withdrew to the shadows of the antechamber to undress. As he hauled his shirt over his head, he noticed Elizabeth's clothing lying there, the skirts and riding coat draped neatly over the back of a chair. On impulse, he reached out and touched a hand to the cloth, measuring the texture of the heavy brocade against his fingertips.

She had been right, he knew. Earlier that evening, when he had returned from the taproom to discover her asleep at her bath, he should have woken her, should have allowed her to dress in privacy. Any gentleman would have, but somehow, he hadn't been able to help himself. Instead he had stood staring at her in the firelight. Even now, with just the very thought of her, his blood seemed to grow warmer.

He was a fool. He was a complete and utter idiot to be thinking such thoughts about her. Tempting though she may be, she was still the daughter of the Duke of Sudeleigh, a spoiled, pampered princess who thought the world turned only for her.

Hadn't she tried to manipulate him into a sham marriage just so she could horrify her father with a poor Scotsman for a son-in-law? She could never understand him, the things that mattered to him. Her life was fancy balls, pleasure gardens, and afternoon tea. His way of life, his *Scottish* life, would never be a life for her. He was daft to even consider it could. His thoughts should focus only on the getting rid of her, and the quicker, the better. *Dunakin. Home.* That was where his thoughts should be, high above the Kyle of Akin on Skye's eastern shore.

Douglas took up the woolen blanket Màiri had left for him and headed for the other room. Elizabeth was no longer in the chair by the fire. Instead she was curled upon the middle of the bed, huddled beneath a nest of bedcoverings, her hair fanned out against the pillow beneath her head, asleep.

Dropping his pillow onto the floor, Douglas eased to the carpet that would serve as his bed. As he rolled onto his side and lay quietly in the darkness, listening to her breathing, he could only hope that the next two months would pass quickly.

"'Tis time to wake, lass. The hour grows late. The road beckons."

Douglas had been shuffling about the room for over an hour, trying not very subtly to stir her. They had miles to cover, and he was eager to be on the road to home, back to familiar ground. At home, he told himself, he would feel more himself. He could put aside the oddness of the past few days and occupy himself with matters needing his attention.

He watched her as she stirred, her hair mussed from sleep. She was slow to waken, like a sunflower that slowly lifted its face to the sun. Her expression was lost in a fog of wakening; he wondered if she'd had as restless a night as he. He hadn't slept more than a wink all night on that rug on the floor, had passed the hours staring at the ceiling, listening to her wrestle with her dreams.

As the glow of morning streaked across her face, Elizabeth opened her eyes and peered at him.

She blinked.

"There is food," he said, "on the table by the fire. Porridge, warm bannocks, fresh tea. Màiri brought them a little while ago. Are you hungry?"

She nodded. "Famished."

Elizabeth glanced to the small window across the room. "The sun, it has been out for some time. Why did you not waken me earlier?"

Douglas lied, "I was more tired than I thought I was. I slept late. 'Tis all right, though, the day promises clear so we'll make good time."

In truth, he had risen at dawn, ready to quit the place.

They ate their breakfast quickly and were on their way.

While Douglas went off to see to the horses, Elizabeth dressed, choosing a simple riding habit of black bombazine with a frothy cravat and tricorne. She was relieved to find a pair of stays that laced up the front among the things in her traveling valise, for she had no intention of asking Douglas to help her dress every morning. Unaccustomed to the dressing of her own hair, she simply brushed it free of tangles and plaited it down her back, tying it off with a snip of black riband.

The next few hours, and for that matter, the next few days, passed quickly enough, uneventful but for the occasional rain shower or lumbering flock of sheep. Elizabeth spent her time drinking in the Scottish countryside—the cragged hills, the brilliant heather—it fascinated her unlike anything she had ever seen before.

The further they rode from England, it seemed, the more rugged the landscape became. Fine whitewashed stone cottages with quaint windows and bright flower boxes gave way to crude thatched huts tucked against stark mountain faces. Trees became sparse, almost impossible to find in some places, and the roads narrowed to little more than meandering pathways. An hour, sometimes several, would pass without seeing another living soul. When they did encounter anyone, it was most often barefoot urchins or hopeless mothers pulling carts filled with their only possessions.

These were the true victims of the failed rebellion. They would speak to Douglas in Gaelic, telling him how they had been driven from the hills, their homes put to ruin by the marauding English troops. It didn't matter that they hadn't joined the rebellion. The Duke of Cumberland, son of George II and leader of the English forces that had quashed the Jacobites, intended to ensure there would never be another rebellion in Scotland. Ever. They were Highlanders, and thus they were to be punished.

It was one night at an inn where they stayed deep in the Highlands that Douglas met up with a familiar face.

"Roderick!"

He was a young man, very near to Douglas in age. His hair was a sandy auburn and he was dressed in a dark coat and a plaid woven in shades of dark green and blue. His face was handsome—not in the rugged way of Douglas, but with finer features, his eyes softly gray.

When Douglas introduced him, Elizabeth found herself taken aback.

"Your brother? But I thought you told me your brother had . . . you said he . . ."

"That was my brother Iain. Roderick is my *foster* brother. He is a MacKenzie but we were raised together after my mother died. Roderick, this is Elizabeth." He stared at him. "My wife."

If the man found it astonishing to find Douglas suddenly in possession of a wife—an English wife at that— he didn't outwardly show it.

"Indeed?" He glanced at Douglas, but that was all, then bowed over her hand. "A pleasure to meet you, my lady."

"Elizabeth," Douglas said then, "I've some things I need to discuss with Roderick. We'll likely be up half the night, so why don't you go on to bed? It's been a long day and we've another, longer one on the morrow."

No doubt Douglas sought to explain the situation and her father's odd stipulation of the next two months. Elizabeth really had no wish to hear it again. She nodded. "Good night then, gentlemen."

When she had retired to their room, Roderick motioned to a table in the far corner of the inn's taproom where they could speak more freely. It was then Douglas heard the first true details of the fall of the Jacobites at Culloden.

"From what I have heard, they never stood any chance of victory. The battle, if you can call it that, was over within the hour. Thousands dead, or left to die on that bloody moor. Others taken prisoner or simply shot on the spot. I heard tell of dozens they locked in a barn and simply set it afire. 'Tis a bloody, dirty business, this rebellion."

"How many dead?"

"The rebels? To hear it told, all of them. But that isna possible. The prince escaped, as did others, although most of those who were in the thick of the fighting did fall, or were cut down as they fled. The only consolation is there weren't that many who made it there to fight as it was. After Stirling, some had gone home to the Highlands to check on their families. They received the call to battle too late. Others simply deserted because they realized the cause was lost after the retreat from Derby."

Douglas nodded. He had heard the reports himself while in London. In early December, the Scottish forces had made it into England, taking the town of Derby just one hundred and twenty-five miles from London. They had been on the very brink of victory; George II had given orders for his household to be removed from Kensington Palace—until a messenger had arrived bringing news to the prince's camp that Cumberland and an army of nine thousand was fast on their heels. On the advice of his advisors, and against his better judgment, Charles had ordered the retreat. It would prove the turning point in the rebellion, and the beginning of the end for the Jacobites. It would also prove to be a grievous mistake—particularly when the report of Cumberland and his nine thousand men turned out to be fictitious.

"Whoever made it off that battlefield alive will be taken prisoner when they're found," Douglas said.

"Or killed." Roderick took a swig of ale, grimacing more from the bitterness of his words than the drink. "The king's son, that butcher, is giving no quarter to those they find afterward. He's a bloody fiend. He's put a price of thirty thousand pounds on the prince's head, aye, but it might as well be a hundred thousand. No one will betray him."

Roderick looked at Douglas, then, realizing he was scarcely even listening to him. "Ye're thinking of young Iain, aye?"

Douglas nodded on a frown.

"Dinna take the news of his death to heart, Douglas. Tha' brither of yours, he widna be one to fall on a field o' battle. You can be sure of that. He's a survivor, that one. Always has been. Likely he'll be there to greet you at Dunakin when you arrive, that idiotic grin pasted on his face and a story or two to tell over a dram."

"I still hold out hope, Roderick. He's all I have left now."

They fell silent, taking swallows from their tankards as they each lost themselves to their thoughts. The fire behind them cracked and popped as someone tossed on a fresh peat. The ale flowed. From the shadows, a serving girl giggled.

Finally, it was Roderick who spoke.

"Well, I've been waitin' for you to say it on your own, but it looks like I'll have to ask. D'you wish to tell me what the de'il you're doin' married to a Sassenach lady when ye're already promised to Muirne MacLean of Carsaig?"

Douglas looked across the table. "'Tis a long story, Roderick."

"Aye, the best ones are. I'm for hearing it, too, afore you even think of going off to your bed."

Douglas knew he would have to tell Roderick everything. Truth be told, he wanted to tell someone, and there was no one he trusted better than this man. Taking a deep draw from his ale, Douglas swallowed it down, and began.

"It started when I came across a coach mired on the side of the road . . ."

When he finished the tale fully three quarters of an hour later, Roderick leaned back in his chair with a sorry shake of his head.

"Och, but you have a certain predilection for finding yourself a mess of trouble, Douglas MacKinnon. And that's what that one sleeping abovestairs is. *Trouble.* You've just to take one look at the lass to know that."

"Aye. I don't plan to keep her long enough to get myself into any trouble. Two months. That's all."

"And what'll you do if the MacLeans find her out? 'Tis bad enough the MacKinnons and the MacLeans have been feuding for all these years now. With your taking Muirne to wife agreed upon long ago, Malcolm MacLean will certainly not look kindly on your already having one wife when he brings his daughter to you to wed."

"MacLean need never know." Douglas looked at Roderick closely, and repeated, "He need never know. 'Twas Maclean who stipulated I must secure Dunakin afore he'd grant me Muirne's hand to end the feud. Keeping this Sassenach lass for the next two months is the only way I am going to get Dunakin back. It will work. All I need do is keep her out of sight till her da comes for her. She doesna know I am laird at Dunakin, so I'll set her up in the croft, away from the castle, and put Eithne to the task of looking after her. Set her to weaving or beating the dust from the rugs. The life of a crofter's wife is no life for a Sassenach noble lady. By the time these next two months are past, she'll be begging to return to her da. I'll make certain of it. I'll get the annulment and, more important, I'll get Dunakin. The marriage to Muirne will just have to wait a bit longer. I've no choice in the matter."

Chapter Twelve

It took a week's time, shelter in a dank cave when they'd met with a sudden storm, constant itching from the midges, and a detour around a rain-swollen river, but they made it at last across the rugged Highlands to Scotland's western coast.

With the exception of the one squalling storm, the weather had held uncharacteristically fine, skies dappled with sunlight, and the occasional mist, showering only at night, as if Mother Nature herself was making every effort to assure their swift passage. The scenery was breath-stealing. Elizabeth often found herself stopping to indulge in one view after another, awed by the stark beauty of the austere mountains, humbled by the still peace of a woodland glade kissed by an overnight rain shower. Sylvan lochs glistened beneath an onyx night sky, set to twinkling by the milky light of the Highland moon. The unspoiled solitude, the untamed beauty, it was easy to understand why Douglas felt so fiercely proud of his homeland.

As he had since the beginning of their journey, Douglas had led them on a route away from the main roads, through tiny crofting settlements and thickly wooded passes that only someone closely familiar with the landscape could ever possibly navigate. Since inns were scarce they'd stayed at the homes of strangers and acquaintances alike, wherever they happened to find the glow of candlelight beckoning through the windows.

It was awkward at first for Elizabeth, this arriving unexpected upon the doorsteps of strangers, but according to Douglas, it was a custom longstanding for the Scots that hospitality should be extended to anyone in need. Questions were not asked of the visitor until after he had been offered food and drink, even an enemy was safe while beneath the protection of his host's roof. It was a matter of tradition. A matter of honor.

Twice during the journey they had come within firing distance of the English soldiers, but Douglas had quickly found them shelter until it was safe to proceed. Sometime along the way, Douglas had learned that the prince had been chased to the outer Hebrides, and thus the focus of the search for him had shifted to the sea, making it far easier for them to travel from glen to glen unnoticed.

But grim evidence of the devastation that had been wrought on the Scots by the English government had been left in the soldiers' wake. They saw carcasses of cattle and sheep, hundreds of them, had been killed not for their meat, but to prevent their ever being of use to feed the Scottish peasantry. They littered the stark fields, rotting in the sunlight. In quiet glens far removed from the main towns, cottages had been raided and burned at random. Crops were destroyed, trampled or put to the torch, and any who protested were often shot on the spot. Yet despite the ruthless tactics, English to Scot, no one they encountered ever treated Elizabeth with anything but kindness and hospitality. They had every reason to be wary of her, but she was Douglas's wife . . . at least in name. Thus she fell under their protection.

Not since that first night at the border inn had they again shared a bedchamber. Elizabeth had no notion of where Douglas slept, or if he slept at all. He always stayed awake when she went off to bed, chatting in Gaelic with their hosts by the light of the peat fire; when she emerged the next morn, he was dressed and waiting for her to leave.

Elizabeth wondered how he managed to keep from nodding off in the saddle as she so often found herself doing, lulled by the forest birdsong, the gentle sway of the horse, and the empty, endless track that seemed to stretch forever in front of them.

It had seemed as if they might never make it to Skye, until finally they stood upon the last rise, looking down on the misty Hebrides.

"Look there, the closest isle," Douglas said as he pointed out Skye in the distance. His voice was thick with the pride she often heard in the voice of her father when he spoke of Drayton Hall.

Douglas was anxious to be home, back among his own people. For this last night, however, they would have to stay on the mainland, in a tiny seaside village called Glenelg.

They had just taken the lone road that gave access to the remote glen and its village when they were met with a patrol of British soldiers guarding the pass before them. They came out onto the path as Douglas and Elizabeth approached, their red coats conspicuous against the dusk sky.

Douglas had expected this and turned to look at Elizabeth behind him, his eyes dark with unease. "Put up the hood of your cloak, lass, and stay well behind me. Say nothing. I will do the talking."

Elizabeth did as he'd bid, trying to ignore the way her heart was hammering in her throat as she followed him to where the soldiers awaited.

"Halt you there," called the first of them, a squat, beefy man who narrowed his eyes from beneath a forlorn excuse for a powdered wig. "Where d'ya think ye're going now?"

Douglas pulled his horse to a slow halt. "Och, we're for Skye on the morrow, my gude mon, on the ferry fro' Glenelg."

He'd assumed a thick brogue, rolling his R's and punctuating his words in the way of the country folk.

The second soldier came forward, taller than his companion, but no less belligerent. His nose seemed to wrinkle in distaste as he took in Douglas's simple Scottish clothing and travel-worn appearance. Neither man gave Elizabeth more than a cursory glance as she sat atop her horse, her face shielded by the hood of her cloak.

"Skye, eh?" The tall one scowled. "And what business would ye be having on that filthy bit o' rock? 'Tis a place fit for naught but thieves and rabble." The soldier looked directly at Douglas as he spat in the dirt at the horses' hooves, trying to provoke a response.

Elizabeth saw Douglas stiffen in the saddle. Her fingers tightened nervously on the reins.

"I make my hame an' my living on Skye, and I mean to return there," he said.

Douglas had moved his horse in front of her so that she couldn't clearly see, so Elizabeth nudged her horse closer, moving to the side. It was then she noticed the taller of the two soldiers studying the pistol and sword that hung at Douglas's side. He glanced at his comrade, gesturing with his eyes. The other nodded and slowly edged his way back as they started grilling Douglas with questions to divert him. They meant to overtake him, she realized, perhaps provoke him into a confrontation so they would have just cause to fire.

Elizabeth looked at Douglas, trying to get his attention, but his back was to her. She had to do *something*, and quickly. So she did the only thing she could think of to distract the two men from making any further move.

"Kind sirs," she said suddenly, urging her horse forward as she shrugged back her hood, "we understand the need for your vigilance in patrolling the area after the recent uprising, but we have only just traveled into Scotland. We are newly wedded and seek only to arrive home as swiftly as possible."

Douglas turned to look at Elizabeth, but said nothing. Nothing at all. What could he say? If he had anything handy at that moment—a glove, a stocking even—he'd stuff it into her mouth and gag her with it. He'd been afraid of this. Curse her! Why couldn't she have just listened to him?

If the soldiers had seen them simply as the Scottish farmer and wife he presented them to be, he had hoped they would allow them to pass without much questioning. And he'd almost succeeded in doing it, but now, with her proper speech and genteel accent, Elizabeth had just earned them a second, closer look.

The shorter of the two, and the one who seemed to be the more in charge, turned to Douglas then. "What be your name, Highlander?"

Douglas sat straighter in the saddle. "Douglas Mac-Kinnon."

The soldiers glanced at one another. "We've been informed of an Iain MacKinnon from these parts, son of the traitor Lachlan MacKinnon of Dunakin, who is wanted for treason against His Majesty King George. Perhaps you would have knowledge of their whereabouts?"

"I'm told my brother is dead." Douglas chose his words carefully. "As is my father."

"Is that so? It is reported they were both at Culloden leading a charge of MacKinnons against the king's forces."

"That is impossible," Douglas replied. "My father has been in France some five-and-twenty years past."

"Your father and your brother are known traitors to the Crown. What does that make you?"

Douglas's voice lowered. "I did not take part in the rebellion. I have been in London. I then traveled to Northumberland to retrieve my wife before making my way here."

"And what would a Scotsman be about in London?

Hoping for a chance to cut the king's throat with your *skian dhu*?"

It was a serious charge, and one that could easily be pressed just for the fact that Douglas had been in London and had had the opportunity. Fear ran rampant in the rebellion. The authorities had detained men in the Tower for simply the suspicion of treason, sometimes for years. The fact that Douglas was Scottish was suspicion enough.

"I think perhaps we should take you both in to speak with our commanding officer." The squat soldier shrugged, adding, " 'Course, Colonel Lyon doesn't care much for talking to Scottish rabble on Tuesdays, so you'll have to wait till he can see you. You needn't worry, though. We've accommodation good enough for you in yon Bernera Barracks."

He gestured in the distance behind him to where a series of bleak gray stone buildings were huddled in a position of some authority over the whole of the village below. Once they were inside the Hanoverian post, Douglas knew they would never be released alive. He had only one option left.

He moved his left hand slowly for his pistol and had almost gotten to it when Elizabeth, damn her, urged her horse forward, deliberately placing herself between him and the two soldiers.

"Elizabeth . . ."

She ignored him. "Did I hear you mention a Colonel Lyon, Corporal?" she asked the taller soldier. "Would that perchance be Colonel Emery Lyon? Of Lyon's Foot Regiment?"

What in bloody hell was she doing? Was she daft?

The soldier turned his full attention to her. "Aye, it would."

"Indeed. Well, then, yes, please do take us to see him at once. In fact, we would be most obliged to you if you would."

Apparently she *was* daft. And completely out of her mind as well.

She glanced at Douglas. Their eyes locked for a single moment, hazel on blue, as he searched for some explanation of what she was doing.

Trust me, her eyes seemed to say.

And for some inexplicable reason, he did.

Douglas lowered his hand to his side again.

The soldier glared at Elizabeth. "And just who might you be, that you think you're due the honor of the colonel's company?"

Elizabeth sat up straighter in the saddle, lifting her chin in a gesture reminiscent of her father. The stare she fixed on the man was filled with every measure of noble arrogance she could muster. When next she spoke, it was with the voice of the daughter of the Duke of Sudeleigh.

"Please tell Colonel Lyon that Lady Elizabeth Drayton would like to see him." And then she added with the slightest of smiles. "His goddaughter."

Colonel Lord Emery Lyon came striding out of his offices not two moments after his aide-de-camp had gone to tell him that Elizabeth awaited him.

"Elizabeth, my dear child, what in the name of heaven are you doing here in the Highlands of all places? Good God, has something happened at Drayton Hall? Is your father unwell?"

At two-and-fifty, he was a vast bear of a man, standing a good six feet in height and surely half that in breadth across his shoulders. His hair, once golden blond but now faded to the color of tarnished silver, was impeccably dressed, pulled back in a trim queue. His clothing was neat, his manner faultless. He had known the Duke of Sudeleigh since their days at Eton, had spent summers at Drayton Hall, and had taken the grand tour on the Continent with Elizabeth's father. For as long as Elizabeth could remember, he had always been a great jolly "uncle" to her, the one who had fostered her love of poetry and who had taught her to ride almost as soon as she had been out of leading strings. But it was his military prowess that had gained him his highest distinction, earning him the command of his own regiment, one whose reputation for valor and honor were unmatched among the English army.

The colonel took Elizabeth in a warm embrace as she kissed him once on each cheek.

"It seems ages since I've seen you," he said, taking in her every feature with the skillful observation of a life-long soldier. "How old are you now? Nineteen? Twenty?"

"I'm four-and-twenty," she said, grinning, "and you know that perfectly well for you sat and listened as my father bemoaned my likely path to spinsterhood the last time he was in London." She looked him direct in the eye. "Am I correct in saying that?"

The colonel nodded. "Aye, that you are." He took her hand and turned to where Douglas stood watching the exchange. "But I see now that all his bemoaning was for naught. Here you appear from out of nowhere . . . and with a husband in tow."

Elizabeth made the introductions, "My lord, allow me to introduce to you my husband, Douglas Dubh MacKinnon of Skye."

The expression on the British colonel's face went from one of genuine pleasure to one of mixed confusion and disbelief. Douglas could easily imagine the direction of his thoughts—the goddaughter he'd thought never to wed, suddenly appearing with a husband, untitled and Scottish at that.

But the colonel recovered soon enough to offer Douglas the appropriate response. "Mr. MacKinnon," he said on a nod, offering his hand. "A pleasure."

Douglas returned the greeting.

"So tell me, Elizabeth," the colonel asked, trying to be casual, "when did all this happen? And why wasn't I invited to the wedding? I admit I've been a bit occupied, what with quelling the rebellion and all, but surely you could have at least sent me a piece of the cake."

Douglas stood back and listened quietly as Elizabeth spun the colonel quite a tale of their meeting and subsequent marriage, one with but a grain of truth amidst a wilderness of falsehood.

"So you met when your carriage broke a wheel, were set upon by brigands, and Mr. MacKinnon here came to your rescue?"

"Yes," Elizabeth assured him, with a smile to Douglas.

"Incredible, my dear."

"Yes, it does sound so, doesn't it? And you know I've never been one of those ladies who dreamed of getting swept off my feet, but that is precisely what happened. We were married at an inn near the Scottish border and went home immediately to Drayton Hall where Douglas met the family."

"That must have been quite an interesting reunion. Tell me, how exactly did your father take the news?"

"Oh, Father was of course quite flustered at first, but once he met Douglas and spent time getting to know him, he was very pleased and welcomed him into the family."

And *that* was when Elizabeth took the tale too far. In trying to paint a picture of contentment and bliss, she had forgotten to consider that she was talking to the one person who knew her father better than anyone else, even her mother.

"I see," said the colonel, seeing all too well, but he decided to wait before passing any real judgment on the matter. He turned to Douglas. "My aide tells me the patrol stopped you on the way to Glenelg? You had hoped to ferry across to Skye in the morning?"

"Yes," Douglas answered, "but your men seemed to think there might be some problem with that."

The colonel nodded. "We've been instructed to keep a throttlehold on all ports until they find and apprehend the Stuart. You no doubt have heard by now that the Jacobites were routed at Culloden?"

"Yes, we did," Elizabeth cut in, "although I cannot think what any of it should have to do with us. Douglas is not a Jacobite. He's had nothing to do with the rebellion."

A page came forward to the colonel then bearing a packet of papers. The colonel excused himself, taking a moment to look them over.

"MacKinnon," he said, looking up from whatever it

was he'd read. "Would your father be Lachlan MacKinnon of Dunakin?"

Douglas inclined his head. "Aye."

"And your brother, Iain MacKinnon, is presently being sought for crimes against the Crown in this rebellion?"

"Aye."

The colonel narrowed his gaze, searching. "But you yourself are not a Jacobite?"

"No, my lord. I did not come out for the prin—" he corrected, "the *Pretender*. As for my brother, I cannot speak for him."

The colonel looked at him closely. "Would you consent to a search of your belongings and your person?"

Elizabeth spoke up. "My lord, really, is that necessary? I have been with my husband every moment of the past fortnight. I give you my word as the daughter of the Duke of Sudeleigh that he is no more a Jacobite than . . . than I am. Or my father for that matter."

Douglas stared at his wife, but wisely kept his mouth shut.

"All we wish to do," Elizabeth went on, "is end a very long and exhausting journey. Can you not assist us by granting us passage to the isle so that I may settle in at my new home?"

The colonel looked at Elizabeth for a long moment. Finally he said, "Very well. If I cannot trust my own goddaughter, then who can I trust?" He looked at Douglas. "You will be given papers by my man Duff here assuring your safe passage and also protecting your property against the invasions which His Grace the Duke of Cumberland has ordered against the homes of the known rebels. I'll arrange for the ferry. You may leave in the morning, but I insist that you stay here tonight as my guests and have supper with us. The inn at Glenelg is not the best choice for a young lady like yourself, Elizabeth, and Lady Lyon would never forgive me if she didn't get the chance to see you and congratulate you on your marriage. So you'll stay?"

Elizabeth glanced at Douglas before giving the only response she could. "Of course."

Douglas could only appease himself with the knowledge that oftentimes the best hiding place was the one that was right out in the open.

Lady Lucinda Lyon was warm, welcoming, and possessed of a discretion her husband had not shown. She did not reveal the slightest hint of distress at the news of Elizabeth's marriage to Douglas when they were introduced later that evening, this despite the fact that her husband was, after all, in command of a regiment that had been sent to the Highlands on a mission to subdue and quell.

Instead, Lady Lyon, who was as petite as her husband was large, whose rounded cheeks dimpled deeply when she smiled, and who despite her noble title had traveled with her husband from the comforts of the London drawing rooms to the "wilds" of the Scottish Highlands, greeted Douglas with a genuine and easy manner.

"Mr. MacKinnon, it is a pleasure to meet you." She offered her hand.

Douglas took it and inclined his head as he bowed to her. "The pleasure is mine, Lady Lyon."

"And you, Elizabeth, how dare you come to us after all this time suddenly married and without the slightest hint

of it beforehand? Just look at you. I swear you've grown
a foot in height since we saw you last, which isn't possible I know, but still. You look so grown up of a sudden.
Whatever happened to my six-year-old goddaughter who
stood with her hands on her hips and her chin in the air,
proclaiming to none other than King George himself—
much to your mother's horror I might add—that she
would never ever marry?"

Elizabeth managed a flush, a most appealing flush,
too. "Do cease your teasing, my lady. If you'll recall I
also intended when I was six to be the next queen of England, ruling alone, of course. And we all know that isn't
going to happen either."

Lady Lyon laughed at the memory. "Oh, it was quite a
sight, considering King George had just celebrated his
coronation, and there you were, all of six, laying claim to
his throne! You should have seen her, Mr. MacKinnon."

Douglas was seized by an image of Elizabeth, tall,
skinny, with her red-gold hair, standing before the periwigged Hanoverian, proclaiming herself the next virgin
queen while her mother suffered a fit of the vapors behind her.

"Shall we go in to supper?" Lady Lyon asked.

And the two couples repaired to a sizeable dining
room set off by a long mahogany table that seated eight
and gleamed like polished glass. Elegant carved armchairs lined each side. Chinaware and silver sparkled in
the candlelight. Paintings hung in gilt frames from the
walls, and a fire blazed in a massive stone hearth. The
room could have easily been part of a country house instead of attached to an austere military fortification in the
Scottish Highlands.

After they were seated, two liveried and bewigged footmen served generous helpings of cockle soup, roast pullet and greens, topped off by a gooseberry pudding that was a perfect mix of sweet and sour.

After a week of nothing but porridge, bannocks, and stew, it was a veritable banquet. Still Douglas couldn't help but think that while they sat there enjoying the delicious food and elegant surroundings, elsewhere, just a few hundred yards away, the men under the colonel's command—the same men who had risked their lives on the field of battle to assure a throne for George II—were sitting on hard benches, eating out of wooden trenchers. Instead of warm bread and creamy butter and gooseberry pudding, they were being served hard biscuits and gruel—and if they were fortunate, salted beef that had been dried to the toughness of leather. No charming conversation or liveried footmen to serve them, but grumbles of dissent and the occasional squabble. In the clan system, when circumstances called for their gathering together in one place, the chieftain ate, slept and marched beside his men. He fought with them, risking his life just as they.

And they called the Scots the barbarians.

"Do you have family on Skye, Mr. MacKinnon?"

Lady Lyon's inquiry broke Douglas from his thoughts.

"I've a brother, Iain, though it is my understanding that he was one of the many who fell at Culloden."

It did not escape Douglas's notice that, though the odds were slight, at that same moment he could be sitting across the table from the man who had fired the shot that killed his brother. Iain had been on that desolate, doomed moor, as had the colonel, facing each other on opposite sides. The irony had apparently not escaped the colonel's notice either. At just the mention of that terrible battle, the man's eyes had grown dim and his expression seemed a degree more strained than it had been moments before.

Lady Lyon endeavored to break the sudden silence. "We are sorry to hear of your loss, Mr. MacKinnon. I lost a brother, too, not so very long ago. Though his passing was the result of a duel, it still came with the honor of defending what he believed was right. It is a loss one never truly gets over."

Douglas read the sincerity in her eyes. "Thank you, my lady."

The remainder of the evening passed pleasantly enough, with the gentlemen enjoying a bottle of port by hearthlight while Lady Lyon sang and Elizabeth played at the pianoforte. She was an accomplished pianist, Douglas could see, her fingers moving deftly over the keys in a complicated *capriccio*. With her hair burnished by the candlelight and her face focused on the keys before her, she presented a picture of elegant determination.

When the candles began to gutter and the clock suddenly struck one, Colonel Lyon rose from his armchair, signaling his wife.

She rose and said, "Come, Elizabeth, Mr. MacKinnon, and I'll show you to your room."

She led them down one hall, then another, before opening the door onto a tiny chamber that fit a bed barely wide enough for two—and nothing else, not even a hearth.

"I'm afraid it's not much, but the barracks weren't built with a mind for entertaining. One must make do when circumstances call. You're newly wedded, so I'm sure you won't mind the cramped quarters. It's not much bigger than you'd have found at the inn, but I can assure you 'tis clean and the sheets are free from vermin. We'll see you at breakfast, dear. Mr. MacKinnon. Good night."

And with that, she turned, closing the door behind her.

"But where are you going to sleep?" Elizabeth asked the moment they were alone.

Douglas looked at her blandly. "In the bed, lass."

"With me?"

"Unless you're planning to sleep on that narrow strip of cold stone floor, aye, I am. I've been over a week in the saddle and sleeping on dirt floors. A stone floor like that will do me in. Now, are you going to stand there gaping at me while I get undressed?"

"Undressed?"

"Aye." He pulled off his shirt. "I sleep in my skin. If the sight of a man's body offends you, then I'd suggest you put out that light and climb into the bed within the next ten seconds." He reached for the fastening of his trews.

She was in the bed, the candle snuffed, before he could count to three.

The room fell dark. There was but a small window on the wall, far from sufficient to allow in the moonlight. Douglas shrugged off his trews and found the bed, lowering onto the mattress. Elizabeth was as stiff as a board beside him, pressed as far to the side as she possibly could be without wedging herself between the wall and the bed.

She said nothing, but he could hear her rapid breathing as she lay there, too shocked by the fact that she was but inches away from a naked man, to even remember to be frightened of the dark.

Douglas closed his eyes and slept.

Chapter Thirteen

Early the next morning Elizabeth awoke with her cheek at rest on Douglas's shoulder. It was a warm shoulder, actually, nice and firm, and as her vision cleared, the small amount of light the tiny window afforded gave her a remarkably clear view of his mouth.

He slept quietly, barely making a sound. Elizabeth didn't immediately move, but lay still, studying his chin, the slant of his nose, the thick lashes that lay at rest against his cheeks. Much as she'd never admit it aloud, his was a handsome face, in fact, more handsome than she'd at first acknowledged. His hair was not really as black as it appeared, more a rich walnut, one small lock of which seemed intent upon falling over his eyes. She lifted a hand, pushing that stray lock back. She noticed a small white scar, long healed, that cut a crooked C on the underside of his chin. Elizabeth touched a fingertip to it, tracing its shape while wondering at what mischief he must have worked in childhood to have left behind the mark.

When he didn't stir at her touch, Elizabeth shifted closer, studying his mouth, the shape and fullness of his lips, the dip of his chin. She remembered the way her sister Matilda had sighed the first time she'd seen the Scotsman, remarking that she thought his mouth *sensuous*. Mattie quite obviously was spending too much time reading cloying romantic poetry.

Elizabeth's gaze slipped to the thick cords of Douglas's neck, his shoulders, the muscles of his broad chest that tapered down across the rippling lines of his middle to delve beneath the bedsheet. She watched the slow rise and fall of his chest as he breathed and wondered if he dreamed. Then she wondered what his dreams could be.

She traced her finger lightly over his arm to his chest, pleased that he was so sound a sleeper. She studied the textures of him, the angles of him, sharp and solid, the straight grainy line of his jaw, the rugged slant of his nose.

She scarce realized she had replaced her fingers with her lips, touching them to his jaw, tasting the salt of his skin, breathing in the very scent of him. Knowing she could do something so daring as to touch him, kiss him, without him even realizing, was a heady, wonderful thing.

This would likely be the only time in her life that she would ever be this close to a living, breathing man without him being aware of her. Once the two months had passed and she returned to live out the rest of her life in England, she would never marry, and thus would never wake with a man beside her in her bed.

She had studied anatomy, yes, poring over books that described the male body in detail. But this—lying so closely to a man, surrounded by the potent warmth of him—this was far more intriguing than any book.

A book was only parchment and ink.

This was real.

He was real.

Douglas had seen every inch of her in that tub. Wasn't it only right that she should, in turn, be given the chance to see him?

All of him?

Elizabeth slipped her fingers beneath the edge of the sheet and slowly started to lift it away . . .

She was on her back a moment later, pinned beneath the man who was her husband.

The very *naked* man who was her husband.

"I was—"

His mouth covered hers, cutting her off. He possessed her, he consumed her, overwhelming her, trapping her with his mouth and his body and his tongue as he teased her every sense, until she was clinging to his shoulders and doubted she could even blink.

Every inch of her felt alive. The taste of him, the scent of him, filled her head, and when she felt that first touch of his tongue on hers, she drew back, startled, but then she gave herself over to the unfamiliar sensation of it, the exciting newness of it, and kissed him back.

She felt his hips, the hardness of him, pressing against her and it wasn't enough. She wanted to feel his hands on her, the way she had touched him. She wanted to feel more, take more. She wanted to *know* more.

Not until he pulled away, breaking the kiss, did the

colors and the feelings that had swirled in a tumult around her begin to ebb. Daylight returned in harsh, undeniable measure. When finally she found the will to open her eyes, Elizabeth met his stare. She saw desire there, a man for a woman. And she knew he wanted her, knew it to her soul.

But she saw something else there, too. She saw refusal.

"You should not begin what you do not intend to finish."

His voice was low, unnerving. She should say something, but the words, any words, somehow escaped her.

Elizabeth, who was known for her quick tongue and frank opinion, couldn't think of a single thing to say. She simply closed her eyes and willed herself to vanish. It was the only thing she could do.

Elizabeth felt the bed shift beneath her as he got up. She lay still, willing him away, wishing she could take back the last minutes as she listened to the sounds of him dressing, moving about the room.

"The ferry should soon be ready to leave."

She did not answer.

"I will await you outside."

Elizabeth waited until she heard the door close behind him before she opened her eyes again. She stared up at the ceiling, awash with humiliation.

What had possessed her to look at him like that? To touch him like that? She was the daughter of the Duke of Sudeleigh, not a common strumpet. All her life she had been determined never to allow a man dominance over her heart and body. With dominance came vulnerability, and with vulnerability came weakness. It was the one thing she'd learned from studying women throughout history.

Elizabeth had grown up surrounded by the cream of English genteel society, earls, dukes, even royal princes. She had spent her formative years observing the manner of the world into which she'd been born. At an early age, she knew not precisely when, she had begun to question the way in which the women of her world seemed to lose their every freedom, their individuality, not to mention their every possession the moment they were wed.

Elizabeth had been witness to acquaintances of her mother, nobly born women who had been reduced to little better than beggars, utterly dependent upon the agreeableness of their husbands. If the man they wed revealed himself to be a boor, the lady could not so much as buy herself a book to read, or quills for letter writing. Instead she was made to ask permission for these small conveniences, and though a lady likely brought a healthy dowry to the marriage, if her husband had hidden a propensity for drink or gambling, she might find herself penniless, threatened with debtor's prison even before her first child was born.

Lady Wolfton, one of the duchess's closest contemporaries, had once quipped at afternoon tea that she'd been on more familiar terms with her modiste than she'd been with her husband the earl when they'd wed. The Marchioness of Thurston, who came from a long line of distinguished nobility, had had to flee to France with her children in the dead of night after discovering that Lord Thurston had lost their home, their fortune, and even their fine town carriage all on a single roll of the dice.

Elizabeth had resolved early on that she would never

allow herself to be placed in such a position. She alone would determine her own destiny. And the simplest way she had seen to do that was to avoid that one peril so many others had fallen victim to before her.

Elizabeth had vowed never to fall in love.

But that was before Douglas Dubh MacKinnon had walked into her life.

Two hours later, Douglas and Elizabeth boarded the small ferry that would take them across Kyle Rhea to Skye.

From where they stood on the pier in Glenelg, the verdant shoreside hills of Skye loomed softly on the morning mist, looking close enough to skip to across the water. In fact, the boatman, a wizened sort named Niall MacRae, told Elizabeth of how when the tide was slack, the drovers would tie their beasts together in fives, nose-to-tail, using heather rope. With a single skiff, they could swim upwards of one hundred head of cattle across to the mainland in a day. Ponies, he added, would make the crossing as well, but because of their high-spiritedness, they would have to be lashed to the boats by halters and withies.

As they crossed, Douglas passed the time chatting with the boatman in Gaelic. Though she couldn't understand them, Elizabeth knew it was no casual conversation. They spoke in hushed tones and Niall MacRae cast her a wary glance on more than one occasion.

When they arrived on the Skye shore, they were stopped briefly by a waiting detachment of militia. As soon as Douglas presented the safe-conduct the colonel had given them, the soldiers nodded and allowed them to continue onto shore. Douglas left Elizabeth at the stone jetty that served as pier, returning a short while later with three sturdy ponies.

"Is it much farther to your croft from here?" she asked. She was anxious now to reach the end of their journey. It would be such a treat to sleep more than one night in the same bed after so many days of traveling.

"We'll be there afore long," Douglas answered, as he secured their belongings onto one of the ponies.

They started out on a drovers' road that wound its way inland through heather-dusted hills from the shore. It was no more than an obscure pathway, really, but Douglas knew every turn, every pitch, even though at times the trail seemed to vanish into the very landscape that surrounded them.

Douglas's wariness, which had been keen throughout their journey across the Highlands, seemed to have relaxed now that they had arrived on his home isle. He no longer sat stiffly in the saddle, and his hold on the pony's reins was slack as they shuffled over the hills heading toward the great rocky crags in the distance.

Elizabeth noticed that everyone they encountered, fishermen at the shore and farmers on the glen, all knew Douglas on sight. They offered him greetings in Gaelic while looking on her with curious suspicion. She searched the hills around them for sign of the place that would be her home, and as they came into a glen that stretched downward toward a rippling burn, it began to rain, not heavily, but enough to have Elizabeth pulling up the hood of her cloak. Soft thunder rumbled through the low patch of clouds, startling a pair of curlews from the tall grass. The wind seemed to shift and surge since there were no trees to buffer it, racing down the hillsides to meet them.

After a while, Elizabeth noticed a stone tower, lone and tall with small overhanging turrets on each corner. "That castle there? What is it?"

"That is Dunakin," he answered. "Seat of a MacKinnon chieftain."

"MacKinnon? Does that mean we are drawing near to the croft?"

"Aye, lass. We should be there before much longer."

As he watched her face, Douglas couldn't help but think that had they wed under any other circumstances, he would be taking her to that same distant tower, continuing a tradition of MacKinnon brides from centuries past. Deep inside, he couldn't help but admit to a certain regret that circumstances were so different. At the time, back when the duke had first told Douglas his plan for Elizabeth, Douglas had been angry at having been trapped into a marriage he'd never wanted, and angrier still that he couldn't immediately get out of it. He'd never expected her to make the entire journey to Skye, but that she would wilt within the first few miles and beg him to take her back.

But she hadn't.

Instead she had withstood the rigors of over a week's worth of riding across harsh terrain. She hadn't once complained. She had endured it all—the rain, the midges, an attack by two vagrants—without giving in. It was a thing a good many men couldn't have done. Appreciating that she could have made the past days a living hell for him only made the task Douglas now faced a far less agreeable one.

"We are arrived, madam."

The rain had stopped and the clouds had drifted over the hills, sparking the glen with dewy tears that glistened in the sunlight. The wind carried mingling scents of heather and rain, sea and turf. Beyond the hills, the sounds of the sea echoed softly.

Douglas watched as Elizabeth pushed back the hood from her face to look around, searching the landscape.

At first, her gaze skipped completely past the crude croft house. Built as it was of the same rugged sandstone as the barren hill it lay nestled against, it was an easy thing to miss. The roof was turfed over so that but for the small windows and door, the place vanished against the landscape. There was no other dwelling in sight, so she looked again, more carefully this time.

Douglas knew the moment she saw it. Though she tried hard to mask it, her eyes gave her away.

As a child, Douglas had lived in that same cottage, scurrying across the glen in play, acting out tales with Roderick and Iain of the great warriors who had once walked these same hills. But now, for the first time in his life, Douglas suddenly saw his childhood home through the eyes of someone who had never known a day of want, who had been surrounded by every luxury of life, and who had never been required to do anything more than look lovely, speak pleasantly, and behave in a dignified manner.

Elizabeth would never last here. Not even for two months. Whether the duke liked it or not, Douglas knew he needed to tell her the truth.

"Elizabeth, I . . ."

She turned to look at him, her face set and determined. "Where do we stable the ponies?"

Douglas looked at her, puzzled. "There is a byre behind the house, but lass, really . . ."

"Shall I see to the pony myself? I assume we are on our own here for the next two months."

And then Douglas realized that this woman would go through just about anything to meet her end of the bargain she'd made with the duke. Her freedom meant that much to her.

"I will see to the ponies. Just drop the reins. He'll not roam."

She nodded. "Well, then, I guess I'm ready to see my new home."

Elizabeth waited while Douglas dismounted and then came to help her from the back of her pony. He took her gently about the waist and eased her to the ground in front of him. It was the closest they'd been since that morning, when he'd awoken to find her touching him. He frowned when he felt her stiffen against his hands.

They walked to the small house on a crooked path Douglas had cut countless times in his boyhood. Suddenly, Elizabeth stopped, rooted to the very spot.

She wasn't going to go through with it. Truth be told, he couldn't fault her for it.

"Lass . . . ?"

"There is a goat on top of our house."

Douglas looked to see a small kid standing atop the turfed roof of the cottage, contentedly munching on a patch of sod.

"*Truis!*" he said, shooing it away in Gaelic.

The goat took one look at him and let out a plaintive *naaa.*

Douglas glanced at Elizabeth. "He's a breed that live in the wild. He'll come down on his own. Let us get inside. I feel the rain starting again."

At least the place was clean inside, everything neat and tidy, and fresh linens had been brought for the bedding. The press had been stocked with the necessaries, flour, tea, sugar.

Elizabeth's trunks were set in the middle of the floor. Apparently the boat carrying them had made it safely to Dunakin, for he had sent along a letter with them to his foster mother, Eithne, asking that she prepare the cottage for their arrival. He'd been worried the boat would have been captured on the seas because of the reports he'd heard of the heightened patrols. It was for that same reason he'd insisted he and Elizabeth travel by land. He was glad to see they had arrived safely.

Elizabeth was standing before her trunks, her mouth screwed into a frown.

"Is something the matter?"

"Yes, something is the matter. One of my trunks is missing."

"Missing? You are certain?"

She opened the two trunks, searching through layers of stockings and petticoats and flounces.

"Yes. My books are not here." She looked at him, clearly perturbed. "Douglas, I packed them myself in a separate trunk with all my writing paper and quills. It was the smallest of the trunks. And it's not here anywhere."

Douglas shrugged. "Well, at least it was only the books and not your dresses."

"*Only* the books?" She spun around to face him. "I couldn't care less about the dresses. My books . . . they are more important to me than a bunch of lace and satin! They mean everything to me—and now they are gone!"

Douglas was afraid she might cry. He'd never met a woman—and an English woman no less—whose sun didn't rise and set upon the state of her wardrobe. It was all they could think about, all they could talk about.

But not so Elizabeth. It was clear from the way she was tossing stockings and slips aside, digging deeply through each trunk, that the loss of her books was far more distressing.

"I will go and inquire as to what happened with the trunk," he said. "Perhaps they haven't yet brought it."

"Yes." Her eyes lightened immediately. "It was quite heavy. Perhaps they needed a cart to bring it and haven't yet managed. You are right, Douglas. Thank you. And I would be very grateful to you if you would inquire after it." She looked at him. "*Now.*"

"Right now?"

She nodded.

"But it is raining . . ."

She frowned. "The rain didn't stop you an hour ago from riding across the glen."

Douglas took a deep breath, then let it out slowly. He wasn't of a mind to argue with her. "I'll go. I need to let the others know we are safely arrived anyway. You'll be all right here alone while I go?"

"Certainly. I'll brew some tea and unpack my clothing"—she glanced at the garments she'd strewn about the room—"whilst you are away."

Before he left, Douglas quickly stoked a fire and showed Elizabeth where to fetch the water from the barrel outside for tea. He set the kettle upon its hook to boil and ferreted out a pewter cup and spoon from the wall cabinet before then heading out the door—into the rain.

"We were pursued by a naval cutter, laird. Sixteen guns at least. We had no choice but to dump the trunk overboard. It was too heavy in that small skiff with all those books inside. It was weighing us down."

Seated by the light of a crackling fire in the study at Dunakin, Douglas nodded to the man, Thomas MacKinnon, who stood fretfully giving his report. He understood perfectly the reasons his crew had abandoned the trunk to the depths of the Minch—if they hadn't, they would certainly have been arrested by the English patrol and possibly imprisoned.

It didn't, however, make the task of breaking the news to Elizabeth any more palatable.

"Have you heard from the others?"

Thomas relaxed enough to take the chair beside him. "The word from MacDonald of Dunvegan is that the prince is afoot in the outer isles. There are rumors he has been spotted on Benbecula, Lewis, even Uist. The Minch is teeming with Sassenach cutters looking to capture him, and they're raiding the estates of any clan known to have been out in the rebellion in hopes of rooting him out. Thus far, the worst of what they've done was at Raasay."

"Old MacLeod?"

"Aye. They didna kill him. He wasna there, but they did lay waste to the isle. They killed the sheep and all the cattle. They burned everything from castle to cottage. They violated the women, laird, lassies and nursing mothers alike, and killed any who dared protest. They thought it would force someone to reveal the prince's whereabouts. They are that desperate to find him."

Douglas's throat tightened at the news. The MacKinnons and the MacLeods of Raasay were allied through the marriage of his uncle, Iain Dubh, the MacKinnon chief, to his second wife, Janet, daughter of MacLeod of Raasay. Thus an affront to the MacLeods was an affront to the MacKinnons as well. "Who ordered this?"

"A Captain John Fergusson of H.M.S. Furnace. They burned Raasay House, Brochel Castle, laid waste to whatever crossed their path. 'Twas followed by a militia raid headed by a Captain Caroline Scott. His men simply finished the job begun by Fergusson's men. They are working their way through the isles, laird. It is only a matter of time afore they come to Dunakin to do the same."

"They will not find the people of Dunakin as powerless as those on Raasay."

Douglas looked into the fire, knowing the next question he had to ask, but fearing the answer. "Anything of my brother?"

"Nae, not as yet. But young Iain was not at Culloden, laird."

This bit of news took Douglas by surprise. "He was not?"

"Nae. I have heard it from the others that Iain had been sent north with a detachment of MacKinnons to join Cromarty's forces in search of Jacobite gold. The rebellion was lost long afore they ever knew it."

"And my uncle?"

"Iain Dubh was among the other chiefs attempting to rally the clans after Culloden. The prince had already decided to give up the fight and advised every man to survive as best he could. I'm told the chief returned home to Kilmarie a fortnight ago."

Douglas closed his eyes. His brother was alive, and his uncle had returned to Skye. And the MacKinnon chief was the one person who would know where Iain was hiding. He looked at Thomas. "We'll head for Kilmarie on the morrow. 'Tis time I spoke with my uncle."

Chapter Fourteen

Early the next morning, Elizabeth came into the cottage to find Douglas preparing to leave.

"Are we going somewhere?" She had been in the byre searching unsuccessfully for a tub—she would give just about *anything* for the luxury of a bath—and had come hoping Douglas could tell her where to find one. Certainly there must be one somewhere for doing the laundry. At this point, she would settle for a large bucket. Instead she stood and watched him as he collected his things in the dim firelight inside the cottage.

He fastened his sword around his waist and shrugged on his coat over his cambric shirt. "*We* are not going anywhere, lass. I'm to ride to another part of the isle for a time today. I should return by nightfall. You're to stay here."

"Nightfall?" Elizabeth looked out the small window onto the muted light of the horizon where the sun was just rising. "But day has barely broken."

"Aye." Douglas took a swig of tea from the pewter cup on the table beside him. "I had intended to be away afore the sun's rise, but I didna wake early enough."

"You're going to leave me here . . . alone? What am I to do whilst you're away?" she asked. "I haven't any books to read, nothing with which to write. Everything I had is lost. I cannot even write to my family to assure them we have safely arrived."

Douglas looked at her, his voice softening. "I very much regret the loss of your things, lass. As I told you last night, it was unavoidable. The men did their best to save them, but in the end they had to save themselves. I cannot swim to the bottom of the Minch to retrieve them. This isn't Edinburgh or London. Books are scarce, so replacing them won't be possible right now."

Elizabeth simply stared at him.

Finally, he sighed. "I will see if I might at least get hold of some foolscap and quills when I return today so that you may write to your family. Until then . . ." He looked around the cottage, gesturing toward a twig broom that stood leaning against the bare stone wall. "Perhaps you might busy yourself with sweeping the floor."

"Sweeping the . . . ?" He might as well have just suggested she paint the Mona Lisa. "But it is a *dirt* floor!"

"Aye."

"You want me to sweep a *dirt* floor?"

"Aye."

Elizabeth stared at him. "Do you really not comprehend the ridiculousness of your suggestion?"

Blank as a fresh page, Douglas shrugged. "Well, if not the floor, then I'm sure you'll find something to occupy your time. There is always much to do on a croft." He took up his pistol, pulled on his cockaded bonnet, and made for the door.

"I've put the kettle on for tea," he said over his shoulder, "but I'm afraid you'll have to fetch the milk yourself. There's some meal and a bit of cheese in the cupboard for breakfast and extra peats for the fire outside the door. Dinna expect me for supper. I'll not likely be back for it."

Elizabeth stood watching, mute as a swan, as Douglas walked out the door. Even after he'd gone, she remained standing for some time, staring at the closed door from the middle of the room with her brow creased in utter disbelief.

Supper. Surely he didn't expect *her* to cook his supper?

Now he was joking. Other than to poke her head in to ask the cook for tea when one of the other servants wasn't at hand to do it for her, Elizabeth had never once stepped foot in the kitchens at Drayton Hall. It had been a hot, smoky cave of a place, filled with clashing smells and noise and clutter. She was Elizabeth of Drayton Hall, after all, a lady of quality and refinement. She was the daughter of England's most powerful duke . . .

She was also the wife of a Highland farmer, at least for the next two months.

Elizabeth thought of her father, of how he'd refused an immediate annulment because he intended her to learn what it was to be a wife. *A wife.* In all honesty, when he'd said that, offering her the arrangement of two months with Douglas in exchange for her freedom, she hadn't really considered exactly what being a wife might entail. In her experience, having spent four-and-twenty years watching her mother, the role of wife had hinged mainly upon stitching pillow covers, walking in the garden, driving about the estate to chat benevolently with the tenants, instructing the servants, and otherwise smiling pleasantly while saying "Yes, dear" when her father was in a temper. That was the role of a duke's wife.

"But I'm not a duke's wife, am I?" she said aloud to herself. "I am a farmer's wife, a *Scottish* farmer's wife, and that is a very different sort of wife altogether."

Elizabeth noticed a column of steam rising from the kettle's spout and went to take it from its hook above the fire with a pair of iron tongs. Tea, she thought, now that was something she could do quite effortlessly. She'd been making and serving and drinking tea since she'd been all of five years old.

Elizabeth found the tea caddy and a spoon with which to measure out the leaves. She scoured the cupboard for something to eat and found a small sack of meal, but she hadn't the first clue to how to prepare it. She imagined she should mix it with something—milk, water probably—but at that moment, she couldn't bring herself to attempt it. Her only other find was a small chunk of cheese that was wrapped inside a cloth.

Elizabeth looked around for the milk, which she took with her tea, before she remembered that Douglas had told her she'd need to fetch it. Fetch it from where? Perhaps there was a jug outside, so she pulled on a woolen blanket to use as a wrap and quickly crossed the room.

Outside, the air was damp and kissed with the earthy scent of the hills, the salt of the sea hidden just over the braes. A cuckoo called out from the tall grass, its familiar song echoing across the still glen.

How odd, she thought, that but a few hundred miles away, a team of gardeners worked day and night to trim and clip and shape a garden made of perfect angles and lines. Here, on this untamed swath of craggy hills, colors soft and dark mixed one into the other in a place where ghosts of ancient warriors and the spirits of fierce beasts were equally at home.

Pulling the edges of the blanket around her, Elizabeth searched for the milk, but found nothing even remotely resembling a jug. She walked around to the side of the cottage, only to find a small drystone enclosure. Standing in the midst of it was a shaggy orange figure of a cow.

Elizabeth blinked at the cow.

The cow blinked at her, letting out a most plaintive *mooo*.

And then Elizabeth realized what Douglas had meant when he'd said she would need to *fetch* the milk for herself.

He expected her to milk the cow.

Elizabeth could very well have forgone the milk in her tea, and at first, that was her every intention. She even started to leave. It hardly seemed worth the effort, but then, as she turned and headed back for the cottage door, she found herself wondering whether Douglas had purposely left her the task as a challenge, as if he didn't quite believe she could do something as simple as milk a cow.

Well she had every intention of milking that cow; in

fact she'd have buckets full of the stuff waiting for him when he returned.

How difficult could it be, milking one cow?

The cow gave her a cursory glance as she approached, then lowered its head to breakfast upon a small patch of grass at its feet. The closer she came to the shaggy beast, however, the more Elizabeth's confidence flagged.

How, exactly, did one milk a cow? She'd never really, actually seen the thing done, had only read about it in books, farming manuals, and the like. Was she supposed to get acquainted with the beast first? Offer her some sort of food? Elizabeth came to a halt two feet from the animal and extended her hand in shy greeting.

"Good morning," she said, eying the beast warily. "Pay me no mind. You just continue to enjoy your breakfast whilst I crouch down here beside you—"

Elizabeth set the bucket on the ground directly beneath the cow's swollen udder. She was not so cosseted as to think that was all it took. After all, even a well had to be worked to give water. So she bent at the waist, reaching out her hand while trying not to tumble forward—

She yelped when the cow swished its slender tail, swatting her right on the cheek.

"What was that about?"

A chortling *naaa* sounded suddenly from behind her. Elizabeth turned and saw the same goat that had been gnawing on the turf roof the day before. The beast was now standing several yards away, watching her from the shelter of the byre. It was white, one horn shorter than the other, with a whiskery beard and floppy ears. Though her intellect told her differently, she would have sworn the little fiend was grinning.

"And I suppose you could do any better," she muttered, ready to turn back to the cow for another try, until she noticed a small wooden stool set against the wall of the byre. That would certainly make things a lot easier, so she went to fetch it, tossing the goat a sour look.

"Do you expect me to believe you were trying to tell me where this stool was?"

The goat simply blinked. "*Naaa.*"

"Oh, do be quiet."

Elizabeth took up the stool and started back for the cow, only the cow had abandoned that particular spot, knocking over her bucket in the process. She now stood several yards away.

Snatching up the pail with the stool propped under one arm, Elizabeth tromped after the beast, holding her skirts aloft and stepping carefully through the tufted grass. Once she reached the cow, she placed the bucket back underneath its belly, situated the stool alongside, and then attempted to lower herself onto it, no easy task given the bulk of her panniered skirts. But she wasn't giving up. Oh, no. Not now.

After several rather ungraceful attempts that would have sent her mother into a certain fit of hysterics, Elizabeth managed to perch herself upon the stool. Her skirts billowed on either side of her, puffed up like a syllabub. And when she reached for the cow, the beast shifted its weight to one side, knocking Elizabeth back off the stool and onto her rump in a *swoosh* of ruffled petticoats.

Elizabeth clamped her jaw tight, biting back a curse. Her face grew flushed as she watched the cow amble further away, leaving her—and the very dry bucket—behind.

Naaa.

Elizabeth turned murderous eyes on the goat. It had come closer, but was still standing out of reach.

"Go eat a roof, then, and leave me in peace."

A half hour—and three more failed attempts later— Elizabeth managed to loop a rope she'd found around the cow's neck so that she could tether it to a tree. Her skirts were muddied, her hair was falling out of its braid, but she was as determined as ever to accomplish this one simple task.

Dropping onto the stool easily now, Elizabeth reached with two hands for the cow's belly. She grasped hold of the teat with conviction, took a deep breath, and gave a healthy pull, then another . . .

Nothing, not even a drop, issued forth for her effort.

And then she heard that all too familiar *naaa*'ing come from behind.

Elizabeth simply dropped her head forward against the cow's girth and willed herself not to burst into tears. She was an educated woman, by heavens. She could decipher Latin texts and tabulate multiple columns of figures in her head. So why, *why* couldn't she manage something as simple as the milking of a single cow?

"You can try singin' to her a bit," came a voice suddenly from behind. "Tha' always seems to help when they're stubborn of givin' their milk."

Please, God, please tell me that it isn't the goat who's talking to me.

Elizabeth slowly lifted her head as a figure advanced from the shelter of the byre. It wasn't the goat, thank the saints. It was a woman. She looked to be of middling years with soft brown hair and softer brown eyes that smiled from behind a careworn face. A white kerchief of sorts covered the back of her hair, twisted and knotted upon the crown of her head. In her arms she carried a basket, and she wore no shoes beneath her tattered tartan skirts.

"Good day t' you," she said, smiling as she stepped easily through the rutted pasture. "I'm Eithne MacKenzie."

Her voice was soft, lilting, the sort that could soothe the distress of a crying babe. It certainly soothed Elizabeth.

"You must be Roderick's mother, then?" Elizabeth caught herself staring at the petite woman with the kind face who looked so like the young man they had met at the Highland inn.

"Aye, that I am. Douglas's foster mother, too."

"I'm Elizabeth. Douglas's wife."

"Indeed?" The woman looked intrigued. "Well, I've come t' see how you're settling in and to bring you some things you might be needin'." She looked to the cottage. "Douglas is no' at home?"

"He said he had to go to another part of the isle. He thought he might not return till nightfall."

"Nightfall?" Eithne shook her head and clucked her tongue softly. "The mon's got rocks in 'is heid, he does, leaving you alone 'ere with naught but that cow for company."

The goat lifted its head from the end of the rope it was chewing to offer a protesting *naaa*.

"*Truis!*" Eithne called to it, the same name Douglas had used the day before. The goat nickered, then trotted off to the shelter of the byre, flicking its short tail.

Eithne joined Elizabeth beside the cow. "Well, afore you can milk this sweet lady, lass, you've got to get better acquainted with 'er. Here—" She took up Elizabeth's hand and helped her to stand, drawing her toward the cow's shaggy head. "Her name is Honeysuckle." Eithne placed Elizabeth's hand flat against the cow's shaggy brow, then scratched her behind her ears, murmuring, "*Tairis,* sweet Hinny. There's a good girl."

The cow lifted its nose, sniffed. Finding nothing to eat, it lowered to the grass once again.

"Now, to milk her, 'tis best to sit on her left side, like this." Eithne crooked her legs and positioned herself effortlessly on the stool, leaning her face full against the cow's girth as she reached underneath. She grasped on with both hands, closing her eyes as she pressed into the creature's warm belly. Softly she started murmuring a tune.

> *A maiden sang sweetly*
> *As a bird on a tree,*
> *Cro' Chaillean, Cro' Chaillean,*
> *Cro' Chaillean for me!*
>
> *In the morning they wander*
> *To their pastures afar,*
> *Where the grass grows the greenest*
> *By corrie and scaur.*
>
> *They wander the uplands*
> *Where the soft breezes blow,*
> *And they drink from the fountain*
> *Where the sweet cresses grow.*

> *But so far as they wander,*
> *Dappled, dun, brown, and grey,*
> *They return to the milking*
> *At the close of the day.*
>
> *Thus a maiden sang sweetly*
> *As a bird on a tree,*
> *Cro' Chaillean, Cro' Chaillean,*
> *Cro' Chaillean for me.*

Elizabeth watched in mute wonder as the milk flowed effortlessly from Eithne's fingers quickly filling the bottom of the pail.

When she'd finished with the song, Eithne turned to Elizabeth. "Now 'tis your turn to try."

Elizabeth took an immediate step backward. "Oh, no, I don't believe I know that song."

Eithne laughed. "Och, lass, any song will do. 'Tis just the cadence of your voice that will coax her to milkin' for you. Surely you must know a song. Come, now. You must try it."

Elizabeth approached the stool tentatively, taking a great deal longer than Eithne to situate herself with her hooped skirts. Eithne cast a curious eye at Elizabeth's gown, but said nothing. She simply persuaded her to lean her cheek against the cow's side and reach underneath her belly. Elizabeth soon got past feeling foolish and found the animal's coat to be soft, not at all wiry as it looked. The beast smelled pleasantly of grass and heather, and her hide was warm against Elizabeth's cheek.

When she'd found a comfortable position, Elizabeth

closed her eyes, took a deep breath, and began an old ditty she'd learned as a child . . .

An outlandish knight came from the northlands;
And he came wooing to me;
He said he would take me to foreign lands
And he would marry me. . . .

When next she opened her eyes, she couldn't believe what she saw.

"She is doing it! She is giving me the milk."

Eithne chuckled. "Nae, lass, 'tis you who are milking her. And very well, too! Come, now, once that pail is better filled, we'll have us a fine breakfast feast."

A short time later, Elizabeth and Eithne walked together across the pasture, eggs tucked in the basket from the hens, milk sloshing in the pail. They chatted pleasantly as they approached the cottage while the goat trotted along beside them. The sun had climbed high in the sky above them, bathing the glen with its soft light. The birds were trilling. The heather was blooming. Summer had come to the Highlands.

"Ordinarily, many of us women would be away in the shielings at this time of the year."

"Shielings?" Elizabeth asked.

"Aye, they are small bothy shelters where we live while tending to the flocks in the hills. While we're away, the crops grow here on the crofts. But with the king's soldiers prowling these hills in search of the bonnie prince, we must keep close to home for safety's sake. 'Twill bring us a leaner winter, it will, keeping the stock here in the lowlands."

"Do you think they will capture the prince?" Elizabeth asked.

Eithne smiled softly. "They'll not catch him."

"We heard in some of the places we passed through on our way here that they've offered a reward of thirty thousand pounds to any who will reveal him. Thirty thousand pounds is a lot of money. There would be no worries over lean crops and cold winters with a sum like that."

"Aye, but a true Highlandman's honor canna be bought or sold, lass. Not for any sum."

It was much the same thing Douglas had said.

"I would ask you to join me for tea," Elizabeth said when they'd ducked inside the cottage's low door, "but I'm afraid the water is long cold by now."

She gestured to the table where the kettle sat untouched since earlier that morning.

"Och, 'tis easy enough to remedy, child."

Elizabeth watched as Eithne crossed to the hearth, taking up the tongs to remove a small, flat stone from the fire. She brought it to the table, opened the lid of the teapot, and dropped the stone inside with a soft *clunk*.

"Tha' should warm the water soon enough. Now let us see if we can make us some porridge."

Elizabeth looked at her. "I've not much experience in the kitchen. I do not know how to make porridge."

"Och, so the man leaves you to go hungry as well, does he?" Eithne shook her head. "You'd think he'd been raised by dogs. Come, lass, I'll teach you the way my mither taught me. 'Tis simple, it is, once you get the way of it."

A half an hour later, there was a pot of tasty porridge bubbling over the fire, and soft round bannocks fresh off the *gridheal*. Eithne showed Elizabeth how to skim the cream off the milk they'd drawn that morning using a scallop shell with holes pierced through it, then how to form the meal into a heap with a small pool of milk in its center to mix and form the bannocks.

Eithne had brought gooseberry preserves and fresh butter in her basket, and they sat together sharing a pot of tea while Eithne showed Elizabeth the proper "Scots" way to enjoy her porridge.

"You take up your spoonful of hot porridge and dip it into your milk bowl afore taking it to your mouth. 'Tis how you get their best flavor."

Elizabeth took a spoonful, closing her eyes as the warmth of the oats soothed her hungry stomach. It was delicious, and she even gave a small bit of what was left over to the goat, which was nickering at the door.

The two ladies spent the better part of the day seeing to the various tasks about the croft. Eithne instructed while Elizabeth took it all in. They walked to the burn that ran along the back of the croft near the hills, and Eithne showed Elizabeth how to use sand and branches of heather to scrub out their breakfast dishes. While the bowls and trenchers dried in the sunlight, they collected tall reeds for weaving into baskets and wickerwork, and wildflowers and herbs to freshen the cottage inside. They took potatoes, carrots, kail, and some of the dried haddies Eithne had brought with her to make a thick soup that would simmer over the fire till supper. And all the while, Eithne passed the time with tales about life at Dunakin and Douglas's childhood.

"Och, a stubborn lad was he," Eithne said as she sorted the oak apples they had gathered for boiling. They would make ink, and Eithne had promised to show Elizabeth how to cut a quill from a goose feather so she could write letters. " 'Twas difficult on him, it was, losing his father and his mither at such a young age."

Since Eithne seemed so willing to talk, Elizabeth took the opportunity to learn more. "So Douglas was not a Jacobite, whilst his brother Iain was?"

"Aye. 'Tis the way of this rebellion, lass, brother fighting against brother, clan to clan. It has been most troubling to Douglas, though, since the MacKinnons have been loyal to the Scottish kings since time first began."

"Then why did Douglas not take up arms for the Young Pretender?"

Whether Eithne sought to protect Douglas or simply didn't know, she only smiled and said in response, "That, lass, would be a question for Douglas himself."

The sun had moved into the afternoon sky when Eithne finally took up her basket and prepared to leave.

"Must you go?" Elizabeth asked. She had enjoyed their time together and she didn't relish the idea of being alone.

"Aye, lass, tomorrow I must rise early, for it is the day for the *nigh*."

"The *nigh*?"

Eithne grinned. "Washing day."

"Would you . . ." Elizabeth hesitated. "Mind if I joined you?"

"Of course you can come, lass. I'll be by t' fetch you after breakfast then."

And with that, Eithne MacKenzie took her leave.

Chapter Fifteen

Kilmarie House, Strathaird, Skye

Douglas strode into the private study of his father's eldest brother, the twenty-ninth MacKinnon chief, Iain Dubh MacKinnon of Strathaird.

His uncle sat against tall windows that faced out onto the scarred blue basalt face of *Bla Bheinn* mountain. The sun was shining and Iain Dubh was dozing as Douglas entered the room. He had apparently fallen asleep while reading, for his graying head was bent to the open pages of his book, and his chin was at rest against his chest.

This man, more than any other, had been a father to Douglas, taking the place of the one who'd been sent away. He'd taught him to shoot, to wield the broadsword. He'd shown him what it meant to be a chieftain. When Douglas had cried at the loss of his mother and infant sister, Iain Dubh had held him. He'd seen to his education, his upbringing. Most importantly, he'd given him honor.

Douglas cleared his throat and the chief awoke with a start.

"Douglas." The older man rose from his chair to take his nephew in a heartfelt embrace.

The rebellion had taken its toll on the MacKinnon chief. His face looked older, scored by the past months since Douglas had watched him ride off to join the bonnie prince in Edinburgh. His hair, once peppery, was now gray. His eyes, the bonnie blue of the MacKinnons, now looked dim and deeply tired.

"It is good to see you, nephew."

" 'Tis I should be saying that to you, sir."

In truth, the last time Douglas had seen his uncle, he had thought it would be the last.

"I was sorry to hear of the loss at Culloden. The last word I'd had was that the Jacobites were in Derby and on the verge of victory. I was in London waiting for the prince's army to march victorious through the city gates. It seems impossible that events should have taken such a decided turn."

Iain Dubh shook his head. " 'Twas a different rebellion than the others, Douglas. Far, far different. So much bloodshed. So much loss. We were ill prepared, and ill advised."

Douglas gave a solemn nod. "There is no hope of another rally?"

The chief returned to his chair, motioning Douglas to the other. "Nae. 'Tis over. 'Twas over afore it began, a doomed venture from the start. Without the French, we could do nothing. I stayed close after the battle, to see if the clans would gather again, but their hearts just weren't in it. Those that didna die or fall prisoner to that butcher son of the Hanoverian, fled for the hills with the government troops hot on their heels."

"Iain?" Douglas asked. "I have heard he was else-where on the day of the battle."

"Aye, he wasn't at Culloden," the chief confirmed. "I foresaw the end, so I sent him north into MacKay coun-try afore the battle had begun."

"He is safe then?"

"Aye."

"Where?"

"On Skye." The chief looked at his nephew, easily reading his thoughts. "He was young, Douglas, foolish, his head filled with the romance of the battle. He could not understand your reasons for refusing to join. He saw it only as a betrayal to the clan. He didna mean the words he spoke. He is a far different lad than he was months ago."

Douglas was seized by the memory of the last time he had seen his younger brother, standing before him in the dusk of morning on the courtyard at Dunakin. He had looked like a lad bent on conquering the world, his sword polished, his eyes determined. He'd asked his brother one last time to join them. Douglas had tried to explain his reasons for refusing, but Iain would hear none of it. Douglas would never forget the bitter words they had exchanged when he'd had to make the most dif-ficult decision in his life, refusing to join his clan and fight for the prince's cause.

"I've another war to fight, brother," Douglas had told him. "The war to see what is rightfully ours—what is yours and mine, what was our father's—restored to us."

He had done it for Dunakin, for the legacy of the clan

and the memory of their father, so that MacKinnons would not become a clan of the past.

But Iain MacKinnon hadn't understood.

"This place, it is naught but rock and ghosts," he'd said. "Honor is something a man carries with him no matter where he chooses to lie down at night. Honor lives forever."

Iain had renounced Douglas as a brother that day, naming him a coward and a disgrace to the clan before turning away to leave for what Douglas had felt certain was the last time. But it hadn't been the words that struck Douglas so deeply as he'd watched his brother turn away from him that day. It had been the disappointment that had colored the eyes of the lad who had grown up looking on Douglas as his hero.

A sudden knocking on the door behind him pulled Douglas from his thoughts. He turned, hoping for a fleeting moment that it was Iain.

His hopes were dashed, however, when he recognized the unwelcome figure of Malcolm Maclean—chieftain of the Macleans of Carsaig, and his future father-in-law.

Iain Dubh rose from his chair. "Maclean, 'tis good it is to see you. How do things fare at Carsaig?"

The Maclean chieftain strode into the room with all the confidence and swagger of a man who felt his importance in the world—and who felt it more substantially than it warranted. He was a clan chieftain like Douglas, but Maclean ruled his sept with a fist of iron, a merciless sword, and a heart of impermeable rock. The fact that he often settled disputes with his dirk instead of his wits showed in the many scars that marked him, face, hands, and arms. His brown hair hung loose, unkempt and wild, and his eyes were always narrowed, the eyes of a wolf.

"Come, sit," Iain Dubh said to Maclean. "Let us get you a brandy. Douglas and I were just catching up on the past months."

Maclean lowered himself into the chair offered, his hand resting on the basket hilt of his sword. He took a swig of the brandy offered, wiping his mouth with the back of his hand. He fixed Douglas a fierce stare.

"What of your efforts in the south? Were you successful in gaining an audience with the Hanoverian?"

Douglas had to fight from showing his aversion for the man. "In a matter of speaking, aye."

"What do you mean, MacKinnon? Were you or were you not able to secure your right to Dunakin?" He turned immediately to Iain Dubh without waiting for Douglas's answer. "There'll be no wedding, MacKinnon, and with it no alliance of our clans without the assurance of that land."

"Now, Maclean, ease your temper . . ."

"That was the arrangement!" He pounded his fist on the side table, upsetting his glass. "I'll not wed my Muirne to a landless whelp without so much as a pissing pot to his name—"

"I did not succeed in gaining an ear at Kensington," Douglas interrupted, drawing the attention of both men back to himself, "but within two months' time, I will have recovered Dunakin and the forfeited earldom—without restriction." He glanced at his uncle. "Through other means."

Maclean was immediately suspicious. "What do you

mean by 'other means?' Why the need for this secrecy if we're to be kin?"

The thought of the man as kin sickened Douglas to the depths of his stomach.

"A moment, Maclean." Iain Dubh looked at his nephew, more intrigued than suspicious of this unexpected announcement. "Do you care to say more of what these 'other means' are, Douglas?"

Knowing the danger the truth could bring, Douglas decided not to tell his uncle of his arrangement with the duke. If it were somehow discovered and there was to be retribution for it, Douglas wanted it directed at himself and no one else.

"All I can ask is that you trust my word in this. Dunakin will be ours again in two months' time. The how of it is inconsequential."

He hated having to mislead him, but there was no helping it.

Iain Dubh nodded. "That is all the assurance I need. If Douglas says he will have Dunakin, then he shall. It will be a winter wedding, Maclean, and your Muirne will be a countess. Now, come, my lovely Janet has prepared a supper feast. Let us break a bannock and have a toast together to celebrate an end to the feud that has rifted the Macleans of Carsaig and the MacKinnons of Strathaird for too long."

It was dark when Douglas arrived at Eithne's cottage, the night sky lit by a partial moon that was veiled behind a thin layer of clouds. He ducked his head under the low lintel as he knocked softly upon the door to enter.

He knew she would be waiting up for him, waiting

and expecting explanations. In the letter he'd sent with the packet boat, he'd only told her to prepare the croft and not to come to any conclusions—no matter what she saw—until he had explained everything to her. He owed her the truth and could trust her to keep it, but he had delayed in coming to see her all day. Deep inside he knew what her reaction would be.

"'Tis time you returned," was all she said, rising from her spinning wheel to fetch him a cup of the tea she had simmering over the fire. The cottage smelled of fresh rushes and peat smoke and a savory stew she had prepared for her supper.

Douglas watched as Eithne pressed a hand to the small of her back as she poured to ease the ache from the past hours she'd no doubt spent spinning the wool over the dull light of her cruisie lamp. Her hair was down, falling to her waist, and she wore her nightclothes, a heavy shift beneath a fringed woolen shawl that fell past her hips. Her feet were bare on the dirt floor, and though her face was cast in the shadows of the firelight, Douglas could tell from the set of her shoulders that she was cross.

"I was to Kilmarie," he said as she handed him the cup, swallowing down a good half of the tea before sinking into his favorite chair by the fire. It soothed the ache that had been throbbing in his head for hours. "My uncle sends his regards."

"Aye."

Eithne took up her spinning, feeding the carded wool onto the whirling spindle of the wheel. She waited, saying nothing, nothing at all, just went on with her spinning, settling into her own easy rhythm while she waited for Douglas to go on.

"He says Iain is safe. He says he is on Skye."

"Is he now?" Eithne lifted a brow. "So why hasna the lad come to show his face then?"

Douglas frowned. "I think you already know the answer to that."

"Och." She shook her head in disgust. "He is your brother, is he no'? I've known that lad since he was a wee thing, always spouting off his mouth afore thinking. His temper is fierce, but his heart is true. He willna bear this bitter grudge against his own blood, especially after all you've both been through these months." She waited, sensing the tension in Douglas. "There is more?"

Douglas nodded. "Maclean was at Kilmarie."

"Filthy *messan.*" She frowned, looking as if she'd swallowed something foul with her tea. "The man will make you a miserable father-in-law, you know."

"Aye, 'tis true, but I've no choice in the matter. 'Twas arranged an age ago. The feud a'tween our clans will seem like naught but a wee spat in comparison to the certain war that will be waged if I dinna wed his Muirne now."

"Bah. There has been ill blood a'tween the two clans for nigh on four hundred years, since one of those rummle-skeerie Macleans took the life of a MacKinnon o'er some imagined affront or another. Yet we've all of us lived peacefully amongst one another. Let it lie, Douglas. You canno' change what has been for so long. You should no' be wedding into that brood. There's foul blood bred into their bones, those Macleans of Carsaig. Foul blood that will be the blood of your sons."

Douglas finished his tea. He set the cup on the hearth-stone with a frown. "I canna do that, and you know it. If I dinna wed Muirne Maclean, MacKinnon blood will be spilled."

Eithne's foot was working furiously on the treadle of her wheel now. "Two wives are one too many, Douglas MacKinnon. E'en for a braw Scotsman like yourself."

Douglas frowned at the mention of Elizabeth. In truth, thoughts of her had kept him frowning through most of the day. More than once he had found himself stopping in his review of the estate accounts to stare out the window onto the distant hill, picturing the croft that lay tucked away on its other side. And for one of those moments, he'd even allowed himself to imagine Elizabeth staying on past the two months . . . staying on forever.

"Douglas MacKinnon, have you run deaf? Do you no' hear me talking to you? Roderick told me what happened, how you came to be married to the lass. 'Tis an ill-faur'd thing, this trickery you've agreed to with her da. I dinna know what ye're about agreeing to do such a thing, but I winna lie to the lass."

"I don't like having to play this deception any more than you like me playing it. It is her da's arrangement. I have no choice. It is the only way I'm to recover Dunakin. And I cannot do it without your help. I am not asking you to lie to her. All I ask is that you help me keep her out of sight till her father comes for her. For her own safety, as well as ours."

Eithne stared at Douglas through the flickering of the fire.

"Aye, you are right. 'Tis better that she doesna know the truth of it. But it still does not sit well with me,

Douglas MacKinnon. She is a good lass, a true lass. She'd be a better wife to you than that Muirne Maclean."

Douglas looked at Eithne as if she'd just been spinning nonsense along with her wool on that wheel.

"Any thought of us remaining wed after these two months is naught but nonsense. Even she would tell you that."

"But I am not asking her, Douglas. I am asking you." Eithne softened her voice. "Look me in the eyes, right now, and tell me truthfully, if you can, that you feel nothing for this lass, nothing at all. Tell me you have no' thought of her, have no' looked into her eyes just once and wondered what could be if she were no' a Sassenach lady, but a simple Scottish lass . . ."

Douglas stared into the eyes of the only true mother he'd ever known and could say nothing, nothing at all.

" 'Tis as I thought."

"It doesna matter." Douglas got up to leave, shrugging on his coat. "None of it matters. She *is* a lady, the daughter of a *Sassenach* duke. She was not intended for a life in the Highlands. She was raised to a life of privilege and ease, with a team of servants standing ready to see to her every wish. Her hands have never known a moment of true work."

Eithne's mouth pressed into a tight line. "You're a muckle blind man, Douglas MacKinnon. Tell me one thing then, and I will ne'er speak of this again. If she was so happy with her life of privilege and ease and servants ready to see to her every wish, why then did she end up in your bed?"

Douglas looked at her. "It was the whisky."

"Och, it wasna the whisky, you daft lad. She could

have chosen anyone, Douglas, anyone at all. Yet she chose you."

"Enough," Douglas finished. "This talk a'tween us is not doing any good. It is late, and I must go."

Douglas lowered his head to kiss her on the temple, then turned to leave.

Eithne stood and watched him go. He was as dear to her as her own son, but sweet *Dia*, how she wanted to clout him sometimes.

Chapter Sixteen

By the time Douglas left Eithne's cottage, it was raining. The clouds had moved in off the Minch, gathering and swelling, muting the moonlight to a dull distant glow. The air was thick, heavy with the damp as it churned and lashed a twisting path across the mist-shrouded strath.

He hadn't been aware of the rain while he'd been tucked away inside Eithne's cozy cottage. Judging from the depth his foot sank with each step, a steady downpour had been falling for some time. He trudged across the soggy glen, impervious to the rain soaking through his plaid; He found himself thinking back on Eithne's words, and frowning against the bite of the wind.

Look me in the eyes, right this moment, and tell me truthfully, if you can, that you feel nothing for this lass, nothing at all. Tell me you have no' thought of her, have no' looked into her eyes just once and wondered what could be if she were no' a Sassenach lady, but a simple Scottish lass. . . .

It didn't sit well with him that she'd been able to see through him so clearly, that she could sense such thoughts, thoughts that he had refused to acknowledge himself. The truth was that he *had* looked into Elizabeth's eyes, more than once, and he'd seen something more than the eyes of a noble daughter. He'd seen pride and he'd seen intelligence, two things he respected, particularly in a woman. But he'd seen something else. He'd seen life.

Douglas thought back to the last time he had seen Muirne Maclean, at a meeting at Kilmarie House shortly before the rebellion had begun. It had been early summer, the heather was just coming into bloom, and Douglas had sat listening while his uncle and Malcolm Maclean had debated the various conditions of their impending marriage.

Muirne had been perched on the edge of a chair beside her father, her feet tucked together, her hands folded gently in her lap. She had always been a lovely girl, with dark hair and a comely face. It was a thing Douglas knew had been passed to her from her mother, a once celebrated beauty on the isle.

More than once that day Douglas had glanced to Muirne, for a glimpse of who she really was. Their eyes had met once, for the briefest of moments, but she'd looked away. He couldn't recall what she'd worn, whether her gown had been light or dark. But he remembered other things, the way she kept her head bowed shielding the lifelessness that had clouded the lovely pale blue of her eyes.

Douglas had long ago accepted that he would wed the Maclean daughter for the good of the MacKinnons. It made sense to put an end to the feud that had estranged the two clans for centuries.

At the time, while Muirne sat so mutely, Douglas had merely thought her as disinterested as he. The terms were clear. They neither of them had any choice in the matter. Only now did Douglas realize that it hadn't been disinterest at all. It had been hopeless, forlorn surrender.

Douglas paused a moment as he reached the hill above the cottage. The rain fell heavily and a gleam of lightning slashed the black sky, a jagged thrust of silver against the night. The hour was late, well past midnight, and he expected Elizabeth to be abed. He would slip in quietly, would change his clothes, and would sleep for a couple of hours. He would be up afore the dawn. With any luck he could be away long afore she ever woke.

The fire was not lit when Douglas came into the cottage, nor was there a lamp burning. The place was shadowed like a cave inside, silent as one, too, with just the sound of the rain trickling through the thatch overhead, puddling on the doorstep outside.

Douglas stepped inside, crossing the room to the cupboard to find a candle. He nearly jerked out of his trews when he heard a voice come suddenly from the far corner of the room.

"I could not find any candles."

"*Dia*, lass. What're you doing sitting alone in the corner like that? The fire is out. 'Tis chill as a tomb in here . . ."

"I know. I could not sleep."

"The storm?" And then Douglas remembered her fear of the dark. "Or was it . . . ?"

"The bed. It is wet."

Douglas felt certain he had just heard her wrong. "Did you say the bed is wet?"

"Yes, I did."

Douglas had made his way to the cupboard, where now he fumbled, opening drawers and feeling in the darkness for a rush wick. He found the flint box and within seconds a single flame was flickering to life. He turned to look at her. He could scarce see her in the darkness, even with the dithering light of the wick.

"I'll tend to the fire and then see about the bedding," Douglas said, and started for the far side of the room where the extra peats were kept.

"While you're at it, you can see about the table, the floor, and the chair in front of the fire. They're all of them soaked."

It was only then Douglas realized he was standing in a shallow puddle. A fat drop of water plopped precisely on the top of his head, running down to the tip of his nose. He dashed it away and looked up. The sounds of the rainfall weren't coming only from outside the cottage. There was a mixture of steady drips leaking from various places overhead.

"The roof."

"Oh, yes," she said. "That idiotic goat has eaten it through. Fortunately, I managed to construct a cover before the place flooded."

Douglas held up the flickering flame of his rushlight. What he saw defied description.

She had suspended her dress panniers from one of the rafters using a stocking garter to tie it. The hoops that she usually wore beneath her skirts were now stretched out in an oblong cone like a voluminous white bell. A lacy stretch of petticoat was draped tent-like to form a canopy just above where she sat.

"At least they are of some use," she said as he stared dumbfounded at the contraption. "They certainly were of no use in milking the cow earlier today."

"You milked the cow?"

She scowled at him. "Of course. That is what you meant when you said I'd have to fetch the milk for my tea, isn't it?"

"No, lass. In truth, I meant you would need to fetch the milk *from the larder* at the back of the cottage. Did you not see it?"

Apparently she had not, but then she could never have known to look for the milk in the larder. All her life, milk for her tea, candles for lighting, a sturdy roof over her head, all of it had simply been *there,* awaiting her pleasure. She'd never had to fetch anything, had simply to ask and it had been provided.

"I'm sorry, lass."

"It doesn't matter." Elizabeth stood. Without the bulk of her panniers, her heavy skirts dragged on the floor behind her. She didn't seem to notice. "I had to do something to pass the time. I made a soup, with Eithne's help, but I'm afraid 'tis long gone cold. The fire was doused some time ago. Then I—"

She fell silent when a slow creaking came suddenly from overhead. And then the roof gave with a giant *whoosh.*

Elizabeth shrieked as Douglas grabbed her by the arm, pulling her away while copious amounts of water, turf, and bits of thatch started showering down around them.

"Come, lass," he called, drawing her underneath the protection of his plaid. He rushed for the door. "We'll not be sleeping here tonight. We'll go to the byre where 'tis warm and dry."

Elizabeth kept herself tucked close to his side as Douglas led them out of the cottage. They stepped quickly along the muddy pathway, splashing as they cut across the yard. Elizabeth could feel mud squishing between her toes and had a fleeting thought that her silk shoes would be ruined.

When they stopped, she heard the sound of a door opening and closing, then felt Douglas release her, though he kept the plaid wrapped tightly around her. The scents of fresh hay and warm animal surrounded her. It was dark. Too dark. Inside the cottage, she had at least had a window and the muted moonlight to comfort her. Now there was nothing but endless, fathomless black.

She heard rustling and a familiar *naa*'ing that sounded from the shadows. But she was too wet and too cold, and it was too terrifyingly dark, for her to care. She stood frozen to the spot where Douglas left her and waited.

Moments later, the warm glow of lamplight sparked to life, illuminating the tiny byre. Elizabeth released the breath she had been holding as Douglas turned to face her.

He looked as pathetic as she felt. His hair was soaked, falling over his eyes and curling around his ears. Mud spattered his legs, and his shirt was plastered to his skin.

"We could run for Eithne's, but it's quite a distance and the rain is falling harder now." His face grew concerned. "Lass, you're trembling like a lamb." He took her hands. "They are like ice. There are spare plaids in the cottage. I'll go fetch them."

Her first impulse was to ask him not to leave her, but she couldn't through the chattering of her teeth. Until he'd said it, Elizabeth hadn't realized how very cold she was. Now her arms began to tremble and her fingers felt as if they might snap like twigs if she tried so much as to bend them.

It seemed to take hours for his return, when in truth it was only minutes.

Douglas ducked under the door with an armful of plaids and a jug which he quickly uncorked. He pushed it into her hands.

"Drink."

"What is it?"

"'Tis whisky."

Elizabeth shook her head. "I d'nt want it."

"Drink it, lass. It will warm you."

Too cold to protest any further, growing colder by the second, Elizabeth lifted the jug to her mouth with trembling hands and took a small swallow. It was enough to send a shock of fire running straight through her insides. She grimaced against it and handed the jug back to Douglas, who tilted it to his own mouth and took a generous swallow.

Douglas led Elizabeth across to the other side of the byre, away from the cow and the goat and the chickens, who were looking at them as if they'd run mad. She stood and waited while he laid out the plaids, making up a bed on a cushion of fresh hay.

Even as she stood there, Elizabeth felt her eyes begin to drift closed as the heaviness of fatigue threatened to overtake her. The whisky had settled in her belly, giving off a dull warmth that wasn't at all unpleasant. She thought of her bed at Drayton Hall, the soft, perfumed pillows, the huge marble hearth that was always burning with a roaring fire. She longed for the feel of fresh sheets just warmed with a pan of hot coals, she dreamed of a steaming teacup in her hands. She didn't realize that Douglas had returned to her until she felt his hands loosening the hooks of her gown.

"What are you doing?"

"Your clothes are soaked, lass. You'll catch ill if you don't get out of them. I'll leave you your shift, but we've got to get you warm and dry afore a fever seizes you."

Elizabeth didn't have the strength to fight him.

In minutes Douglas had removed her gown and stays, and Elizabeth was standing trembling in her chemise. He helped her to lay back upon the hay and draped a heavy plaid over her body. When he doused the lamp, it was dark, but Elizabeth was so tired, she scarcely acknowledged it.

She was half asleep when she felt him lower himself onto the hay beside her. She thought he said something, but she couldn't understand him. The warmth of his body next to hers was immediate and so very inviting that she unwittingly turned into it, burrowing her head against the solid width of his chest. As he folded her into his arms, enveloping her with the heat of his body, she let go a soft, sweet sigh.

Lulled by the steady beating of his heart against her cheek, Elizabeth descended into the arms of Morpheus, never realizing that the body that was pressed so closely to hers was totally, utterly unclothed.

Chapter Seventeen

Everyone who knew Eithne MacKenzie thought her a reasonably sensible woman. She'd raised her son, Roderick, alone, without the support of a husband, rearing him into a fine young man who was as strong as his father, as bright as his mother, and handsome enough to turn the heads of lasses from the age of six to sixty. When her husband died suddenly of an epidemic fever only four months after Roderick's birth, Eithne left the Scottish mainland and her sad memories behind, returning to the place of her birth on Skye, where she could raise her son surrounded by the love and support of her family and friends.

Not many things surprised Eithne. She hadn't endured over half of a century in the Highlands without coming up against her own share of adversity. Still, Eithne would be the first to admit she had been stunned when the MacKinnon chief Iain Dubh had arrived at the door of her snug glen cottage one summer afternoon, asking her to foster his nephews, Douglas and Iain, who had just lost their mother.

"As elder brother to their sire, I will see to their fathering," the MacKinnon chief had said. "Their mothering, however, will require a woman of patience, with a warm and giving heart, a woman of sense and wisdom and endurance."

A woman, Iain Dubh had decided, like Eithne.

It was an honor, she knew, to be chosen by the clan chief, and Eithne had willingly taken on the responsibility. That had been nearly three decades ago. Since then she had raised the two lads as her own, watching as Douglas matured into a man of unrelenting loyalty and honor, trying desperately to live up to the memory of the father he'd never known. Iain was the rash one, always acting on impulse regardless of the consequences. Douglas was the thinker, a man who carefully weighed every possible outcome before setting out on any course of action.

A man of *sense*.

Because of this, he rarely made a questionable decision, which was why, standing as she was at the open door of the byre, Eithne had to wonder if her eyes were somehow deceiving her.

She cocked her head to one side as the sun climbed higher in the morning sky. True, the light was low and the hour was yet early, and her eyes were not quite as clear as they'd once been, but it certainly looked to her as if Douglas was lying asleep on a bed of straw, as naked as the day he was born, and wrapped around a lass he claimed to have no feeling for—the same lass who he claimed had no feeling for him.

A slow smile crept across Eithne's lips as she stood there holding a basket filled with laundry that needed washing and pondered what she should do in the face of this altogether awkward situation. She could turn and leave, she knew, but then anyone else who might be about would happen upon them, and Douglas would be left with some explaining to do.

In fact, Eithne had to admit, she was more than just a little curious as to just why Elizabeth's underthings were hanging from the rafters in the cottage—while these two were out here hanging on to each other.

She glanced at the goat, who had just poked his head in the doorway. "Just what the devil went on here last night, eh?"

The goat blinked and shook his horned head.

In the end, and to spare sensibilities, Eithne decided upon a simple clearing of her throat. It was discreet, and it was civilized, and if that didn't prove adequate enough to wake them, well then, perhaps the cowbell hanging on the wall beside her would.

Eithne gave her quiet little cough and stood back to wait.

Douglas was the first to stir. He'd always been a light sleeper and he rolled slowly onto his back, blinking up at the rafters. Beside him, Elizabeth slept on as if the hounds of hell wouldn't rouse her.

Eithne waited until Douglas sat up before she spoke.

" 'Tis fortunate for you that it was me who found you and not old Lilias. She's ninety-seven years, has lived through five rebellions, single-handedly faced down four of Cromwell's men, birthed sixteen children, and buried three husbands, but I'm quite certain the sight of you lying needle-naked in the byre would be enough to shock her to her grave."

"*Dia!*" Douglas scrambled for a plaid to cover himself. "What the de'il are you doing here at this hour?"

"'Tis I should be asking that of you, Douglas MacKinnon. I'm no' the one sitting there without a stitch to cover myself, now am I?"

Douglas scowled, stood, and wrapped the plaid quickly around his waist. Despite the fact that she was a good two decades older and had wiped his snirty nose as a lad, Eithne had to admit he was a braw fine figure of a man. 'Twas easy to see why the lass would be taken with him.

Eithne watched as Douglas shoveled a hand through his hair, glancing once at the still-sleeping Elizabeth. When he finally spoke, his voice was no higher than a murmur.

"The roof was leaking in the cottage."

"And you thought that by hanging her privy garments from the rafters you could stop it?"

"Nae." Douglas's mouth tightened into a frown as he led her out into the daylight. His face was shadowed by a night's growth of beard, and his hair was mussed, falling about his eyes. His brow drew tight above the bridge of his nose. "'Twas she who rigged it in that way in an effort to keep dry afore I got here last night."

"Well, that might do to explain how the hoops got tied to the ceiling, but it still doesn't explain why you decided to strip down to your *quhillylillie* and—"

"The fire had been out for some time," Douglas cut in. "She was cold and wet and shivering. Her clothing was soaked. I thought she'd catch ill, so I tried to keep her warm with my body heat. My clothes were wet, too, else I would have left them on."

Eithne lifted a skeptical brow. "I see."

"Nothing happened. Nothing."

"Aye, 'twas that same declaration that got you wed to the lass after you woke in her bed the last time, lad."

Douglas fell silent. He could not deny it.

"So why have you come then?" he finally asked.

"I promised the lass I would take her with me to the burn to wash the linens this morn." She gestured toward the basket she had set upon the ground at her feet. "I expected you'd be up and gone by now."

"Aye, that was my every intention, until last night. Now I've got to stay and mend the turf on the roof."

"As well you should."

Eithne stared at Douglas a long moment, then slowly shook her head. Her thoughts, she decided, would be better kept to herself. "Well, I'll take the lass with me to the burn. 'Twill give her something to do whilst you mend the turf. Go, fetch me your washing and find something more to cover yourself with whilst I go in to rouse her."

"So, are you nearly finished with treading those blankets, lass? Lass?"

Though some small part of her might actually have heard Eithne, Elizabeth certainly wasn't attentive to it. She was standing barefoot, calf-deep in a sudsy wooden tub, her skirts hitched up about her waist, diligently employed in the close study of the native landscape—

—the one in which Douglas was standing atop the cottage roof wearing naught but the kilt.

Sweet saints above, the man looked like a veritable divinity.

Even as she was horrified at herself for it, Elizabeth found herself distracted time and again by the sight of him. She told herself she was not fascinated by him. No, she was simply enthralled with the art of his work, the ancient method of turfing a roof with precisely cut sods of moor grass and heather.

But deep down, she knew it was the simple potent strength of him, the way the flatness of his belly rippled in the sunlight when he moved, each muscle defined like solid stone.

How had this happened to her? She was actually, *unbelievably* unable to tear her eyes away from him.

Elizabeth had always thought that if she ever were to actually fall in love with a man, he would have to be her intellectual equal, someone who could discuss politics and philosophy. He wouldn't try to repress her but would encourage her curiosity, respect her opinions no matter if they didn't quite agree with his own. He would be a man of honor and wisdom, a man of patience and compassion . . .

. . . . a man who quite frankly didn't exist.

"Lass, can you hear me?"

"Hmm? Oh, the blankets?" She glanced quickly at Eithne. "Yes, yes, I think they should be finished by now."

Elizabeth stepped from the tub, toes dripping, and padded barefoot to where the burn ran cool and clear over a bed of pebbly stones. Eithne had brought along a spare kirtle for her to wear for the washing, showing her how to wrap the length of her hair beneath a kerchief to keep it off her face while they worked. The airy linen sark and loosely fitting "working" stays had at first felt peculiar, almost improper. But after passing the morning bending and kneeling, scrubbing clothes and treading blankets, comfort had quickly prevailed. Now she didn't think she'd ever willingly don the hoops again.

Elizabeth watched as Eithne paused where she was kneeling at the burn, scrubbing a shirt with a flat, round stone. She stood, flexing her fingers and arching her back to ease the stiffness from washing, then cupped some of the water in her hands and splashed it over her face to cool it.

"Och, lass," Eithne said, "come, douse your face afore it turns as red as a bogberry."

The sun at midday was ablaze in a cloudless sky, and the midges had worked themselves into a full offensive swarm. Earlier, when they had made their way to the burn, Eithne had shown Elizabeth how to pick fresh sprigs of fragrant bog myrtle and fix it to her kerchief to help keep the pests away.

Elizabeth knelt on the bank and dipped in her fingers, touching a hand to her cheek. The water felt like ice against the heat of her skin. In the back of her mind, she heard her mother's voice, urging her to cover her head when she went out of doors lest she freckle.

"You'll end up looking like some sort of brown, spotted native," she would say, referring to a faraway fictional island she'd once read about in a novel where the populace ran around half naked in loincloths and speaking in guttural yelps.

"Ladies should have skin as white as the dewflower and as soft as the finest Chinese silk." The duchess and her sisters had spent many a fine summer's day slather-

ing on concoctions made of purified wax to vinegar,
even the juice of a white lily, in their quest to keep their
faces as pallid as their supper plates. The duchess had
tried, albeit failingly, to instill that same practice in her
eldest daughter. But such measures had rarely done more
than exasperate Elizabeth.

The two women spent the next quarter hour rinsing out
the blankets and then wringing them dry, unfurling the
length between them across the burn and twisting until
every last drop was squeezed from the wool. As they
worked, Eithne softly hummed a pleasant tune while the
omnipresent goat munched happily on tufts of marram
grass and vetch.

The women twisted and coiled, pulled and shook. By
the time they had finished wringing out the last blanket,
Elizabeth's arms felt as limp as tallow.

"Well, I think we're about through with the wash
no'," Eithne said, gathering up the damp clothes for her
basket. "We'll just take these things back to the cottage
and drape them o'er the gorse to dry whilst—"

She never finished her thought.

Elizabeth turned to see what had caused Eithne to fall
silent. She found her staring downstream with a look that
was nothing short of terror.

"Eithne? What is it?" She turned, looking downstream, but saw only the sun reflected in a blinding swell
of light that shifted and faded, shifted and faded with the
ripple of the water.

Eithne didn't answer. Her eyes remained fixed on that
same distant spot. Soon, her hands began to tremble and
she dropped the shirt she had been holding. As Elizabeth
bent to retrieve it, a menacing cloud appeared from be-

hind the hills, drifting across the light of the sun and throwing the whole of the glen in shadow.

"Do you see something there, Eithne? What is it?"

Eithne turned. Her eyes were vacant.

"Se do leine, se do leine ga mi nigheadh . . ."

She chanted in Gaelic, repeating the phrase over and over in a quivering voice. Her eyes were filled with anguish, moist with unshed tears. Elizabeth found herself reaching for her, covering her hands, hoping to ease their shaking.

"Eithne, please, I don't understand you. Can you tell me what you are saying? Can you tell me what has made you so upset?"

But she just shook, mumbling that same peculiar phrase as tears slowly slipped down her cheeks.

"Bean Nighe."

It was all she managed to say before she fainted.

Elizabeth looked up from the fire when the door to Eithne's cottage creaked open behind her.

"You're back."

Douglas had been gone for so long, hours now, she'd begun to fear the worst.

"Aye, lass. It took me some time, but I found him."

Roderick entered the cottage, crossing the room to where his mother sat in a rocking chair, wrapped in a plaid before the fire. He knelt down before her, taking her hands, and spoke to her in Gaelic. The moment she saw him, Eithne's eyes let some of the light in, glistening with unshed tears.

"Come, lass," Douglas said, motioning for Elizabeth to follow him. "We can come away now."

"Will she be all right?" Elizabeth asked as they walked slowly across the shadowed glen. He looked tired, she thought, as if he hadn't slept in days.

"Aye, now that Roderick is there. I'm only sorry it took me so long to find him. He was on the mainland, and the crossing seemed longer than it should have."

Several moments passed, broken only by the sound of their footsteps and the wind fleeting through the tall moor grass. The heady sweet scent of gorse filled the air. Somewhere, the plaintive *baa* of a new lamb called out for its mother. The goat, ears flopping, trudged slowly at Elizabeth's side. He'd been there since the episode with Eithne at the burn, as if he somehow sensed the turmoil. Oddly, Elizabeth found herself comforted by the beast's just being there.

"Douglas, what does *bean nighe* mean?"

Douglas stopped. "Why do you ask?"

"Eithne said it to me right before she fainted."

Douglas looked at her but didn't immediately respond. Finally, he said, "It is Gaelic. For 'washerwoman.'"

Elizabeth knit her brow. "I don't understand. Why would that have upset her so much?"

Douglas studied her face for a long moment. "Do you believe in faeries, lass?"

The question took Elizabeth by surprise. "I suppose I've never really thought about it. I've certainly read of them and other such phenomena. I've never really made any determination." And then she realized why he'd asked. "Is that why Eithne became so upset today? Because she believed she saw something, a faery, at the burn?"

Douglas just looked at her. "There is a belief here in the Highlands, an apparition called the *bean nighe*. It is purported to be the spirit of a woman who died in childbirth, doomed to spend what would have been the rest of her time on earth washing clothes by the river."

"But I still do not understand. Why would that have caused Eithne such distress?"

"It is commonly believed that when the *bean nighe* appears, she washes the clothes of those who are about to die. The words Eithne repeated to you—'*Se do leine, se do leine ga mi nigheadh*'—it is a chant, 'It is your shirt, it is your shirt I am washing'."

"So Eithne believes this spirit she saw was singing the song to warn her?"

"Aye. And she believes the shirt that the *bean nighe* was washing was Roderick's."

A chill swept suddenly through Elizabeth's body. "That is why you were so desperate to find him. But surely Eithne can see Roderick is well, that no danger has befallen him."

"Aye. She still fears he is in danger."

"How horrible for her."

Douglas stopped and looked at her.

"What is it?"

He started to answer, but instead found all he could do was look at her. How could he explain how much she amazed him, how every day she amazed him even more? He'd been reluctant to tell her of the superstition, thinking she would scoff, or ridicule him and the beliefs of his people. But she hadn't.

As he looked at her now, he realized that every day she was looking less and less the stranger to him.

Douglas touched a finger beneath her chin, lifting her face to his. Elizabeth said nothing, but he heard her take in a breath and hold it. He saw so many parts of her as he looked into her eyes—the noble lady, the vulnerable girl afraid to admit her fear of the dark, the gentle lass who stood before him looking more lovely than he ever thought possible.

Without giving it a second thought, he lowered his head to kiss her.

A moment later, he was lost.

Chapter Eighteen

Douglas threw wide the door and crossed the room to the box bed, all the while locked mouth-to-mouth with Elizabeth.

As he lay Elizabeth back upon the mattress, freshly filled with the fragrant heather he'd gathered himself that morning, he thought to himself that he'd never before seen anything more beautiful than this woman . . . his wife. Her eyes were shiny and large, and she said nothing, not a word. Silently, she reached for him, entreating him to kiss her again.

Douglas used his mouth, his tongue, his breath, overwhelming her as completely as she had overwhelmed him. He worked his fingers over the kerchief that covered her hair, unraveling its knot until her hair was loose and falling over her shoulders in a river of red and gold. He kissed along her jaw, her neck, nuzzling the soft skin behind her ear. He fisted his hands in the tangle of her hair and slowly drew back her head so he could kiss her again.

He felt her hands slide upward along his arms, twining her fingers with his. Douglas lifted his head, caught his breath at the sight of her, and brought his mouth down to her breast. He heard her gasp, felt her fingers tighten as she arched her back against his mouth, seeking more. And he gave it. Much, much more.

"I need to see you," he whispered, untangling his fingers from hers. He drew his knuckles down the side of her face, the nape of her neck, pulling the tie on her chemise that would free her to his touch.

"Sweet *Dia* in heaven. You are lovely."

Her breasts were soft, full, and shaped to fit in his hand. He stroked her tender flesh with his fingertips, thumbing her nipple to hardness until he felt her shiver, heard her moan, and whisper his name once, twice.

It was the sweetest sound he had ever heard.

"Close your eyes, *leannan*," he whispered against her cheek. "You needn't fear the dark this night."

He loosened the stays that bound her waist, pulled away her skirts. He slid his hand beneath her and lifted her, sweeping away the petticoats underneath.

She was nearly naked. His breath was coming quickly. His body felt on fire. He sat back on his knees, drinking in the sight of her as she lay scarcely covered by her scrap of chemise. He tugged his shirt over his head, saw her lashes flutter open. He leaned over her until his chest was pressed to hers. He softly kissed her nose.

He kissed her mouth again, long and deep, and felt her body yielding to the pleasure of his touch. As he looked down on her in the moonlight, he could see the rapid rise and fall of her chest as she lay, eyes closed, senses heightened, anticipating something she had never known, could never have suspected . . . but would remember for the rest of her life.

By *Dia* she would remember.

He pulled away, looking at her in the twilight. He could take her, he knew, bury himself within her and end the torment. He could make love to her and lose himself in her softness and her scent. God, how he wanted to do that. Never in his life had he wanted something so badly. But just as much as he wanted, ached for it with a need he'd never known existed, he knew deep inside himself that it could never, ever be. Giving in to his need would change the course of destiny. But he could give her a woman's pleasure so that for as long as she lived, she would have this night, this time . . . and the memory of him.

He settled himself above her, parting her with his hips as his mouth moved down, searing the flesh along her throat, her breasts, nipping at those taut peaks until she cried out his name. He pressed against her, trying to imagine her around him. When he felt her lift her hips, opening to him, wanting him, it nearly did him in. The wool of the kilt was suddenly, unbearably hot, confining, so he fumbled with the buckle until it was loose and he was free, free to cover her, his body to her body, his flesh to her flesh.

He slid his body down, dragging his mouth across her breasts, over her belly, nipping at the angle of her hip. He parted her legs, opening her as he slowly lowered his mouth against her.

When he touched his tongue to her, she lifted off the bed on a strangled half gasp.

"Douglas, we cannot—"

"Shhh," he whispered, urging her back. "And let me love you in the only way I can."

As he spoke, he caressed her with his fingertip, finding that place where all her senses pulsed and tingled. He touched her, and when he slid his finger inside her, he felt her body still as she took in a breath, saw her lips part in wonder, her eyes tightly closed.

He stroked her with his finger, as he eased his body lower. He drew up her knees, opening her to his mouth while his fingers moved yet deeper. He knew when she was ready, felt the tightness in her legs as they squeezed against his shoulders. She lifted her hips, struggling against his constant caress. He felt her rake her fingers through his hair, clutching him tightly. She begged him to go on. He could no more stop pleasuring her than he could cease breathing . . . he could only love her.

Her breath hitched, once, twice . . . and with his next caress he knew she would plummet over the edge. And he gave it to her, that gift, that caress, drawing her hips up into his hands and taking her orgasm into his mouth as she cried out.

Only when her body had stilled and her breathing had quieted did he release her, easing her back as he pulled himself over her and drew her into his arms.

The sun was shining when Elizabeth awoke, stretching her arms over her head as she lazed amidst the bedcovers.

She hadn't felt this good in . . . in truth, she'd *never*

felt this good. Now she knew why young ladies fluttered their lashes and sighed over the prospect of being swept off their feet. She'd been swept off her feet, utterly and completely, and then thrown into a tidal wave of feelings too wonderful to have been believed. Douglas had loved her, he'd loved her in a way she had never thought possible. He'd taken her to a place so precious, so real, it must surely be heaven's model.

He had held her in his arms throughout the night and they had slept the sleep of lovers, breaths mingling, pulses beating together. Had she been any other woman and he any other man, all would have been right in the world. But for one inescapable thing: He might have kissed her, touched her, loved her with his hands and his mouth, but he had not made her his wife.

And she'd wanted him to. Oh, how she'd wanted him to.

Elizabeth sat up on the bed, pushing back the bed-clothes. He was gone. She knew without calling his name. His sword wasn't leaning by the door. His coat was missing. But more noticeably than that, the cottage just felt empty.

She stood and pushed her mussed hair from her eyes, tucking it behind one ear. She crossed the room to the table, taking up the kettle for tea, and it was then she saw them, sitting on the table, waiting just for her.

Books.

Her heart gave a familiar skip as she took them up, running her fingers over the bindings. There was Defoe, Milton, even Chaucer. Some she was not familiar with; others she had already read . . . and would read again.

She didn't know how, but somehow Douglas had gotten these for her, to replace the ones lost to the sea. They were the most thoughtful gift she had ever been given. And she couldn't wait to thank him.

Elizabeth dressed quickly, slipping on a chemise and simple skirt and the stays Eithne had given her to wear. She poured the water for her tea and tried to decide which book to read first. When the tea had been made, she settled into a chair, tucked her feet up beneath her, and opened to the first page.

Hours passed. Morning slipped quickly into day. Day passed into twilight while she read page after delightful page. Only when her stomach gave a hollow grumbling did she tear her attention away long enough to realize she had read the entire day away.

Outside, the sky was darkening. Where could Douglas have gone for so long? It had been hours. And then she realized.

Eithne.

She should have thought of it sooner.

Taking up her shawl, Elizabeth headed off across the glen.

As she walked, she hummed a tune Caroline often played on her spinet. She'd been on Skye nearly a week and hadn't yet sent her sister the letter she'd promised. She reminded herself to ask Douglas about the foolscap and she picked a sprig of fragrant heather to press inside the page.

When she arrived at Eithne's cottage, the sun had dipped to the hilltops, summoning the coming night.

"Good day to you, lass," Eithne said when she noticed Elizabeth's approach on the hill. She was standing outside, beating the dust from her rugs. "I expected to see you long afore now. Did you find something to occupy your day?"

Elizabeth took one end of the rug and helped Eithne to shake it out. "Indeed. I've been reading. When I awoke this morning, I found several books lying on the table. Some poetry, novels . . . I thought perhaps Douglas would be here . . . I wanted to thank him for getting them for me."

"Oh, lass, I dinna think the books could be from Douglas."

"No?"

"Where could he have gotten them so quickly?"

"But if they're not from Douglas, then who could they be from?"

Eithne thought. "Well, the only person I know of around this part of the isle with books would be the laird."

"The laird?"

"Aye, MacKinnon of Dunakin. He's a library filled with them passed down from the MacKinnon clan chief. Likely he heard of the loss of your things and thought you might enjoy the loan of some of his. Someone should be reading them. Otherwise they sit untouched, moldering in that auld empty castle . . ."

"Yes, of course," Elizabeth agreed. "It would have to be the laird, wouldn't it? I have never heard Douglas mention him, so it didn't occur to me that it might be him. Perhaps this MacKinnon of Dunakin brought them to the cottage yesterday whilst we were away?"

Eithne nodded. "Perhaps . . ."

"Yes, that must be it. I should go there, to the castle to thank him."

"Yes, lass, why don't you do that? But not today." She took Elizabeth's hand and urged her toward the cottage. "I've had a stew simmering on the fire a'day. Have a wee bit o' supper wit' me and tell me what you read about in these books, eh?"

As she watched Elizabeth turn and duck inside the door, Eithne couldn't help giving in to a small smile.

She'd told Douglas she wouldn't lie to the lass.

And she hadn't.

Oh, Eithne MacKenzie, you are a muckle clever woman, you are.

Douglas was frowning as he read his uncle's note.

"The prince is on Skye?"

"Aye, so it would seem."

Roderick poured himself a brandy, then filled another for Douglas. He settled into the chair before the hearth, scratching one of the hounds behind the ears.

"He fled Benbecula in the guise of an Irish maid of all things. 'Betty Burke' they called him. Can you believe it? A royal Stuart trussed up in petticoats like a lassie?"

"Better an Irish maid than a dead prince."

"Aye, true. He rowed over, I'm told, with a schoolmaster from Uist and Hugh MacDonald's stepdaughter, Flora."

"Flora MacDonald? But isn't Hugh MacDonald a captain in the king's militia?"

"Aye, he is. As you well know, Douglas, a good many who did not join the rebellion are true Jacobites at heart."

Roderick paused, giving Douglas time to take this all in. "Your uncle has called a meeting of those who can be counted on for support. Two nights hence. It is to be held here, at Dunakin."

This news brought Douglas forward in his chair. "Why Dunakin?"

"If we were all to meet at Kilmarie, 'twould surely arouse suspicion, and would put your uncle and young Iain at great risk for capture."

Douglas could not refute his point. "Who will come?"

"Iain Dubh, of course, Macleod of Raasay, myself . . . and young Iain."

It pleased Douglas to know that he'd finally see his brother. He only wished it was for any other reason. "What of Maclean?"

"Nae. Your uncle was firm on that point. Carsaig is just the sort of man who would betray us all for the prize of thirty thousand pounds." Roderick looked at him. "Douglas, I know you were determined not to take any part in this rebellion . . ."

"Say no more. There is no rebellion any longer. A man's life is at stake. He is being hunted like a beast. Nothing, not even my inheritance, is worth more than saving him."

At the sudden sound outside the cottage, Elizabeth dropped the book she'd been reading, scuttled from her chair, and yanked the door open.

"I was beginning to—"

But it wasn't Douglas. It wasn't Eithne, either. Instead, it was the goat, happily munching one of the stockings she'd just hung out to dry.

"Truis!" she cried. "Drop that stocking before I . . . put you in the stew pot!"

Instead of heeding her, the goat trotted off across the cottage yard, her white stocking fluttering from his mouth like a victory banner.

"Truis!" she called, chasing after him. "You absurd little beast. Bring back my stocking. Why don't you come when I call? Truis! Truis . . ."

She followed him into the byre. "Truis?"

She took in a sharp breath when she saw a figure outlined in the shadows.

"Douglas."

He was standing with her stocking dangling from his fingers.

"Looking for this?"

"Ridiculous creature," she muttered. "The beast doesn't even have the sense to come when he's called."

"Perhaps if you tried giving him a name."

"I did. Did you not hear me? I called him just as you did, '*Truis.*' "

Douglas smiled. "*Truis* is Gaelic for 'begone,' lass. In truth, he was only doing as you instructed."

A horned head appeared from behind a pile of straw, letting out an affirmative *naa*.

Elizabeth walked into the byre, snatching the stolen bit of silk from Douglas's grasp. "You've been gone a long time," she said. "It is . . . too quiet here when I am alone."

Douglas looked at her. "But that is what you were after, isn't it? A house in London, to live in as you please?"

Elizabeth didn't much care for having her words thrown back in her face. "Yes, well at least in London I would have diversion. Museums to visit, books to read, gardens in which to walk . . ."

"Come with me."

Douglas took Elizabeth's hand and walked out of the byre. Up the slope behind the cottage, he led her through the knee-high sprays of heather and broom. He stopped once, and bent to retrieve a single wild rose, six petals of white. He tucked it behind her ear.

"This entire isle is a garden. Can you no' see it? Just fill your breast with the air around you. The sweetness of the heather, the spice of the gorse . . ."

Elizabeth just looked at him, stunned by the poetry of his words.

He took her farther up the slope. "What is it you find in a museum? In books? Antiquities? Stories? You can have those things here, lass. All you need do is open your eyes. The very hills around you are more ancient than any sculpture or pretty painting you'll find in London. If you've an ear to listen, their stories surround you. They are not hidden behind vellum and board."

Douglas spent the afternoon with Elizabeth, walking the hills, showing her ancient stones carved with peculiar symbols, a cairn beneath which a Celtic princess was buried, even a knoll of oddly-shaped hills where faeries were reputed to dance by moonlight. And he was right. Each place, even a seemingly insignificant stone, seemed to tell a story of its own, tales of fierce warriors and beautiful maidens, love lost, honor defended.

They picnicked on bramble and cloudberry, drank water cool and fresh from the burn. The sun shone brightly, and a pleasant breeze drifted in off the coast, sweeping across the hillside like the flutter of a bird's wing. Elizabeth gathered wildflowers—bindweed, willowherb, and thistle—to sweeten the cottage inside. And when the stories had been told and the flowers had been gathered, Douglas netted salmon and they shared a lovely supper as the sun went down over the distant Cuillin hills.

It had been a day both of wonder, and of wondering. What was it that had brought her to that isle? To this man? Why should she want to run *from* Douglas when with him she felt happier than she could ever imagine? When he looked at her, deeply, with those eyes of blue, he reached inside to the very center of her, a place no one else had ever dared touch. He made her question everything she had ever believed about herself. She had always thought she knew what it was she was meant to be. But now, somehow, that life no longer tempted her as it had. What she wanted, what she needed, more than anything now, was to be Douglas's wife.

They had reached the cottage, its stone walls swept a pearly white by the moonlight. The sky above was kissed by stars. The magic of the night embraced them. Elizabeth could think of no better time to tell him that she loved him.

She watched him stoop to kindle the fire in the hearth. "Thank you for today."

"It was a fine day, lass."

She turned, searching for the words—and the courage to say them.

"Douglas, I—"

She noticed him taking up his jacket then, his sword, his pistol. "You are leaving?"

"Aye, I've business to tend to."

At this hour of the night? "For a farmer, you know, you do very little farming."

Douglas paused in gathering his things to look at her. "I've commitments other than this croft."

"But when will you be back?"

"I'm not certain."

"Tonight?"

"Nae."

Elizabeth stared at him. "Tomorrow?"

"Perhaps." He put on his bonnet and started for the door.

"What am I supposed to do whilst you're away?"

Douglas never answered.

He was already gone.

Chapter Nineteen

The face that answered the door upon Elizabeth's knocking was fresh and young and clearly confused.

"Seadh?"

She couldn't have been more than sixteen, although it was difficult to tell from the soot that covered her from nose to her bare big toe.

"How do you do? My name is Lady Elizabeth Dray—" She stopped herself, correcting, "MacKinnon. Is the laird at home?"

Two eyes, wide and white against the grime on her face, blinked curiously back.

"MacKinnon," Elizabeth tried again slowly, "of Dunakin? Do you speak English?"

The girl simply stared. *"Dé?"*

Elizabeth showed her the books she had tucked under her arm. "I am here to return these . . . *books,*" she said, emphasizing the word as if that would somehow make the girl understand. "They are the laird's books," she repeated. "Dunakin? Is he . . . by any chance . . . here?"

She waited a moment, thinking, and then rattled off a string of words in rapid and incomprehensible Gaelic.

Then it was Elizabeth's turn to stare. "I'm sorry. I'm afraid I did not understand you."

The girl said something else, something that in English sounded a bit like "sausage," shook her head, and turned, leaving Elizabeth standing alone at the open door.

"Excuse me? But what should I . . . ?"

She was gone. With any luck to find someone who could speak English. And not, Elizabeth hoped, to fetch her a sausage.

Elizabeth stood before the open door and waited.

And then she waited more.

She felt like a fool, truly, standing outside an open door which clearly no one was going to come to. She looked around the courtyard, wondering if there might be a stablehand, or a steward, or a cook. But there was no one. No one at all.

She thought to leave, set the books right there at the threshold in a neat little pile, but then decided against it. *It wouldn't do*, her mother would say, *to return such a kindness without properly acknowledging it. It just wouldn't do.*

So she waited some more.

When another five minutes had passed, Elizabeth decided she would just leave, return another day, perhaps tomorrow. She turned, readying to go . . .

. . . until the clouds that had been gathering all that

morning suddenly broke above her head, letting loose with a downpour.

Shielding the books beneath her arm, Elizabeth ducked inside the doorway, closing the door behind her.

The place was cold, dank, and smelled of dogs and must.

"Is anyone here? Please, is anyone here?"

No one responded, not even the sooty young girl.

From where she stood, Elizabeth could see there was a narrow flight of stairs leading up, at the end of which she saw a hint of pale light. She started up the stairs and arrived at a landing that opened onto a corridor lit with torches. Several doors fed onto the hall, all of them closed. Elizabeth went to the nearest one, knocked softly. When no one answered, she tried its latch, only to discover a storage closet filled with linens and rugs.

The next door was locked.

The third, however, opened quite easily. Elizabeth gently lifted its latch.

"Excuse me? Is anybody here . . . ?"

There was no one to greet her, just a fire roaring in a huge stone hearth, bare stone walls, and books, countless many of them, stuck in shelves that stretched from the floor all the way to the ceiling, and left in piles on the floor.

She'd apparently found the right place.

A large desk, carved walnut and riddled with papers, stood off to one side beneath windows that were no wider than her arm. Rugs covered the pitted wood floor, and armchairs with small side tables were set at random about the room. A bottle of spirits stood open on the sideboard with a glass awaiting beside it.

The laird, it would appear, was at home.

Elizabeth crossed the room and set the books on a table. She skimmed the shelves, the furnishings, the floor, absentmindedly running a fingertip along the desktop. Perhaps if she waited here for the laird, she could thank him for the loan of his books . . . and maybe even entreat him for the loan of a few more.

She took a book from the nearest shelf, flipped a page, and started reading through the lines of Pope's *Dunciad.*

> Yet, yet a moment, one dim ray of light
> Indulge, dread Chaos, and eternal Night!
> Of darkness visible so much be lent,
> As half to show, half veil, the deep intent.

Elizabeth quickly became so engrossed that she didn't hear the approach of the footsteps behind her.

"What're you doin' there, lassie?"

Elizabeth spun around, nearly dropping the book in her haste. She opened her mouth to speak, but the moment she saw him, the words died in her throat.

The man who stood behind her was younger, no more than twenty-five, far younger than she would have thought for the laird of such a castle. He was tall, with dark hair that was cut about his face in a manner that looked quite as if he'd used a sword and not a pair of scissors to trim it. He wore a tartan jacket and waistcoat in differing colors from his kilt. His bonnet was pulled low over his brow and adorned with the white Jacobite cockade. But it was his eyes . . . eyes that seemed to laugh even though he wore no smile. There was something behind them, familiar somehow, that left her standing and staring.

"Get you gone now and see to your duties, lass. Dunakin willna take kindly to anyone intruding in his lib'ry."

So he wasn't the laird, after all. And he thought she was a servant, so Elizabeth decided to leave him with that. It was easier than trying to explain why she was standing uninvited in the midst of the laird's study, a stranger looking through his belongings.

She set down the book as the man crossed the room and began pouring himself a drink from the open bottle on the sideboard.

"Tha's a good lass. Off wit' ye now."

Elizabeth was so intent upon slipping away that she took a wrong turn out the door and found herself wandering down a corridor that only took her farther into the castle. She realized her error when the stairs she'd thought would lead her to the courtyard instead took her to a bedchamber. Thankfully, it was empty, in fact, it looked as if it had been for at least the past century.

Elizabeth retraced her steps, down the hall, past the study door, slipping silently through the shadows. And she'd almost made it, until she heard a voice that stopped her in her tracks.

"I believe we're all assembled now, gentlemen."

She recognized that voice.

It was Douglas's.

Douglas walked into his study, nodding to his uncle, Iain Dubh, who sat before the fire. In the chair next to him sat MacLeod of Raasay. The two men were kin since the MacKinnon chief had married the MacLeod's daughter, Janet; they had been friends even longer than that.

Roderick stood at the sideboard, pouring a glass of claret. He offered it to Douglas, who took it as he crossed the room to his desk. In the shadows farthest from the door, lurked the figure of Douglas's younger brother, Iain.

It had been nearly a year since they'd seen each other, but the memory of their last meeting, and the bitter look even now in his eyes, kept Douglas from going to his brother. He gave Iain a brief nod that was quickly returned. It was not the sort of reunion he would have hoped for.

"I believe we're all assembled now, gentlemen." Then he said to no one in particular, "What is the news of the prince?"

"A moment, Dunakin," cut in old MacLeod, looking around the room. "Should we not speak in the *Gaidhlig?*"

"Nae," Douglas assured him. "I've sent everyone from the castle except for a simple lass who does not understand the king's tongue. I've set her to brushing out the roasting hearth in the kitchen. She'll no doubt be at it for hours. We'll be safe enough."

"Aye, I saw the lass when I arrived," Iain broke in. "Though in truth I thought her mute. Looked at me as if she expected I'd take a bite from her."

"Saraid is a sweet lass," Douglas said, "attentive to her duties in the kitchen, but simple-minded. We needn't worry she'll cause us any trouble. So what news of the prince?"

"He is on Raasay," answered MacLeod. "I received

word that the prince needed to be placed under my protection. My son, John, and two of our kinsman have taken him to a bothy near the shore. But they cannot stay there. He would be captured for certain."

Iain Dubh spoke up. "Aye, the prince must be moved. I have sent Roderick onto the mainland at Applecross to scout for a landing place, but he reports it is not safe to attempt it. There are too many of the government's troops skulking about. They would be certain to see a sloop attempting a landing. So our only alternative is to bring the prince back here to Skye and then conduct him to the mainland further south. I have sent some of my clansmen out to Mallaig and Knoydart to assess where might be the best place to land him. Time, however, is of the essence. I received word just today that the two boatmen who rowed the prince and the MacDonald lass over from Uist have been detained and have told everything they know. Even now this Captain Fergusson is on his way to Monkstadt to question Kingsburgh and Lady MacDonald for their part in helping the prince."

"I would say that has already been done," Douglas cut in. He held up a folded parchment. "I received a missive from Campbell of Mamore just this morning. He is coming to Dunakin aboard the *Furnace*."

At the outbreak of the rebellion, General John Campbell of Mamore had been put in command of all government forces on the west coast of Scotland. A fair man, he was not generally thought to be unscrupulous like his captains. He was a gentleman and conducted himself in a manner fitting that distinction. Douglas had attended university with his son, John the younger, and on Mamore's advice had sought the counsel of the Duke of

Argyll in his attempts to regain Dunakin. Though many Highlanders resented the Campbells for their power and loyalty to the Hanoverian regime, Douglas had been able to put aside political differences and had maintained an amiable relationship with the clan.

John of Mamore's sudden visit to Dunakin now, however, couldn't have come at a more inopportune time.

As expected, Douglas's announcement brought heated comments from the others. MacLeod suggested they put off the plan to move the prince. Iain called him a coward for even considering it. Doing so would guarantee the royal fugitive's capture.

It was Iain Dubh who finally stood, silencing them all.

"The plan will go on as arranged. We will bring the prince here to Skye and then we will conduct him to the mainland. 'Tis good, this news of Campbell, because whilst we can engage the attentions of the general and his captain here at Dunakin, others of us can slip the prince away to the mainland from Kilmarie."

"It is a good plan," Douglas said. "A sound plan, and—"

The door behind them suddenly swung open and every man present took to his feet, pulling pistols and swords.

The young clansman who stood guard for Iain Dubh came into the room, dragging Elizabeth by the arm behind him.

Douglas swallowed a curse.

"I found this spy lurking outside the door," the guardsman said, propelling her to the rug.

"I am not a spy, you—"

Elizabeth turned, her words dying in her throat as she faced one man after another. She finally settled her gaze on Douglas.

It was Iain who spoke first. "I thought you said she couldn't speak English."

"Who?"

"Your maid."

"She's not the maid."

"Well, she is the same one who was here, in this room earlier, when I arrived."

What the devil was she doing here?

Douglas glanced again at Elizabeth, who sat on the floor, eyes wide, mouth surprisingly shut.

Finally Iain Dubh spoke up. "If she isn't your maid, Douglas, then who is she?"

Douglas glanced to Roderick. Roderick looked blindly back. Elizabeth was staring at Douglas, her eyes beseeching him to free her from the numerous sword points and pistols that were aimed at her head.

Douglas did the only thing he could. He reached out his hand and helped her to her feet. "Gentlemen, allow me to introduce my wife, Lady Elizabeth MacKinnon of Dunakin."

"Your wife?"

Iain nearly choked on his claret. "But what about Mac—"

"It is a complicated tale, brother," Douglas said, cutting him off. "Let us discuss it later."

His brother wisely took the hint and fell silent.

Douglas turned to his uncle. The expression on the elder chief's face was unlike anything he'd ever before seen. It wasn't anger. Nor was it shock. It was disappointment.

"I will explain everything to you. All I ask is that you listen first before passing any judgment."

The chief simply gave a nod.

It took nearly an hour for Douglas to relate the circumstances of his unexpected marriage. Blessedly no one said anything about his betrothal to Muirne Maclean. They had other more pressing matters to consider.

"She's obviously overheard everything we said," Young Iain muttered as he paced the floor. "Her father is a Sassenach duke. She will betray us all. Unless . . ." He stopped pacing then, an idea dawning. "We could take her to St. Kilda, like they did that Grange woman."

"Who is the Grange woman?" Elizabeth asked. Whoever she was, she didn't like the sound of his suggestion.

"She was the wife of the Lord Justice Clerk of Edinburgh," Douglas said. "She and her husband had a turbulent marriage, sparked by public quarrels and a good deal of broken glass. Matters culminated in her threat to expose him for a Jacobite and see him arrested and hanged for treason. Fearing a loss of his position—as well as his head—her husband had her secretly abducted, carried bodily from Edinburgh to the distant isle of Heisker, where she was held before later being moved to the more distant isle of St. Kilda. Back in Edinburgh, her husband staged her mock funeral, playing the grieving spouse in order to conceal his shameful deed. No one thought to consider that the casket buried in the kirkyard might be empty. The lady was left a prisoner thus for some fifteen years, eventually being transported here to

Skye, where she eventually died, just before the onset of the '45, a madwoman wandering the beaches of Waternish."

Elizabeth stared at him in horror.

"I do not believe measures that extreme will be necessary," said the MacKinnon chief. He stared at his unexpected niece. "Although we will have to do something with the lass to ensure that our plans don't go awry."

"We could set her adrift then," suggested Iain. "By the time she lands, the prince will have escaped."

"Or we could lock her in a tower . . ."

"But I can help you."

Everybody turned to stare at Elizabeth.

"What do you mean, lass?" Douglas asked.

"I could help you to divert the general's attentions while he is here. From what I have just learned, you are laird here, so then I am the lady of this castle." She looked at him. "Am I not?"

Douglas nodded.

"Well, I am also the daughter of an English duke, which would make any effort on behalf of the prince even less suspect."

"She makes a good point," said Iain Dubh.

"Aye, but it is that same fact," Old Raasay retorted, "that makes her even more suspect. She could be just tryin' to lay us a trap."

"What you are proposing is treason, Elizabeth."

She looked at Douglas directly. "To hunt down and kill a member—any member—of the royal family is a far worse crime. You forget—this man is my kin."

"Kin?" Young Iain came forward. "What do you mean?"

"Charles Stuart's father descends from Mary, Queen of the Scots, granddaughter of Margaret Tudor, a sister to Henry the Eighth, from whom my own father descends, albeit illegitimately. In any case, we are cousins, the prince and I."

"Aye, but that would make the Hanoverian your cousin as well, my lady," pointed out Iain Dubh. "So the question that remains would be with which of your royal cousins does your loyalty lie?"

Elizabeth heard the muffled voices coming from outside the door. She lay on the bed in the castle chamber she'd been taken to the night before. It was early morning. The sun was up and shining on the water that broke against the rocks below her window. She hadn't seen Douglas at all.

After she'd made her offer to Douglas's uncle to assist them in liberating the prince, the MacKinnon chief had dismissed her, citing the need to consider her proposal and discuss it more thoroughly with the others. His guardsman had brought her to the highest chamber in the castle, with a window that looked out onto the sea, and had sat outside the door to keep her from fleeing.

All the rest of the night Elizabeth had simply waited, expecting that Douglas would come to her, to explain why he had done this, leading her to believe he was a farmer and not the laird of this castle. There had to be a reason. But as the hours passed and she'd seen no sign of him, she had begun to worry that he might not trust her to do as she'd promised, that he would listen to the others and lock her away in this tower. Sometime, she couldn't say when, she must have fallen asleep.

She slipped from the bed and walked quietly to the door, testing the latch. She was hungry and she needed to relieve herself. The latch lifted easily, and she eased the door slightly forward, expecting to see the guardsman still posted there.

He was not.

Perhaps he'd gone to find something to eat, or to relieve himself. Whatever his reasons, he was away, and the voices that had awakened her were still echoing from down the hall. They sounded muffled, angry; likely they were discussing what to do with her. And since she had every right to know, Elizabeth walked quickly to the stairs and descended to the floor below.

As she came to the study door, she could pick out Douglas's voice among them, and another that sounded like the MacKinnon chief. There was a third she did not recognize, but it was the one that was speaking the loudest. She was just about to knock upon the door, to demand to know what they planned to do with her, when she heard the MacKinnon chief say something that had her dropping her hand to her side.

"No one can be more distressed by this turn of events than I am, Maclean, but it matters naught. The lass will be going back to England—where she belongs—at the end of the month. Douglas has explained the situation to me. It was unavoidable. He was unwillingly duped into wedding this girl and then was forced to remain wed in order to regain the rights to Dunakin. It is blackmail pure and true, but her father has agreed that once the two months is up, he will grant an annulment and see that Dunakin and the earldom are restored to Douglas. Douglas will then be free to marry your daughter as was originally planned."

Elizabeth's breath caught and held. Her vision blurred and she had to flatten a hand against the wall when the floor threatened to shift beneath her feet.

Douglas was going to marry someone else?

For the first few moments, she wanted to think that she'd heard them wrong, that they were speaking of someone else. But how could that be? She wanted to scream. Why hadn't Douglas told her this weeks ago when it had all begun? He had kissed her. He had done precious more than just kiss her, all the while knowing that he was promised to another.

What an utter fool she'd been.

Elizabeth yanked the door open. Inside, four pair of eyes turned to stare at her, watching as she crossed the room straight for Douglas, pulled back her hand and cracked him hard against the side of his face.

He didn't even flinch.

"You bastard," she said, horrified with herself that she felt the threat of tears. "You lied."

She saw a flicker of something deep in the blue of his eyes. Pain? Regret? She'd thought it would make her feel better. But it didn't.

Douglas's expression was rigid, marked only by the burning imprint of her hand. "Elizabeth, leave us."

"Why should I wish to do that, my lord? I have always thought it unfair that a person should be discussed in such intimate terms without being present." She turned to the others, quickly setting her sights on the newcomer. "Allow me to introduce myself. I am Lady Elizabeth MacKinnon, *this man's wife.*"

Elizabeth was too upset to realize that the man was looking at her with murder in his eyes.

Douglas muttered. "That will do, Elizabeth."

But she was beyond all sense or reason. "I'm not nearly finished."

Douglas looked like a storm about to break. His eyes had darkened, and his mouth was set in a grim and angry line. He glanced beside himself to where Roderick stood, a spectator to the debacle.

"Roderick, take her to the croft. *Now.*"

Roderick came forward. "Come, my lady."

"I have no intention of leaving this room."

"Please, my lady."

But she folded her arms and planted her feet. She had her pride, after all.

Roderick looked at Douglas.

Douglas nodded.

Before Elizabeth realized what was happening, she was lifted bodily from the floor and thrown over Roderick's shoulder with all the grace and dignity of a sack of oatmeal.

He headed for the door.

"Put me down!"

She kicked and struggled, flailed and bucked, but could not break the Highlander's hold. "You cannot do this to me—"

They were gone.

Douglas stared at the vacant doorway for a very long time, warring with the urge to go after her and the knowledge that if he did, his life and the future of his clan would be ruined.

He had to make Maclean think she meant nothing to

him. If the man so much as suspected Douglas might have any feelings for Elizabeth, he would slay them all by nightfall.

"She will no longer be any trouble," he said, trying to sound as indifferent as he didn't feel.

Across the room, Malcolm Maclean was staring at Douglas. "She'd better not be, MacKinnon. She'd better not be."

Chapter Twenty

Elizabeth yelled all the way out of the castle.

She yelled through the courtyard, past the ancient arched gate covered in ivy, that had heralded the arrival of at least seven Scottish kings. She yelled down the first hill, and then up the next, and all along the pathway that ran beside the shore. She yelled until the castle was a distant, shadowy figure, and she cursed a string of curses so colorful it would have set a sailing man to blushing. All the while Roderick carried her, leaving a trail of astonished faces staring in their wake.

A Dia, Roderick thought, grunting as she pummeled his back with her fists. *'Tis a good thing they none of them spoke the king's tongue.*

He didn't pause, not even to rest, until they reached the croft. In truth, he feared that if he did, she would somehow wriggle free and he'd end up having to chase her all the way back to Dunakin.

Only then, he'd be the one yelling.

At the cottage, Roderick kicked open the door, setting Elizabeth on her feet with a *thunk*. The Sassenach lassie was so furious, even her hair seemed to have turned a shade redder.

"How dare you?" she railed. "How dare you treat me in such a manner? Do you have any idea who my father is?"

Roderick simply looked at her. He was not intimidated by the idea of any Sassenach duke. "My apologies, my lady. I was simply doing as I was told."

"And do you do everything you're told, Mr. MacKenzie?"

Roderick thought for a moment. "Aye, I do."

He watched her pace before him, wringing her hands. He tried to put her at ease. "The laird will come to see you when he is ready."

"When he is . . . ?" Elizabeth took a deep breath as if, if she didn't, she would surely scream. "He will speak to me when I wish him to. Which is now."

She started past him, but Roderick shot out a hand, taking her by the arm.

She glared at him. "Unhand me."

"I'm afraid I canna do that, my lady."

"Doing what you're told again, Mr. MacKenzie?"

"Aye."

She pulled away from him and crossed her arms over her chest. "I'll scream."

Roderick had to smile. "You did that all the way here. Now come, just sit and wait like a good lass. The laird will be here directly."

He led her to a chair, surprised when she sat down without further objection. She frowned at him, scowling so deeply that her eyebrows nearly met. Even so, Roderick had to admit it was easy to see why Douglas was so taken with her.

The lass had spirit.

Roderick turned, crossed the room and closed the door. He slid the cupboard in front of it, just in case she should bolt.

When he turned, she was taking up a wooden trencher, readying to throw it at him.

"Whoa! Now, what'll tha' do, lass, except give me the de'il of a headache and get you tied to that chair?"

Elizabeth thought a moment, then lowered her arm. No doubt she'd save the trencher for Douglas.

Or rather, Douglas's *head*.

By the time Douglas appeared, more than an hour later, Elizabeth had devised thirty-seven different ways in which to torture him. Thirty-eight, actually. The last one, however, had the potential for imprisonment so she decided against it. She might be furious, but she wasn't willing to spend the rest of her life in Newgate for it. All she really wanted was for him to feel as horrible as she did.

"My thanks, Roderick," he said, watching her warily as if he expected her to leap upon him at any moment. "You may leave us."

"You are certain?"

"Aye. I think she is clever enough to realize that killing me will not make matters any better for her. Right now, I'm the only one keeping her from being left on St. Kilda."

Elizabeth simply stared at the floor.

"Perhaps I should tie her up afore I go?" Roderick asked. "Just to be safe."

"Nae, I dinna think that will be necessary."

Douglas waited until Roderick had gone, closing the door behind him. He crossed the room and took up a chair, setting it directly in front of Elizabeth. He sat. She simply frowned at him, but the expression in her eyes told him exactly what she was thinking.

It wasn't anything at all pleasant, either.

"I will explain everything."

"Which version?" She lifted her chin, tilting it stubbornly.

"The truth, Elizabeth."

Blessedly, she listened.

"You have every right to despise me. I have deceived you from the very beginning in more ways than one. Some I did because I had no choice. Some I did because it was the only way I could protect you. Yes, your father and I entered into an agreement whereby if I would stay wed to you for two months, he would help me to regain this estate. It is my birthright, and was forfeited by my father for his part in the Jacobite rebellions of thirty years ago. I had intended to tell you the truth, but your father insisted that I should . . ." He chose his words carefully. ". . . *sustain* your belief that I was a poor Scottish farmer. So I did. At first, I wanted to teach you a lesson every bit as much as he did. Wedding you caused me a great deal of complication."

"Indeed. Particularly since you were already betrothed to another."

"Aye, I was. My betrothal was arranged when I was in the cradle. It is no love match. I dinna even know her. It was a means to put to an end to a feud that has waged between the MacKinnons and the Macleans for three hundred years."

"That is absurd."

"No more absurd than your *Sassenach* marriages arranged for financial or dynastic reasons."

Elizabeth frowned at him. Her parents' marriage had been just such a union.

"You don't understand the Highland way of life," he went on. "My uncle is our clan chief. He is father, king, and leader to us all. His word is never questioned. It was he who arranged the marriage when I was just newly born, and I agreed to honor it for the good of my people. I am a chieftain. The people of Dunakin are my responsibility. My clan is weakening and with each new generation our numbers diminish more. I could have refused to see the marriage through, but I chose to barter my happiness for the well-being, the future of my clan. And I thought I could do that. In fact, I had convinced myself of it. *Until I met you."*

Those four words caused Elizabeth's defenses to buckle. She didn't want to believe him. She wanted to believe he would say anything to keep her from ruining his plans. But she could not deny the light of sincerity she saw in his eyes, the way his voice had softened until it was nearly a whisper.

He looked into her eyes, deeply, completely. "I have never met a woman like you. I, too, judged you wrongly when we first met. I thought you were spoiled, pampered, that you saw me as some sort of a pawn to use in a game against your father. But in the weeks since we have been together, I have seen that you are so much more than that."

Elizabeth closed her eyes, fighting tears. "But I heard what you said, what your uncle said, to that man. You told him you were going to send me back to England."

He kissed her temple, her eyelids, saying against her hair, "I would have said anything to keep you from harm."

The tears came unbidden, rolling down her cheeks. God, how she wanted to believe him.

"I have been nothing but a burden to you," she whispered.

"Oh, but you are mistaken in that."

Douglas stepped away, only far enough to remove something from the pocket of his waistcoat. Through the haze of her tears, Elizabeth saw that it was a ring. A single band of gold.

"I should have given this to you long afore this."

He took up her hand and slipped the ring onto her finger. It fit too loosely, so he closed her fingers around it, then covered her hand with his.

"This ring was my mother's, given to her by my father when they were wed. It is simple and plain, aye, but it was the most precious thing she ever owned. I would ask that you wear it . . . as my wife. Because I love you, *leannan*."

Elizabeth blinked, hoping, praying she had heard him rightly. "But what of my father's stipulation?"

"Damn his conditions." He pressed his fingers to her lips. "It is you who are my wife. Elizabeth MacKinnon of Dunakin. For the rest of my life, it will always be *you*."

Elizabeth felt her throat tighten against her words. "Only in name."

"That, can be remedied."

Douglas lowered his mouth to hers and kissed her deeply, passionately, and with all the love in his heart.

And it felt so right. So very right.

He lifted her into his arms and carried her to the bed.

Douglas lay Elizabeth back, raining kisses on her face, her neck, her mouth. She closed her eyes, letting him love her, giving herself over to him, this man, her husband.

He stood above her, dark, potently male. The room was so still, she swore she could hear his heart beating. Time stopped. Neither spoke. They simply stared at one another, memorizing the moment.

Douglas reached for her, touching her on her face. Elizabeth closed her eyes, and slid her fingers up, covering his as she rested her cheek against the warmth and roughness of his hand.

Her breath hitched when he broke from her and hooked his fingers around her neck to draw her slowly toward him. Elizabeth closed her eyes and waited for the kiss that she knew was coming.

She felt the heat of his breath against her cheek and his lips took hers. She let her head fall back, offering herself to his mouth. She never wanted it to end.

But it did end and Elizabeth opened her eyes to see him standing above her. She blinked once, then eased her hands upward against his thighs, sliding them beneath the woolen hem of his kilt. His body was warm. She heard him suck in his breath sharply, watched him close his eyes as she splayed her fingers over his belly.

He let out a moan that sounded like her name, a desperate, wanting sigh.

Elizabeth moved her hands to his waist, tugging at the wide leather of his belt, releasing its buckle.

The kilt loosened, fell.

She watched him as he lifted his arms and slid away his shirt. She thought she had never before seen anything so perfect, and so male. The hardness of him, beautiful and sexual, stoked an ache deep in her belly.

Slowly she reached out to him and closed her fingers around him.

"Dia . . ."

He dropped back his head and surrendered to her touch.

Elizabeth marveled at him, the size and texture of him, the steel and softness as she stroked her fingers over him. His body hitched and tightened. A moment later, he covered her hands with his, easing them away.

"We've all the time in the world, lass. The rest of our lives."

He reached for her, and soon Elizabeth was naked beneath his gaze.

"You are more beautiful than can be possible, *leannan.*"

He whispered words of love to her in Gaelic as he took her hand and had her kneel on the bed. He kissed her, tenderly, fully, cupping her breast in his hand, caressing her delicate skin, as he slid his arm around her waist and pulled her against him.

They sank to the bed as he nuzzled her neck, fondled her breasts, rubbing his fingers against her taut nipple. He kissed her in sensitive places she'd never imagined . . . the very top of her shoulder, the inside of her wrist. She wanted to touch him as he was touching her, and her hands sought him out, stroking him.

She felt his hand slide between them, gently pressing against her. She opened to him, seeking, needing what she knew he would give her.

She arched, sucking in her breath when his finger entered her slowly and his mouth closed on her taut nipple.

She prayed he never stopped, never realizing she'd spoken the words aloud.

How did he know just what to do, just how to touch her to make her feel as if her very blood and bones and flesh were aching for more? She lifted her hips against the pressure of his hand, climbing, seeking, straining, begging him to bring her to that exquisite place where all she would do was feel . . . feel.

And when he did, when she drew that last breath and held it, gasping out loud as her body convulsed around his touch, he covered her mouth, taking in her soft cry.

She felt as if she might weep from the pleasure of it.

She felt him settle against her, felt the heat and hardness of him pressing to her, and suddenly nothing in the world mattered more than wanting, needing to feel him inside her.

He pulled his mouth away, and she slowly opened her eyes to see him braced on his arms above her.

"Look at me, lass. Tell me you'll be my wife, for now . . . and forever."

Elizabeth gazed into his eyes, and whispered the words that would bind them completely.

"I will, Douglas. Yes, I will."

Douglas thrust his hips forward, stilling when she

gasped out in pain from the sudden tearing of her maidenhead. He waited a moment, until she had accustomed herself to the weight and fullness of him inside of her. He felt her ease, then sigh, and gathered her into his arms, pressing kisses along her throat and neck. He drew back slowly, and the slickness and tightness of her was almost too much to bear.

"Sweet, sweet Elizabeth," he whispered as he pressed forward again. She opened her eyes on another gasp, this time not of pain, but of pure, primitive pleasure.

Douglas drew in a controlled breath as he began to move, slowly at first. She gave herself to him utterly, matching his movements thrust for thrust, deeper and faster until he was breathless above her.

A moan tore from his throat when he climaxed. He buried himself within her, spilling his seed in violent, shuddering tremors. His hands clutched her hips, desperate to feel her as spasm after spasm rolled through his body. It was so fantastic, so wonderful, he had to squeeze his eyes tight against the sting of wondrous tears.

He could not move for what seemed an eternity. He never wanted this sweet oneness with her to end. When he did finally move, pulling up on arms that felt as powerless, as pliant as potter's clay, Douglas drew her into his arms and kissed her tenderly, this woman who was now his wife in the most essential of ways.

Much later, when the skies outside the cottage had dimmed, then darkened with the night, and the bedclothes were tangled hopelessly around them, Elizabeth lay still and quiet, listening to the gentle, even beating of his heart. It was perfect, this moment, kissed by twilight and stars, but there was one thing she suddenly knew she needed to say.

"Douglas," she whispered.

"Aye?"

"I love you."

He tightened his arms around her. "I know, lass."

He pressed his lips against her hair, and kissed her softly on the forehead. Elizabeth drifted to sleep, wrapped in the warmth and safety of her husband's arms, no longer afraid of the shadows.

After Douglas returned to Dunakin, bringing Elizabeth as his wife, they went to see Iain Dubh with the news. Though the MacKinnon chief was not pleased that Douglas would be breaking his betrothal to Muirne Maclean, he could not deny the happiness that the Sassenach lass had given his nephew.

The task of telling Malcolm Maclean, however, would not be so easy.

Together, Douglas, Iain Dubh, Roderick, and Iain decided it would be best to wait to inform him until after they had successfully spirited the prince away from Skye. It would only complicate matters if Maclean decided to seek retribution for what he no doubt would see as an affront to his clan. Whatever action Maclean might eventually take, they would stand as one . . . and they would fight as one.

To engage the attentions of the Hanoverian general John Campbell of Mamore, and his captain, Fergusson, they agreed it was best Elizabeth know as little as possible of the details of their scheme. It was not because they didn't trust her, but rather if she should be brought for questioning, there would be nothing for her to conceal. Her part, they had agreed, would consist only of enter-- taining the visiting men and keeping them occupied by playing the role she had been tutored in since birth, that of noble lady and grand hostess. Other than that, she need know nothing more.

Two days later, Douglas and Elizabeth stood together on the ramparts of Dunakin Castle, watching as the naval cutter *Furnace* sailed through the still waters of the kyle, parting the mist like a hulking spectre as the sun slowly descended on the horizon.

Douglas turned to her. "You are certain you wish to do this? You can change your mind even now, if that is what you wish. I willna think any differently of you."

Elizabeth shook her head. "I do not do this for any other reason than because it is right, Douglas."

Douglas kissed her, embraced her tightly, then walked with her to the courtyard to meet their arriving guests.

Elizabeth watched as a party of men advanced along the seaward path. They were dressed in bright red coats decorated with braiding and buttons, their polished black boots tromping the heather as they approached. They wore black tricorne hats with the distinctive black cockade of the Hanoverian army and swords of gleaming silver at their sides. Their very arrival had brought a sense of foreboding to the glen, sending the people of Dunakin fleeing to the safety of their cottages.

Elizabeth's heart beat rapidly as the company came to a halt before them. Her nervousness must have shown on her face. She felt Douglas's hand slide around her fingers and squeeze reassuringly. She pasted on a pleasant smile and stood unflinchingly at his side.

"MacKinnon," said the general in greeting, shaking Douglas's outstretched hand. "It has been too long since we've seen one another."

John Campbell of Mamore was a gentleman, from the trim and elegant tidiness of his powdered wig to the flawless red uniform that gleamed with honors and decoration.

"Aye, sir," Douglas responded. "It has been too long. How does John fare these days?"

Campbell grinned. "My son is very well. It has been a long time, hasn't it, since your days at university? He is presently at Fort Augustus with the Duke of Cumberland and hoping soon to remove to London."

Douglas nodded. "Give him my best wishes, if you will, when next you see him."

Campbell turned to the other man who had come forward to stand beside him. "Douglas, allow me to introduce Captain John Fergusson of H.M.S. *Furnace*."

Elizabeth watched Douglas meet the man who had been in command of much of the brutal devastation wrought along the Scottish western seaboard.

The captain delivered Douglas a look of bland indifference, marked by the dark eyes of an ambitious man. Captain Fergusson had made it his public vow to capture the fugitive Charles, and had spared little in the way of decency in pursuing that aim. The stories of his viciousness and cruelty throughout the isles had been shocking in the degree of their dishonor. With his support, his men had killed, pillaged, and raped, cloaking it in the guise of casualties of war.

The captain didn't want to, but courtesy demanded,

that he extend his hand to Douglas in greeting. "Mac-Kinnon."

Douglas acknowledged the captain so briefly that it bordered on a slight. Elizabeth recognized the dangerous spark of outrage light the man's eyes as Douglas turned.

"General Campbell, Captain, allow me to introduce to you Lady Elizabeth MacKinnon, my wife."

The general's face registered his surprise. "What is this, you say? Your wife? Tell me, how did this all come about?"

" 'Tis a story better told over brandy, sir."

"Then by all means, let us proceed, Douglas."

As they made their way inside, Douglas spun the general a brief and somewhat modified tale of their meeting, marriage, and misadventures. By the time he finished, they were seated in the castle's great hall, enjoying brandy by the warmth of a roaring fire.

"So your father is the Duke of Sudeleigh?" Campbell asked. "I am acquainted with him. In fact I believe he said he had five daughters . . . ?"

"Indeed, sir. Of whom I am the eldest."

Elizabeth looked up when she saw Eithne standing at the door, nodding silently.

"It seems our supper is ready, gentlemen. Shall we retire to the dining room then?"

Chapter Twenty-one

Elizabeth slipped from the castle and crossed the shadowed courtyard on silent feet, heading for the stables. She glanced behind her once, twice, making certain there was no one following her. The moon was new, cloaking the castle in darkness, with only the distant sounds of the sea echoing on the wind. Before coming, she'd changed from her silk supper gown into one of more serviceable linen that wouldn't *swish* when she moved, so as not to give herself away to the soldiers she knew were posted just outside the castle's barmkin wall.

Supper had been a tense affair. At times, the others had fallen silent, watchful. The air of distrust among them had only thickened as the hours had passed. Elizabeth had done her best to both divert and engage attentions—making conversation, performing at the pianoforte, playing the part she'd watched her mother play countless times before. Finally, during the hour approaching midnight, she'd left the men to their port and their pipes, begging off for her bed with fatigue.

In truth, she had one more guest awaiting her.

She patted one of the hounds who lay before the stable door as she carefully lifted its latch. The door squeaked softly on its hinges when she opened it. She quickly slipped past. Once inside, she daren't light a lamp, so she had to feel her way past the numerous stalls, stepping cautiously along the straw-littered breezeway. A horse nickered softly to her in the darkness, lifting its head to watch her part the shadows as she passed. At the end stall, she paused, then ducked inside.

"Easy, girl," she said to the mare, Caledonia. She set down the basket she carried and stroked the horse's soft muzzle. Gifting her with a sugar lump, Elizabeth sank to her knees and ran her hands lightly through the dirt and straw that littered the ground. Her fingers soon grasped something—a small, twisted piece of rope set into the stable floor. She gave the rope a pull, and felt a breeze of cool air as the hatch lifted free.

Elizabeth swung her legs over the edge of a narrow opening in the floor. She searched with her toes for a foothold, nudging it with her slipper. Taking up her basket, she started down the ladder slowly, descending into total darkness. At the bottom, she turned, and whispered.

"Are you there? 'Tis I, Lady MacKinnon."

A few silent moments later, the glow of lamplight came into view, casting its flickering light on the face of the prince.

"It is safe," she said. "No one saw me come."

It was impossible not to be awed by him. His light auburn hair was tousled, his face shadowed by a slight beard, yet even standing in the ragged clothes of a fugitive, he had the noble bearing of royalty. He was handsome, tall, and it struck her then that he was only twenty-five, nearly the same age as she. Yet his eyes, a pale blue, looked as if they'd witnessed a lifetime.

"I have brought provisions for your journey," she said. "Food, clothing, other things you might need—and this."

She held out the small pouch of coin her mother had given her weeks earlier, the day she'd left Drayton Hall.

The prince took it all from her, bowing his head. "My lady, without friends like you, we would have been lost long ago." He spoke English, but his words carried a distinctly Italian cadence. "I understand from the MacKinnon that you are our cousin."

"Yes, Your Highness. Through the Tudor line, albeit a somewhat shadowed connection."

"The ties of blood know no such incongruity." He breathed a sigh, tired with discontent. "Would that Fate had allowed us to meet at St. James, my lady. Perhaps, one day yet, we shall. Until then, I must leave you with a token, something with which to bestow our gratitude for your kindness and aid."

She watched as the prince rummaged through the pockets of his coat. "That is not necessary, Your Highness—"

He shook his head. "I fear I have nothing left to leave you with . . . except"—he held up a hand—"a moment. Have you anything to write with?"

Elizabeth looked at him. "In the basket. There is ink, quills, some foolscap. I thought you might need them.

The prince searched through the basket, removing

several things. He knelt on the ground, and quickly scribbled something in the shadowy light of his lamp.

When he handed the page to her minutes later, Elizabeth read what appeared to be a recipe.

"An Dram Buidheach," he said in Gaelic.

"An Dram-buie?" she repeated.

"It is a secret recipe that has been passed down in our family for generations, the favored drink of the Stuart kings. No one outside of the Stuart family has ever been allowed to know of it. We can think of no better person to whom we should entrust it than you, our dear cousin. And when the day comes that we are ensconced at our rightful place in St. James, we shall drink a toast together, my Lady MacKinnon. Until then, *an Dram Buidheach."*

The prince was delivered safely to the mainland in a small skiff accompanied by the MacKinnon chief Iain Dubh, Roderick, and Douglas's brother, Iain. As they'd dined on boiled gigot of lamb and a Scottish trifle for dessert, the Hanoverian general Campbell of Mamore and the notorious Captain Fergusson were none the wiser.

It had now been a fortnight since Douglas and Elizabeth had consummated their marriage, a fortnight of days spent walking hand in hand on the shore beneath Dunakin Castle, talking of books, ideas, and times past. They picnicked by the burn and made love on a bed of heather as the sun had eased slowly behind the mountains.

Sometimes late at night, when she lay awake in his arms, Elizabeth still found herself wondering if she could be dreaming. But then Douglas would make love to her with the moon shining its pale light in the window and the sound of the water of the Minch drifting on the soft summer breeze. No longer did nightmares haunt her. In Douglas's arms she felt safe and free, and loved, truly loved, for the woman she was.

The sun was drifting slowly toward midday when Elizabeth stirred to see Douglas getting dressed across the room. When he turned and caught her watching him, a smile crept across his mouth. Elizabeth felt her cheeks flush, yet she didn't look away.

"Keep looking at me like that, woman, and we'll not leave that bed till the morrow."

"Is that a promise, my lord?"

Her cheeky response brought a chuckle from deep in his belly. "Och, but I've wed myself to a wanton, I have," he said. He leaned on the bed and kissed her deeply, a kiss that left her groaning in protest when he finally pulled away.

"You just keep that thought for tonight, lass, when I'll be back from Kilmarie."

"Must you really go?"

"Aye. Iain has returned from the mainland, but he is without my uncle or Roderick. He cannot come here for fear of discovery, so I must go to him to find out the news from the mainland." He smiled at her. "Give me a kiss that will stay with me till I return."

Elizabeth slid from the bed. She rose up on her toes and pulled his head down to hers.

Several moments later, he pulled it back. "I'll be back afore the dusk." His voice was husky with longing.

"I'll be waiting."

Elizabeth walked with him to the door.

"What will you do today, my lady?"

"I thought I might take a walk . . . to the cottage."

"The cottage? But I had everything brought here to the castle for you." He nodded. "Ah, I see. It's that goat you're missing, eh?"

Much as she hated to admit it, Elizabeth nodded. "Well, he certainly cannot chew through the roof of the castle, can he?"

Douglas chuckled, rubbed his knuckles against her cheek. "All right, lass. Fetch the goat, if you'd like, but dinna stay away long. There are troops yet loitering about the isle in failing hope of finding the prince."

An hour later, dressed in a simple chemise and skirts with her Scottish *arisaid,* a ladies' plaid that could be used as shawl, cape, or hood, Elizabeth set out across the glen.

It was a lovely day, the sun high and bright, and as she walked she picked wildflowers, tucking them into a small basket that she'd slung on her arm. She hummed a soft tune and stopped more than once to watch a sea tern soaring overhead. The breeze off the water teased her hair from its ribbon, and the warmth of the sun kissed her cheeks a rosy pink.

When she arrived at the cottage, she didn't see the goat anywhere. She called to him once, twice, then decided to look inside.

As she sat in the chair beside the stone hearth, she thought back on her time there, and found herself smiling at the memory of the night when the roof had leaked from the rain. How ridiculous it must have looked with her panniers strung from the rafters. How wonderful it had been when Douglas had taken her to the byre, lying with her on a bed of sweet straw while warming her with his body as the rain pounded the walls around them.

Had it been then, that night, when she first fell in love with him? Somehow she believed it had been long before that. Perhaps even that first day she'd seen him, laughing at her as she'd been slung over Manfred's back in the middle of that murky bog.

Elizabeth heard a sound outside the door and quickly got up from the chair. "I was wondering when you'd decide to show your face, you little beast."

She froze when a figure ducked inside the doorway.

A war cry rent the air.

"A MacGhille Eoin!"

A moment later, Elizabeth screamed.

Douglas made it back to Dunakin earlier than he'd expected. Which only meant he had that much longer to make love to his wife before supper.

He'd spent the afternoon with Iain, listening as he briefed him on the happenings with the prince on the Scottish mainland. From what he had to tell, things hadn't gone smoothly. Finding a safe place on the coast of Morar, they had sought out the assistance of some of the known Jacobite clan chiefs. Most were hiding in caves and makeshift shelters in the wake of the government's destruction after Culloden. Several of his most ardent supporters, who had stood beside the prince only months before, now refused to take part, fearing the risk to their families.

Iain Dubh and Roderick had stayed on, refusing to leave the prince until he was safely delivered to the ship that would take him to France.

When Douglas arrived back at Dunakin, he immediately went in search of Elizabeth, knowing she would be eager to hear the news.

When he couldn't find any sign of her in the great hall, the study, or their bedchamber in the tower, he headed for the kitchen, where he found Saraid, the young maid whom he'd once set to scrubbing out the roasting hearth. This time, however, she was baking oatcakes.

The lass told him that Elizabeth had left shortly after breakfast and hadn't returned. Trying to ignore his growing apprehension Douglas made for the stables to see if anyone there had seen her.

A quarter of an hour later, that apprehension had turned to panic.

He was saddling one of the horses when he heard someone behind him.

"Maclean has her."

Douglas turned to see Iain standing in the stable doorway.

"How do you know?"

"After you left, soldiers began arriving at Kilmarie. I went to the croft, thinking to take refuge there until they removed. But when I got to the cottage . . . the place was all in chaos, Douglas, chairs overturned, flowers strewn about the floor. That ridiculous goat was standing outside the door, bleating like a bloody banshee. I also found this."

He held out a scrap of tartan that bore the Maclean sett. "She must have torn it from him in the struggle."

Douglas had feared something like this, but he hadn't expected it so soon. Somehow, Maclean had taken his revenge by taking Elizabeth. Douglas couldn't allow himself to think of what a man like Malcolm Maclean could be doing to her.

"Saddle one of the horses, Iain. I need you to come with me."

"Do you know where he's taken her?"

"Aye. To Mull, and that bloody castle of his."

"*Caisteal nan Maoidh?* But isn't it in ruins?"

"Aye. But it yet stands. There is a pit, scarcely wide enough for a man to stand and turn, hollowed out beneath one of its towers. He will lock her in there and leave her there to die."

Iain nodded. "I have heard of it. I met a man who had once run afoul of Maclean in a game of chance. Maclean was heavy into his ale and put that pile of rocks up as his wager. When the man bested him, Maclean was so furious, he put him in that pit dungeon and told him that was the only part of the castle he'd ever lay hands upon. The man said 'twas a terrible, fearsome place, dank and moldering and echoing with the scurry of rats."

"Oh, it willna be the rats that will terrify Elizabeth," Douglas said. "It will be the dark."

Douglas and Iain dipped the oars in wide strokes as they made their way across the sound toward the Isle of Mull's eastern shore. In good weather and with a favorable tide, the crossing could take up to two days. They made it by the following evening.

Maclean would be expecting them from the sea, Douglas knew, so they would put ashore northeast of the castle and make their way on foot through thicket to the base of the tower wall.

The ancient Maclean fortress known as Caisteal nan

Maoidh stood like a menacing beast off the lonely Firth of Lorn. It had been built as a single rectangular tower house, commanding a wide prospect of the open sea. Broad merlons and narrow crenelles cut a jagged crown atop its breadth, adding to the dark aura of evil about the place.

As they approached, a quarter moon shone through the drifting clouds, casting the formidable tower in shadows. They watched, waited, until Douglas signaled Iain with a mock sheep's *baa*. He waited for the signal, then, coming from opposite sides, they closed in on the castle's landward wall.

They found Maclean alone and awaiting them inside.

"Stay here. Guard the entrance!" Douglas walked with purpose into the large central cavity of what had once been the castle's great hall.

Decades of neglect had rotted away the flooring on the upper levels, leaving the chamber exposed to the sky above. Leaves and brush littered the stone floor; the walls, once hung with priceless tapestries, were now covered with creeping ivy. In the center of it all stood Malcolm Maclean, sword drawn, eyes flat and mad with murder.

"You've put her in your hellhole, haven't you, Maclean?"

"Aye, she's in the pit, MacKinnon," he said. "What's left o' her, that is. But you'll hae to get through me to get to her."

Douglas wanted to kill the man. Now.

He lunged.

Maclean lifted his blade, slicing it crossways with both hands. The swords connected, the impact resounding with a deafening clang. They jerked apart, facing each other. The only light was the moon and the heat of their rage.

Douglas charged, slashed, charged and slashed again with such force that there were sparks in the dim light from the clashing blades.

Douglas swung a wide arc, just missing his mark. Maclean lunged, ripping Douglas's jacket and cutting into his shoulder.

Douglas grunted, brought up his arm and tightened his fingers around the hilt of his sword.

Slow down, he told himself. *You will tire too quickly. Focus. Precision.*

Douglas came to Maclean's left side, sword ready.

He charged.

Twice Douglas sliced his sword into Maclean's arm. He felt him weakening. They fought like warriors of old, swinging and wielding the steel of their swords in a battle dance more ancient than time. Douglas aimed his strikes with purpose, determined to prevail. They clashed again, and Douglas twisted his arm around, shoving Maclean hard against the wall. Maclean tried to break free. The end was near now. But Maclean suddenly pulled his dirk from his stocking, dropping his sword as he aimed for Douglas's heart.

Douglas jerked back, nearly tripping on the fallen sword. Dirk raised, Maclean rushed at him. Douglas dropped to his knees, the blade of his sword pointed upward toward the charging Maclean. They met, and collided. The dirk came within inches of Douglas's face. Douglas's sword stuck a foot out of Maclean's back.

Douglas yanked his sword free, yelling, "Iain, come.

She's in the dungeon. It is in one of the towers. But I dinna know which one."

"I'll check the north," Iain said, running.

Douglas headed for the west.

It was in the second tower, down a narrow, winding flight of steps that Douglas finally found the locked door. He charged with his shoulder despite his wound. The door splintered inward.

In the center of the floor was a yawning opening, looking like the mouth of hell.

"Elizabeth?"

There was no answer.

"Elizabeth!" he cried, kneeling at the side of it. Oh, God, he was too late.

"What are you yelling about, my lord?"

Douglas turned to see Elizabeth sitting high above him in the moonlight, tucked into a place where the stone wall of the tower had fallen to ruin. In her lap she held a sizeable stone. Four more of equal size were lined up beside her.

She smiled at him in the moonlight. " 'Tis about time you got here. I had begun to think I was going to have to rescue myself." She pointed to the stones. "I've been waiting for Maclean. I was going to clout him when he returned."

Douglas dropped his sword, still slick with Maclean's blood. It clattered to the floor as he reached to take her by the waist at the same time she slid down.

He grunted when she glanced his wounded arm.

"You're hurt."

" 'Tis nothing." He pressed his face into her hair.

"But how did you get out?"

Elizabeth stepped away, kneeling beside the dungeon's hole. She reached inside and pulled out a rope— a rope fashioned out of petticoats.

"I was able to hook this around the jagged end of that rock and pull myself out."

Douglas could only shake his head and laugh as he gathered her more tightly in his arms.

Epilogue

Early autumn, 1747

They were standing at the boat jetty when the ferry-man's sloop glided to meet them. The wind was brisk, tugging at the fringed ends of Elizabeth's tartan shawl and teasing her hair from its pins. She scarcely noticed. She was standing on her toes, anxiously awaiting the boat's arrival.

Not a moment after the mooring ropes had been secured, three figures disembarked and were racing up the pathway to meet them.

"Bess! We're here!"

Elizabeth took Caroline in a joyous embrace.

"Caroline? It can't be. Oh, look how you've grown. It has been little more than a year since I've gone. What happened to you?"

Gone were the pudgy cheeks, the rounded nose. In the time since Elizabeth had come to Skye, Caroline had grown up. Until she smiled, and the familiar twin dimples dented her cheeks, making her appear once again like the child Elizabeth had left behind.

Mattie and Catherine besieged her next on each side, exchanging kisses and hugs and excited chatter.

"But where is Isabella? And Mother?" She looked to Caroline.

"'Tis Mother . . ."

"Has something happened to them?"

Elizabeth turned just as the duke came to join them. He took her in his arms and kissed her gently on her forehead.

"Father, what has happened to Mother? Has she been injured? Is she unwell?"

"Well, she has been complaining of a queasiness of late in her belly." At Elizabeth's worried look, he smiled. "Odd thing is, it only seems to bother her in the mornings."

It took Elizabeth less than a moment. "Mother . . . is with child? Oh, good heavens!"

Her father beamed. "Aye, and she assures me that this time it is a son. Says only a miniature version of me could be causing her such distress. She wasn't up to the journey, I'm afraid. Isabella stayed with her."

The girls all started to chatter as the duke made his way to where Douglas stood, watching.

"We would have been here yesterday, MacKinnon, but we had to put in somewhere first along the way." He grinned. "He said his wife would have his head if he didn't go to see her first."

Douglas simply looked at the duke. "Iain Dubh?"

"Aye, son, your uncle has come home."

"Oh, Douglas!" Elizabeth threw her arms around his neck. "It is finally over."

It had been a very long year.

After the MacKinnon party had landed Prince Charles safely on the mainland, Iain Dubh had sent his nephew Iain back to the isle, while he and Roderick stayed on. For a fortnight they had skulked about the Highlands. Several times they were within moments of capture, and at one time surely would have been, if not for the heroic Roderick MacKenzie.

One day, as they were hiding out in a cave near Glenmoriston, they found themselves surrounded by a company of government troops. The prince could see no means of escape. It was over . . .

. . . or so it had seemed.

Roderick, who was of similar appearance and build to the prince, would have none of it. Taking to his feet, he ran out of the cave alone, drawing the soldiers' attention. There was no possible chance of escape, and one of the soldiers shot him. As the English surrounded him, he managed to say, "Alas, you have killed your prince. . . ."

The soldiers, unwilling to drag the man's body all the way to Cumberland's headquarters at Fort Augustus, simply cut off the dead man's head as proof to collect their promised reward.

Roderick's quick thinking had saved a prince's life.

It wasn't until weeks later that the Hanoverian general learned the truth, that he'd been duped into looking the ultimate fool, as well as letting the true prince escape to France.

Douglas had been devastated. It had been Eithne who had come to him, taking his hands in hers.

"I knew this would happen," she said, reminding him of the vision she had seen that day at the burn. "I was prepared for it. My son died with honor and courage in the truest sense of the words. He has changed the course of history. Remember him for that, Douglas. Tell your children and their children his story, but do not lament his passing."

It was but a week after Roderick's death that Iain Dubh himself was captured by the British. He was put on board the *Furnace* under the command of the reprehensible Captain Fergusson, taken to London, and imprisoned in the Tower.

It had taken the Duke of Sudeleigh over a year to secure his pardon. As he was leaving the court bound for his home on Skye, the judge asked him what he would do if the Stuart were once again in his power, to which Iain Dubh dryly replied, "I would do to him as you have this day done to me; I would send him back to *his own* country."

"I thank you for your efforts in securing my uncle's pardon," Douglas said to the duke. "If not for you, they would surely have hanged him."

Two nights later, the great hall at Dunakin was aglow with brilliant candlelight, echoing with music from a fiddle and whistle as a great celebration, the likes of which hadn't been seen since the previous century, was held.

At the table that stretched through the middle of the room, Douglas and Elizabeth sat with their son Roderick, born just the month before. Beside them was Eithne, who had recently agreed to take rooms in the castle to help Elizabeth with the wee one's care. They looked on, laughing and cheering, as Iain Dubh and his wife danced a lively jig and MacLeod of Raasay sat clapping his hands in time to the music. Elizabeth's father and her three sisters were all sampling the haggis and whisky; even little Caroline had been given a taste, though she declared it quite nasty and pulled a funny face.

But there was one missing among the many gathered. He soon emerged from the shadows, bringing another with him.

"Iain," said Douglas, "we were wondering where you'd run off to."

"I am sorry for being late. I hope you won't mind that I invited another guest."

A dark-haired young girl stood beside him, peering meekly at Douglas from behind his brother's shoulder.

"Muirne?"

Elizabeth spoke up then, answering her husband's unspoken question. "Iain and I have offered Muirne the use of the croft cottage, Douglas."

Douglas looked at her, unable to believe that both his wife and his former betrothed were standing together in front of him.

"Aye," added Iain. "Mull has proven to be too far away for planning a wedding."

"Wedding?" Douglas looked from his wife to his brother. "You?"

Iain didn't even have to answer. He just looked at Muirne and his eyes went soft with emotion. "I have asked and Muirne has agreed to become my wife."

Elizabeth leaned her head against her husband's shoulder. "He wasn't sure how you would feel about it, so he came to me first, to ask what I would think if he asked for Muirne's hand. I told him I thought it simply wonderful."

Douglas took his wife into his arms, whirling her around until she was giggling out loud.

He couldn't have agreed with her more.

Author's Note

Dear Reader:

I hope you have enjoyed reading Douglas and Elizabeth's adventure as much as I have enjoyed writing it. While the story itself is purely the work of my overactive imagination, a good deal of the events around which it is set are factual.

While Douglas Dubh MacKinnon is a character of my creation, the place where he made his home, now in ruins, can be seen to this day. Caisteal Maol, once known as Dunakin, sits on a lonely promontory near the present day village of Kyleakin on the eastern shore of Skye. Built by a Norse princess and her MacKinnon husband, it has stood looking out on the Scottish mainland for more than one thousand years. It is the only MacKinnon possession still in clan hands.

There was indeed a MacKinnon chief named Iain Dubh who lived on the isle of Skye during those turbulent times. Although he didn't, to my knowledge, have a nephew named Douglas, he did take a substantial role in the Jacobite rebellion of 1745. His actions, as they affected the events of history, have been portrayed in this story as true to life as I have been able to determine. From all accounts I have found of him, he was a great and honorable man.

In the aftermath of the Jacobite rebellion, the MacKinnon clan was vital in helping the prince, Charles Edward Stuart, escape to the mainland and eventually back to France. There is a legend surrounding these events which contends that the prince did indeed give Lady MacKinnon the gift of a recipe for a special blend of whisky. That drink, the Drambuie liqueur, is still bottled today by descendants of the MacKinnon clan, and each bottle bears the inscription, *Cuimhnich an tabhartas Prionnsa*—Remember the gift of the prince.

When traveling through Scotland it is almost impossible to miss the many monuments and historical markers that record the various events of that fateful final rebellion. One such marker, found on a lonely stretch of roadway, lies deep in the Highlands where the prince hid for his life that long ago summer. At the edge of the Beinneun Forest near Glenmoriston, a cairn was erected in honor of a fallen Jacobite hero who gave his life to save a bonnie prince. The inscription upon it reads:

At this spot in 1746 died Roderick MacKenzie an Officer in the Army of Prince Charles Edward Stuart of the same size and similar resemblance to his Royal Prince when surrounded and overpowered by the troops of the Duke of Cumberland gallantly died in attempting to save his fugitive leader from further pursuit.

Across the roadway, nearly hidden in the trees, an unadorned cross marks his place of final rest. On it is simply carved R.M. 1746.

In concluding this story, I wish to thank first and foremost my editor, Hilary Ross, whose patience and understanding while I created this tale never once wavered. To Susan King, with whom I traversed the Highlands of Scotland on a journey during which this story first took root. Thanks for the wonderful memories and your constant friendship. And lastly, to my readers. Thank you for your letters and e-mails. They are a treasure to me. I hope you'll watch for my next story, in which Elizabeth's younger sister Isabella finds herself swept up in a whirlwind adventure that takes her straight into the arms of another handsome Highland hero.

Until then . . .

J.R.

**Please read on for
an excerpt from Jaclyn Reding's next
Highland Heroes novel**

The Adventurer

coming from Signet in November 2002

Versailles, 1748

Lady Isabella Drayton was sitting by the fire in their apartment at the palace, curled against the cushions of a carved armchair. She was reading by candlelight when a soft scratching noise sounded at the door.

She opened the door slowly onto the face of one of the palace footmen.

"Pour vous, mademoiselle."

In his hands he bore a small silver tray, atop which lay a folded note. Isabella took the note, and thanked the footman. He bowed his head, backing away as she turned from the door to read.

Mademoiselle Drayton,

There is a matter about which I find I must speak to you before your departure on the morrow. My request might seem peculiar, since we have only just met, and I beg your understanding in this. Please meet me in the Gallerie de Glaces precisely at midnight. I give you my word as a gentleman I intend nothing dishonorable.

Yours, Le Comte de St. Germain

Isabella glanced at the ormolu clock on the mantel. It read a quarter hour before midnight.

She knew very well she should not be meeting a man alone, let alone meeting a man she'd only just met alone and at midnight. Still, despite this, something—some strange, unknown impulse—prompted her to rise from her chair and make ready to leave.

She glanced across the room to where Aunt Idonia was snoring softly in the shadows of her bed. A sound sleeper, she would never notice if Isabella slipped from the room for a brief walk through the palace. And she wasn't going all that far. Only to the Gallerie, one floor below and in the wing adjoining their apartment.

She wouldn't have the time to lace into her stays, so Isabella just slipped on her skirts and the jacket of one of her riding habits, buttoning it over the white of her nightrail. Her hair was down, just brushed for the night, and she left it that way, spilling over her shoulders in a twist of dark curls that wound its way nearly to her waist. She slipped on a pair of shoes with a soft sole and a low heel that would allow her to walk quietly across the palace's marble floors. Then, with a quick glance behind, she headed for the door.

She gathered the bulk of her skirts in her hand and made her way quietly along the corridor. There was no one about, not even the footman who had brought her the message. Only darkness and the pale, pale light of the moon shining through arched and mullioned windows. Somewhere, from behind the cover of a closed door, she heard a woman giggle seductively.

Isabella passed through a door at the end of the hallway, descending into the darkness of a curving stairwell. Within minutes, she was standing at one end of the lengthy and elegant Gallerie des Glaces.

The moonlight was brilliant, glittering on the myriad crystals that hung from the chandeliers overhead. They reflected in the seventeen arched windows, and an equal number of magnificent mirrors that lined the opposite wall for which the room was named, making her feel as if she was standing in the midst of a star shower.

Isabella walked along the polished parquet floor, studying the various works of art in the moonlight, the ceilings painted by

Le Brun celebrating the reign of the Sun King, the sculptures that stood like soldiers standing at guard along its length. When she had first arrived at the palace earlier that day, the room had been so crowded with courtiers, she hadn't been able to see all the elegant statuary and polished marble that graced the magnificent room. Standing alone now in the near darkness, the vast room seemed to whisper with ghosts of masked balls and stately processions from an earlier era.

Until the comte stepped suddenly from the shadows, and Isabella nearly jumped from her own skin.

"Mademoiselle, l am pleased you decided to come."

Isabella took a slow breath to steady her pounding heart. "*Oui, monsieur.* Your message seemed quite urgent."

"Indeed, it is." The comte took her hand and led her away from the windows, further into the shadows. "You see, I have been waiting for you for some time, Mademoiselle Drayton. Many, many years."

Isabella's skin prickled at his touch, not from fear, but in anticipation. "But you did not know me before today, sir."

"This is true. But I did know *of* you. I have always known of you."

"I'm afraid I do not understand."

"Mayhap this will help to explain."

Isabella watched with eyes wide as the comte reached inside his coat. A moment later, he removed something, something that hung from the length of a silver chain. It was a stone, crystal in appearance, encased in crisscrossed bands of engraved silver. It was uncut, in its natural state, yet deep within, it glowed with a milky fire that even the darkness of the night could not subdue.

The oddest thing of it was that the stone had a sense of familiarity about it, as if she'd seen it somewhere, sometime before. But that was impossible. And she knew it.

"What is it?" she asked, even as she took it, feeling the weight of it against her hand.

"This stone was once the property of the kings of the Gaels. And it is more ancient than anyone can accurately trace. It is said to have been given to the Mac Aoidh centuries ago by a faery queen. Its powers are many, both healing and mystical, and as such it is sought after by many who would abuse it. It was taken from Caledonia, from the Mac Aoidh some time ago. And since that time, all has not been right. A great fog of unrest has descended, and continues to grow even now. The stone must be returned, else hope will be lost forever."

It was just the sort of story that Isabella could get lost in.

"It is a fascinating tale, monsieur, but what does any of this have to do with me?"

"In each age, mademoiselle, there are powers at work, powers higher than anything we of this earth can command. For each transgression, there is a virtue, the natural order of things that keeps the balance between the elements of earth, wind, water, and fire. There was a transgression when this stone was taken. And as such there must be a virtue to restore it. I believe *you* are that virtue, Madmoiselle Drayton. You must take this stone, and you must return it to the rightful Mac Aoidh. There is, however, a complication."

"Isn't there always?" Isabella asked, at once fascinated and frightened of the comte's ominous words.

"There are three of the Mac Aoidh, not one, and it is your task, my dear mademoiselle, to choose among them. Choose correctly, and all will be as it should. Choose wrongly, and you shall shift the course of history."

Isabella had been so engrossed in the comte's evocative words, she hadn't even noticed when he slipped the chain around her neck.

"Wait . . . no . . . this is not—I don't even know who . . ."

Her words fell to silence as she lifted the stone up by its chain and stared at it in the moonlight. It was mesmerizing, hypnotic, as if filled with thousands of sparks of brilliant light. As soon as she wrapped the weight of it in her fingers, the stone began to glow, as if lit by a fire deep inside. First blue, then a pale red. It was no trick of the light. It was real, for it felt warm, almost hot against her skin.

"Heed the stone, my lady. It is telling you what you must do. It will lead you to Scotland, and once you are there, all will come to you . . . in time. Until then—and please heed me well— you must not let loose the stone. Not until you have found the true Mac Aoidh. Only then must you release the stone. Only unto him."

And then, as if he'd been a wisp on the wind, a trick of the moonlight, the comte vanished.

And was gone.

"Monsieur? Monsieur le comte? Where have you—"

But she was speaking to the shadows.

Isabella stood for several moments, trying to decide whether the past several moments had truly happened. Had it been a dream? Had she walked in her sleep to find herself here in the Gallerie alone? But, no, she couldn't have because the weight of the stone was heavy on her neck even now.

As she made her way slowly back to her apartment, Isabella wondered if she should just take the chain from around her neck, give the stone to a palace footman to return to the comte the next day after she had gone, and forget all about this meeting and this night. But something in his words gave her pause.

It must be returned, else hope will be lost forever.

It was no ordinary stone, for even now, as she climbed the dark stairwell, it held a glow that couldn't be explained. Who was this Mac Aoidh he had charged her with finding? And why had he chosen her?

To Scotland, and once you are there, all will come to you . . . in time.

And then she knew what she would do. She would ask Elizabeth and Douglas when she saw them in Edinburgh. Douglas would know what to do, would know who this Mac Aoidh was.

Until then, she would keep the stone around her neck, just as the comte had urged her to do.

Edinburgh, one week later

"Mac Aoidh is a clan, Bella, not a person," Douglas said, without the slightest hesitation and just as soon as Isabella finished telling him her story. "It is the clan MacKay. Their chief hails from up in Sutherland on the northernmost coast of the Highlands."

They were sitting in the coffee room of the White Horse Inn, just off the High Street near the palace of Holyrood. Her ship had arrived at the port of Leith earlier that morning and Isabella had waited until after they had arrived in the Scottish capital city before telling her sister and brother-in-law about her encounter with mysterious St. Germain.

Elizabeth sat beside her, holding the stone and examining it closely.

"But the comte said there were *three*," Isabella said.

"Aye, and that there are. The current MacKay chief has no heirs of his own body, so next in line to head the clan would have been his brother, until the man died in the rebellion of 1715. He did, however, leave behind a wife who was with child, which, if it proved a son, was duly chosen to be the old chief's heir."

Isabella was sitting forward, waiting for him to go on. "And?"

"The widow bore three sons."

"Triplets?"

"Aye. Instead of one, the chief suddenly had three heirs. Typically, the chief would have named the first one pulled from the womb his heir, since it had been born first. However, the midwife confused the bairns while she was birthing them. They were identical and she couldn't say with any certainty which had been taken before the others. A disagreement ensued among the chieftains who had been named each to foster a lad, as to just who should be named the next heir. Sides were taken. Words were exchanged. The lads were separated, each raised to treat his brothers with contempt and suspicion."

Isabella thought of the closeness she had with her own four sisters. She couldn't imagine there being anything but love and devotion among them. "I'm afraid to ask what happened next."

"Time passed. The chief, pressed continually to name his heir and troubled by the ill will that was unraveling the very fabric of his clan, finally declared he would climb alone to the summit of Ben Hope to counsel with the spirits of the clan chiefs who had ruled before him. He vowed to settle upon an heir at his return. But while he was away, sleeping 'neath the stars on the top of that mountain, the chief was said to have had a dream, a vision in which the clan charm stone, which had vanished mysteriously when the lads' father was felled on the field of battle, was returned to determine the rightful heir and bring peace once again to the clan of MacKay."

Isabella was taken by a chill, even though their table was near to the hearth. "It's an incredible tale."

"Aye, considering . . ."

"Considering what, Douglas?"

Douglas looked directly at Isabella then. "Considering that in his dream, the MacKay said 'twas a dark-haired maiden who brought the stone back."